Also by Jade Everhart

Taber Tigers

I Blame the Dimples

I Blame the Alcohol

I Blame the Club

I Blame the Rival

I Blame the Rival

Jade Everhart

To anyone who has ever fallen down and gotten back up for someone else.

Here's to having someone worth fighting for.

Note

This book contains subject matters that may be difficult for some readers including anger management, domestic abuse, emotional abuse, drug use, violence, flashback of rape (consent withdrawn), sexual harassment, sexual violence, and references to self-harm.

If any of these issues rung true to you or a loved one, please seek help from professional psychiatrists, psychologists, and other scholarly resources to find the support needed.

Prologue

1 year earlier...

Skylar

I slip into our rival's locker room.

Ducking my head, I avoid eye contact with the guys wearing orange and black jerseys. It's the first tournament of the season and Taber University has home field advantage. The rough edge of my poster digs into my hands as I duck past the rows of lockers, my grip on the rolled-up piece of paper tightening until I make it to the safety of Silverwood's lacrosse team.

At the far end of the locker room, the Sabers are jostling each other, their laughter and high spirits helping to take some of the tension out of my shoulders.

If everyone is in a good mood then maybe today will be okay.

Pushing back the grey hood of my sweater, I nod to a couple of the familiar faces who smile at me. I've never been particularly friendly with the varsity team, most of the guys on it are overly aggressive and use their sport as an excuse to beat the shit out of their opponents.

The worst of them being my older brother.

The tension returns when I come to a stop in front him, my eyes raking over his body language to determine whether today will be a good day. Calm fingers make quick work of his cleats, the steadiness of his hands and relaxed posture giving me a flicker of hope.

"Are you going to keep it under control today?"

Stark blue eyes glance at me, an amused smile painting his face, "Depends if the Tigers are in the mood to play or not."

"You promised to be better this year."

The smile slips, "I red-shirted last year to work on *keeping things under control.*" He hisses out the words and the threat in his voice has a few of the Saber players glancing over, "I've put in my time, Sky. Stop being such a mother hen."

I stare back at him, wishing his words were true.

My brother sighs, shoving his shoulder-length blonde hair out of the way, "Look, I'm going to try my best, okay? I can't do more than that."

His best is bullshit and we both know it.

I remain silent, choosing to keep the fighting words buried deep inside me. Over the years my silence has saved a lot of pain, and today doesn't appear to be an exception.

"Baby Vin, would you mind giving our all-star some space? Man needs to get his head in the game if we're going to slaughter some Tigers."

The Silverwood player closest to us slaps a locker and I flinch, making him laugh. The dark-haired player has barely caught his breath when my brother stands up and grabs him by the jersey. The locker room goes deathly silent as Silverwood's leading forward leans in with a snarl.

"Show some fucking respect or the only person being slaughtered on that field today will be you." Vector turns and flashes his teeth to the rest of the team, "That goes for all of you. The next person who looks at my little brother the wrong way will have me to answer to."

Shame washes over me as each player mumbles some sort of an agreement. Vector turns back to me with a satisfied gleam in his eyes and nausea creeps up my throat.

He's just like our father.

Vector drops down on a bench across from where I'm standing. I drop my gaze, not wanting to see the fire burning in his eyes.

Today isn't going to be a good day.

"Don't be like that, Sky." There's a bite to my brother's tone, "Can't you see everything I do is for you?"

Another bullshit excuse.

"Can you at least show me the masterpiece you drew for me?" Vector tilts his head, trying to catch my eye, "I heard you drawing late into the night. I know it's going to be a good one."

He's offering me an olive branch and because I'm weak, I take it. A strong sense of self-loathing washes over me as I hand over the poster and watch my brother carefully unroll it. Delight fills his eyes as he takes in the carnage I disposed on the black piece of paper.

"It's beautiful."

He runs a hand over the slaughtered tiger, the darkness of its blood and mutilated organs bringing out the metallic colour of the blade slicing it right down the middle.

"That's fucking horrifying." Walsh, another forward player, bends over Vector's shoulder to get a closer look, "You drew this?"

He glances my way and I give him a short nod.

"Damn. Your little bro's got talent." He slaps Vector on the back and gives me a toothy smile, "I'll hit you up the next time I want a violent piece done, yeah?"

My shoulders tense and I quickly look away.

At the end of the day, it doesn't matter that I don't use my physical strength to hurt people. My temper is just as unhinged as my brother's, the only difference is I direct mine to the ink on a page. I don't hurt people, but no matter how hard I try, I can't escape the monster inside me. The rage that controlled my father now controls my brother, and I'm terrified that one day it will control me too.

"I can't wait to see the Tigers' faces when they see it." Vector passes my poster back and I take it with a dry throat.

"I didn't draw it for them. I did it for you."

"And now they get the chance to admire your artistry. It's a win win." Pulling me in for a quick hug, he whispers in my ear,

"Hold it up high so I can see it from the field. Might help keep me under control."

I know exactly what he's doing, so I don't respond when he releases me. Heart burning with broken shards, I turn and head back towards the exit door without another word.

I push through the door and almost make it outside when a black and orange jersey crashes into me. I stumble sideways and a muscular arm quickly reaches out to steady me.

"Sorry about that, my head is all over the place this morning. Should have checked where I was going."

A concerned look takes over the guy's face, his blonde fauxhawk giving him an inch or two over me, "Are you okay?"

I stare back at the Tiger's team captain, wishing I could tell him to run before my brother is unleashed on his team.

"I'm okay."

"Good. Wouldn't want the Sabers losing any fans before the game starts." Cody glances at my team hoodie and casts a smile at me.

He has a kind smile. One that doesn't have menace or violence behind it.

"Yeah."

He gives me one last smile before disappearing through the door I just came out of. I stare after him, hoping with all my heart that I was wrong.

Today will be a good day.

Vector doesn't hit the field until halftime. It had been a close game with the Tigers one point ahead, but the excitement I was feeling cheering on the Sabers quickly turns into dread when I see my brother walk towards the front line.

He casts a glance at the crowd, and I know when he sees me – or rather, the poster I made him – because he gives me a grin that does nothing except increase my nerves. I watch the next few plays with eagle eyes, wincing when Vector makes an aggressive cross check, but his temper remains in check, and he leaves the poor guy alone.

Just like he promised.

Relief hits my chest when I see the uninjured Tiger player get pulled off the ground by Cody, the captain I bumped into earlier, and a dark-haired rookie. The defenseman shoves them off with a laugh and walks back to his starting position.

And that's when it goes to shit.

The bleachers are too loud for me to hear what's being said between the teams lined up on the field, but I can tell something is wrong. Vector yanks his helmet down over his face and staggers back to his position. The ref blows his whistle, and the players take off, my brother's fumbling movements making me drop my poster and scream.

"VECTOR NO!"

His graceful athleticism is long gone when he goes charging towards the rookie running for the ball. I squeeze my eyes shut, knowing Vector isn't thinking about stealing the ball right now.

He's out for blood.

The crowd gasps as the ref blows his whistle again, and I peel my eyes open, forcing myself to look at the damage my brother left behind. The breath gets knocked out of my lungs when I register it isn't the rookie lying unconscious on the ground.

It's the Tiger's captain.

The one with the kind smile.

"CODY!" A piercing scream cuts through the bleachers as a girl goes running for the field. I can't tear my eyes away as she sprints past the medics and drops to her knees beside him. My stomach surges and soon I'm running as well, except I'm running in the opposite direction.

Away from my brother's carnage and my equally horrifying poster.

I make it to the parking lot before nausea takes a hold of me. I collapse to the ground, throwing up the breakfast I'd eaten hours before. I heave until there's nothing left then crawl along the pavement towards my car. It takes me a few tries to get my door unlocked and even more tries to drag my shaking body into the driver's seat.

I don't touch the ignition once I get inside. I just sit there, trembling as I watch the ambulance pull into the stadium through my cracked windshield.

It doesn't matter what I do, or who I try to become.

The monster will always find me.

Chapter 1

Present day...

Lacey

I wake up to the sound of clapping.

And not the good kind.

"YES! Right there, baby. Hit me right there." Cecelia's moans float through our adjourning wall and I shudder, pulling my blankets over my head to try and block out the noise.

"Harder, baby! I'm getting close."

I throw my blankets back down and glare at the patchy ceiling above me. This isn't the first time Cecelia has woken me up with a front row seat to the porn show and I doubt it's going to be the last. Cursing whoever was in charge of roommate distribution, I cross my arms and wait for the sound of slapping skin to fade, half-heartedly listening to my roommate's squeals of ecstasy.

My God. Does it really take that long to come?

Doing my best to ignore the masculine grunts drifting through my wall, I roll over and grab the book from my nightstand. There's just enough light streaming in through the dusty window that I can see the words on the page in front of me.

Naturally, I stopped reading the night before on a sex scene.

"I'M COMING!"

I snap my book shut and fling it across my first-year dorm room. It slaps the window and falls face down onto the gross beige carpet. Regret fills me immediately and I abandon my warm bed to retrieve the fallen soldier.

Carefully smoothing the corners back into place, I put the book back on my nightstand and turn to look at my makeshift bookshelf above the small desk pushed tight against the wall.

I run my finger along the colourful spines, the fourteen books I managed to squish in between the drawers holding my school supplies putting a warm feeling in my chest. There is nothing like a pretty bookshelf, however small.

Especially when each novel contains a happy ending.

The screams from the next door finally fade into an un-rhythmic pattern of heavy breathing. I turn my attention to the envelope tucked between my favourite romance novels. Gently pulling it out of its hiding spot, I open it up and pull out the first photograph.

"Mi amor? You in there?"

A loud knock on the main door has me hurrying to put the envelope back in its hiding spot.

"Coming!" Wincing at my word choice, I leave my bedroom and walk through the tiny living room to open the main door that connects to the residence building. Nico Montez grins back at me, his pink polo shirt unbuttoned to show off the tanned, lean chest underneath.

I smile, giving his bare torso a glance, "Isn't it a little early for a strip tease?"

"Babe, it's never too early for a strip tease. Maurice would know."

He winks and I laugh, picturing Nico's brooding partner. The two of them met last summer when Mo came back to help coach Taber's lacrosse team. It took a few fights and a drunken standoff, but finally the enemies-to-lovers became an official couple a few weeks ago.

The sound of my laughter puts a bright smile on his face and the familiar sting of guilt hits me. Both Nico and my brother try to hide the fact they still worry about me, but the obvious attempts at keeping me light-hearted are a dead giveaway.

Not that I can blame them. If I had a little sister who tried to commit suicide I'd do everything I could to make her laugh as well.

"As much as I love taking off my clothes, that's not why I'm here." Nico conspicuously looks over each shoulder before dropping his voice to a whisper, "It's time to put our plan in motion."

"OTB?"

"OTB."

I smile, leading him into the dorm. Nico follows close on my heels, his anxiousness to get to the safety of my room making me laugh.

"Cecelia is occupied with an overnight visitor. There's no need to fear."

"Until that woman stops dying her hair green and piercing her septum for fun, there will always be something to fear." Nico leans against my closed door and blows out a breath, "I will never forgive Housing Services for making Lucifer's offspring your wallmate."

I bite back a laugh, "That's a little on the dramatic side."

"Is it though?"

He sweeps his eyes around my room, and I do the same, noting the unmade duvet and the desk cluttered with every succulent imaginable. My heart skips a beat when I see the white edge of the envelope peeking out of its hiding spot, but Nico doesn't seem to notice.

"Green hair and piercings don't qualify as demon qualities, Nico."

"Maybe not, but the woman their attached to does."

I shake my head and walk over to grab my plant mister. The glass spray bottle catches a ray of sunlight and the adorable flower design etched along the side sparkles back at me.

Nico makes himself comfortable on my bed while I tend to my plant babies, carefully looking them over for any dead stems or dry spots. Just like the bookshelf, my indoor garden is limited by Taber University's tight residence quarters, but I make the most of the little space I have.

"Don't be mean."

He heaves a sigh, adjusting my pillow beneath him, "You need to be less kind, Lace. Did she wake you up with another sex fest?"

My eyes flick to our adjoining wall, waiting to hear Cecelia shout some sort of response. Her side of the dorm stays silent, so I cross my heart and hope she fell back asleep.

I nod with a sigh, "I needed to get up anyways. We've got lots to do today."

"Have you figured out if she's a dominatrix yet?"

"Nico!"

He grins, "What? It's an innocent question. If you're gonna hear what's going on, you may as well learn something from it."

The smile slips from his lips and he jerks upright on the bed, "Shit. I didn't mean to-

"It's fine." I cut him off, not wanting to go down the same rabbit hole we've been down countless times before, "What's the next step for Operation Trip's Birthday?"

Nico falls silent, his dark eyes scanning my face for the broken girl I became two years ago.

"We've got to grab the cupcakes and set up shop. I'm thinking we go hard on the decorations and hope they make up for the lack of people in attendance." He hesitates, "I really am sorry, mi amor. I didn't mean to call you out like that."

I point the spray bottle in his direction, "If I was really upset, I would have misted you. Now, get out of here so I can change and we can hit the road."

Nico rolls off my bed and saunters over to give me a hug. Tucking my head beneath his chin, I close my eyes and fight to keep the tears at bay.

He squeezes me tightly, the familiar scent of his cologne reminding me of all the memories we wouldn't have had together if the pills had worked.

"You are perfect, Lace. Never let anybody, including my dumbass, make you feel any different, okay?"

"Okay." I whisper, afraid that anything louder will make the cracks appear.

He smacks a kiss atop my head, "You've got thirty minutes and then we're on our way to Party Central. Got it?"

"Got it."

I wait until he's gone before I walk over and pull the envelope out of my bookshelf.

As much as Nico and my brother shower me with support, they don't understand what it's like to be the broken girl. To be composed of shards so sharp that sometimes I wonder whether this is my punishment. To be stuck with a darkness that never goes away, a past people are too scared to talk about, and thoughts too dark to voice aloud. I've been surrounded by love and support these last few years, but I've never felt so alone.

Until I met her.

Opening the envelope, I let the photographs fall onto my desk. At first glance, they look like pictures I took of my therapist's sunshine yellow tissues – each one marked with a daily quote of inspiration – but if you look closer, you can see the handwriting covering the back of each one.

Happiness is not by chance but by choice.

But what if that choice doesn't belong to you?

Then maybe it's time to make it your own again.

I run a finger over the photo, tracing our first correspondence. I had found the tissue by accident, the bright yellow material had caught my eye before one of my therapy sessions and I had hastily written a reply, filled with hope that this stranger might be the friend I've been looking for. It seemed silly to take a photo of the tissue, but I wanted proof that I wasn't alone, something to hold on to in case I never heard from her again.

Turns out, it was a good thing I took the photo because my mystery friend left me a new tissue the following week, but the original one had disappeared.

Don't wish for it. Work for it.

Who took the choice from you?

A boy who didn't deserve my time or affection. So, who is currently keeping your happiness just out of reach?

Some people look for a beautiful place. Others make a place beautiful.

A guy as well, although I have the misfortune of being related to him. Was your happiness-stealer a first love or just a tragic one?

First love. I was your typical naïve girl who fell for the wrong guy.

Every day may not be good, but there is good in every day.

I'm sure it wasn't that simple.

You're right, it wasn't that simple, but it was embarrassing. Sometimes I think back on the girl I was and I get so angry it feels like I can't breathe. The worst part is, I'm not even angry at the guy who hurt me. I'm angry at how easily I let myself be manipulated. I'm sorry, you probably don't want to hear this.

A little improvement goes a long way. Take it day by day.

Never apologize for speaking your mind. Few people speak the honest truth, and it is not something to be ashamed of. As for your TedTalk, well, I really enjoyed it. Anger has always played a present part in my household, so I know a thing or two about feeling trapped in your own skin.

Honestly, I'm normally not this open with people. Karen has helped my communication skills (as I'm sure you know) but I don't normally talk to strangers about my past. And yet here I am, opening up to someone whose name I don't even know.

Even the smallest action can make a difference.

If it's any consolation, I don't normally talk to people like this either. My name is Skylar, by the way.

Skylar

It's nice to meet you Skylar, my name is Lacey. I have to say, your name is almost as pretty as your handwriting. Are you an artist?

I tilt my head, rereading the girl's response. There's something strange about it, some sort of misassumption that I can't quite put my finger on. I study the yellow tissue intently, as if it might conjure up an image of the girl I've spent the last few weeks talking to.

A girl named Lacey.

For the past year, Silverwood's one and only therapist has done her best to get me to open up, to share the horrors of my childhood so we can fix the damaged pieces inside of me. Karen went through every trick in the book, even letting me bring my sketchbook to our sessions so I can try and communicate with her that way. Nothing seemed to work until I met her.

A girl named Lacey.

When I first saw her writing, her resilient response to my dark question, it felt like I was being seen for the first time. Finally, I had found someone who understood what it was like to walk on the dark side and come out a little bit shattered.

It's not Karen's fault that our sessions are unproductive. She just doesn't understand that not all broken things can be fixed.

But Lacey does.

Pulling out the sunshine tissue from my pocket, I let it unfold out in front of me. The bold letters of today's quote scream back at me, but I pay the words no attention as I flip it over and pull the pen from my sketchbook.

Pretty is not normally what people say when they find out my name, but yes, I do like to draw. I find sketching helps relieve some of the pressure inside me.

I carefully fold the yellow tissue and bend down to tuck it between the rocks in the flowerbed outside of Karen's building. Originally, I started leaving my thoughts as a way to amuse myself after the emotional garburator these therapy sessions put me through. Eventually it became a sort of solace. A safe space to leave my lingering questions and inner demons after Karen's intrusive line of questioning.

Now, I look forward to these sunshine tissues. Reading Lacey's responses has somehow become the motivation I need to get through the hard days. The days I feel more broken than normal.

Clipping my pen back onto the ring binding of my sketchbook, I tuck it under my arm and walk back down the gravel path. The beige building that holds Karen's counselling sessions sits on the far edge of Silverwood, the very tip of the small town I grew up in. The main street can be seen from the nearby parking lot, the mom-and-pop shops and the little boutiques running along a road that has four streetlights and two stop signs.

The bottoms of my sneakers have just hit the rough edge of the concrete parking lot when a red hatchback pulls in. My shoulders tense when I register who's sitting in the passenger seat, the platinum blonde hair telling me Silverwood's biggest rival has arrived.

Stella O'Brien hops out of the car with a tight smile, her dainty features and lean frame a polar opposite to her fierce personality. Like me, Stella's older brother is well-known in the lacrosse circuit except hers shines in a positive light. Mighty Mo helped lead his team to four consecutive championships while Vector became known for putting his opponents in the hospital.

I'm not surprised that students from Taber University wind up in enemy territory. Given the small size of both university towns, Karen is the only certified therapist within a 100km radius.

What is surprising, however, is that someone like Stella attends therapy. From what I've seen, her family lives and breathes competition and success, and that type of personality doesn't normally leave much room for mental health.

Guess you can never tell though.

I shift the sketchbook under my arm, hoping to make it past her ride without being spotted. Hunching my shoulders to hide my face, I've almost made it to the sidewalk when the driver's door opens and a familiar face gets out.

My hurried steps falter when I register the blonde fauxhawk attached to the guy walking around the vehicle to give Stella a hug. I stare, watching Taber's old lacrosse captain whisper something in her ear that makes her laugh.

He's okay.

Blood roars in my ears as I change course and start walking towards the couple. There are so many things I want to say to him but I don't know if I'll be able to say anything at all.

I'm so focused on the uninjured captain that I don't notice Stella's glare until I'm ten feet away. I freeze, heart pounding, as I take in the venom in her eyes. The accusations are right there, reflecting back at me through someone else who was hurt by my brother's actions.

It doesn't matter that it wasn't me on the lacrosse field that day. My last name holds me responsible.

Cody turns his head and I quickly duck mine, not wanting him to see me for what I truly am. Pulling up the hood of my Sabers sweater, I turn away from my demons and start the long trek home.

"Your boss called. He needs you to take the late shift tomorrow night." Vector glances at me from the kitchen table, "I told him you were free."

Rainwater drips from my hood onto my face while a puddle starts to form on the floor. I'm completely drenched, the thick cotton of my hoodie no match for the downpour that started halfway through my walk home. I pull my sketchbook out from under my t-shirt and assess the damage.

"Did you hear me? I said you could work tomorrow night."

I nod, flipping through the damp pages. Most of the ink got smeared or bled right through the page, destroying the sketches I had completed the week before.

Frustration burns through me as I toss the ruined book onto the kitchen table. The number of hours I spent filling those pages are all gone. Destroyed, ruined, because of a simple walk in the rain.

The moment you think you have something good life steals it away.

Or someone else ruins it for you.

Bitterness fills my mouth as I pull out a chair and sit down across from my brother. I stare at him, observing the way he slouches over his laptop. His long hair is pulled back into a low ponytail and the grey Sabers t-shirt he's wearing makes him look like a normal person.

Rage burns through my body as I look at the person who has almost single-handedly ruined the family name. He has no right to look like a normal person.

Not when I can barely see straight.

"I saw Cody Ellsworth today."

"Oh yeah?" Vector grins, "How'd he look? He was rocking a wicked black eye for a while."

"He looked healthy. Not that you would care." I stare him down, waiting for the fire to alight. My brother meets my stare head-on, his gaze steady and focused.

"If the old Tiger captain is back on his feet then there's no need to have regrets."

My teeth snap together, "You're fucking sick. You can't just go around hurting people."

A spark hits Vector's eyes and suddenly I've got the fight I was looking for. He leans forward and places his muscular forearms on the table.

"Watch yourself, Sky. Don't forget who stepped up when it came time to kick dad out."

"And look how that turned out. Now you're just a bully on a lacrosse field."

A screech fills the air when Vector pushes back his chair and stands up. The fire in his eyes is blazing, matching the one running through my veins. I shove my chair aside and stand up, the rage linking us together making the air between us crack with tension.

"What are you going to do? Hit me?" I spit out the words, the jagged edges of my heart throbbing painfully, "Do it. Break me into fucking pieces, I don't care."

Vector stares at me but doesn't move from his place across the table. I glare at him, burning a hole through his skull while I wait for him to make a move.

I want him to hurt me.

Then only one of us will be a monster.

"Come on, Vin. Hit me." My voice cracks and tears start to leak out of my eyes, "Show me what it's like to be broken."

Vector walks towards me with slow measured steps. I squeeze my eyes shut once he's within reach and brace myself for impact.

"What is going on in here?" My mother's gasp echoes through the kitchen, "Skylar, honey, did you walk home in the rain?"

I blink my eyes open and see Amber Vin rushing towards me. My brother is two feet away with an unreadable expression on his face.

"You're going to catch a cold in those wet clothes! Why didn't you call me? I could have picked you up."

"I wasn't thinking."

She shakes her head, "Next time call me. Vector, go run and turn the shower on hot for your brother. We need to get him warm."

Amber turns and walks away, the limp in her gait as prominent as the day we brought her home from the hospital. I glance over and see Vector watching her as well, the pained expression on his face identical to the one I'm feeling.

He catches me staring, but before I can say a word, he steps forward and wraps me in a hug. I try to pull away but he doesn't let me. Strong arms pull me tight against him, the soaked state of my clothes starting to soak through his.

"I'll buy you a new sketchbook, Sky. Today is going to be a good day."

Chapter 2

Lacey

"HAPPY BIRTHDAY!"

Trip's jaw drops as she enters the study room, a deep blush hitting her cheeks before she turns to my brother with a scowl.

"You told me you were keeping it low key!"

Wesley grins, popping out his dimples, "I'll take that as a thank you."

Trip rolls her eyes before turning to the rest of us with a shy smile. There's only six of us in the small study room, but Trip gets nervous being the center of attention. Unlike my brother, she struggles to feel comfortable in social situations, although she has come a long way since they started dating last year.

As if reading my thoughts, Stella lets out a shriek and runs over to give her roommate a hug. Cody watches the interaction with a grin, the old lacrosse captain waiting to take his turn to wish the birthday girl a good day.

Nico sighs beside me, the birthday hat pinned to his dark hair perfectly matching the stripped dress shirt he's wearing.

"My idea was so much cooler. I said we should throw a rave in the library."

I pat his shoulder in sympathy, "Your party ideas are legendary, but this is perfect for Trip. I'm surprised Wesley resisted inviting all his friends."

"Babe, that's what happens when you're pussy whipped."

I adjust my party hat and give him a knowing smile, "You're just mad Mo couldn't make it. Where is he anyways?"

Nico sighs, "Working. But at least I'll get to play out my CEO fantasy later."

"Mo's a CEO now?" Cody joins us with a juice box in hand, the tiny carton a comical contrast to the stocky build beneath the plain white t-shirt he's wearing.

"Hell no. My man's a financial advisor but we like to role play."

Wesley lets out a groan, "Dude. What did we say about keeping the sex talk to a minimum? It's disturbing when it's our assistant coach."

"And my older brother." Stella chirps in hopping up on the desk beside Cody and stealing his juice box. Her platinum blonde hair hangs in loose waves, the ends brushing the top of her leggings.

Both the O'Brien siblings are attractive in very different ways. Where Mo is tall and built like a gladiator, Stella is small and lean.

Wesley and me, on the other hand, have been mistaken for twins on countless occasions. I missed out on the dimples, but the midnight-coloured curls and green eyes make it hard to convince people he was adopted.

Nico waves his party blower like it's his royal sceptre, "Taber University is so small it's one giant incestuous pool. You either fuck a friend's sibling or your own."

Cody chokes and Stella slaps him on the back.

Wesley does a full-body shudder, "Too vivid, man. Take it down a notch."

Trip tilts her head thoughtfully, "He's not wrong. We all ended up being related to each other in some way."

"See? This right here is why the birthday girl is my favourite." Nico grins and saunters over to give her a kiss on the cheek, "Happy Birthday, Gorgeous. Thanks for putting up with our class clown."

My brother flips him off and I laugh.

"Can we get to the presents now? I've been dying for her to open them." Stella shimmies on the table, her hands clapping with excitement.

"Presents? You guys didn't need to get me anything."

The flush returns to Trip's cheeks, but before it can give way to discomfort, Wesley swoops in and picks her off the ground. He swings her around, Disney-movie style, and by the time her feet are back on the ground, there's a smile shining in her grey eyes.

"Don't worry, there's only a couple of things for you to unwrap." Wesley grins, planting a kiss on her lips, "Until later anyways."

"Wait. He can talk about sex, but I can't?" Nico sniffs, crossing his arms, "I'm calling double standard."

I lean over and tap his shoulder, "If it makes you feel any better, I just threw up in my mouth."

"That does make me feel better, thank you."

He grins at me, and I can't help but smile back. Wesley and Nico have been best friends since the second grade, but Nico has always been a brother to me as well.

"Quiet down everybody! It's time for the birthday girl to open her presents." Stella claps her hands and Cody stifles a laugh.

Nico raises his hand, "Are we doing the big one or little one first?"

Wesley groans, "Dude. We went over this."

"When did we go over this?"

"Yesterday. You were in the shower, remember?"

"Why would you tell me important details when I'm in the shower? You know that's not when my brain is in active mode."

I catch Trip smothering a giggle across from me. Cody is biting his lip and Stella looks like she's about two seconds away from pummelling the both of them.

"So, when you say the big one first do you mean the actual big one or the other one? Fuck, now I'm confused."

Wesley shakes his head remorsefully, "This is why we can't have nice things."

"Because of me?"

Taking matters into my own hands, I ignore the bickering friends and walk over to the makeshift cupcake display. Nico insisted everything had to match, from the tablecloths to the frosting on the cupcakes, so it took us over two hours to hunt down the appropriate party favours and a plastic tray big enough to hold a dozen cupcakes.

The end result was worth it, though. The High School Musical theme Wesley wanted works perfectly with the small study room, with East High streamers dangling from the light fixtures and cute pictures of Troy and Gabriella taped to the wall.

I grab the white envelope from the table and walk over to where Trip is standing. She doesn't give me a chance to say anything before she pulls me in for a hug.

I smile into her oversized t-shirt, "Happy Birthday, Trip."

"Thanks Lacey." She pulls back and looks at me with a smile, "Are you enjoying your first semester at Taber?"

I hesitate, the truth catching in my throat. I thought moving away from the people who hurt me would help me move on, but so far all I've felt is alone. Besides Nico, the only friend I've made this year is Skylar and we only talk once a week.

Forcing my lips into a smile, I give her a nod, "It's been good. I'm lucky to be here."

Grey eyes scan my face, but before she can respond, Stella lets out an impatient huff, "Can we please get back to the present opening? Wes and Nico, if you two don't stop fighting I'm going to get Cody to kick your ass."

Cody grins, "Newly appointed ass-kicker, at your service."

Trip holds up the envelope I handed her and glances around the room, "Just to be clear, it's okay if I open this one first?"

A chorus of "YES" goes around only for Nico to scrunch his nose.

"So, the little one goes first?"

Stella's eyes start to bulge and Nico throws up his hands, "Just kidding! Rip her up, Trip."

Trip shoots a glance at my brother who gives her an enthusiastic thumbs up. She rolls her eyes and opens the envelope, pulling out two concert tickets.

"What is... OH MY GOD!"

Stella laughs, her body vibrating with excitement, "Do you know what it is?"

Trip nods, tears glistening in her eyes, "*When We Were Young* is the biggest annual rock festival. It's held in Las Vegas every year."

Nico grins, "You know what that means."

Wesley pumps his fist in the air, "We're going to Vegas, baby!"

I laugh, watching the mismatched group celebrate together. There's something beautiful about a group of people who end up together by choice instead of circumstance.

Making myself comfortable on a desk in the corner, I watch the couples intermingle and let my mind wander. As always, I end up thinking about Skylar and the last message she left me.

Pretty is not normally what people say when they find out my name but yes, I do like to draw. I find sketching helps relieve some of the pressure inside me.

By pressure, do you mean anger?

I didn't want to assume, so I thought it would be better to ask the question outright. Skylar had hinted at being familiar with anger in one of our earlier correspondences, so it felt like a safe guess on my part.

I wonder what my friend looks like. Whether she's tall or short, an extravert or an introvert. Maybe she likes reading romance novels like me.

Although she probably doesn't cross out the sex scenes like I do.

Before my train of thought can get any darker, I hop off the desk and wander over to start lighting the candles. I light the first cupcake and pause, a hopeful idea glowing in front of me.

Sneaking a glance over my shoulder, I turn back to the burning candle and make a wish. Blowing it out as fast as I can, I take out the used candle and replace it with a new one before anybody can notice.

Skylar

"Are you an albino or something?"

The man squints at me, his receding hairline blocking my vision as he leans in closer, "Pretty sure white hair and weird eyes make you an albino."

I hold back a sigh and look at my watch. Three more hours until closing.

"I'm not an albino. Is there anything else I can help you with?"

"The hell is wrong with your eyes then?"

"Heterochromia."

"Hetero what?"

I don't bother smothering my sigh this time, "It means I have two different coloured eyes. Now, if that's everything..."

"That's not normal." The man squints at me again, as if he can't comprehend why one iris doesn't match the other.

I stare at him, wondering why strangers feel the need to voice unwanted opinions. My pale hair and mismatched eyes are unusual, but when you compare them to the rest of my life, suddenly they seem pretty mundane.

The man shakes his head, "You gotta get that checked out. Can't be healthy."

"I'll keep that in mind. Are you looking to purchase that?"

Pointing to the piece of shiplap in his hands, I manage to distract him long enough to ring up his order and send him on his way. Pulling up the inventory list, I cross out the latest supply and abandon the till to head towards the warehouse.

Brock's Bolts & Beams is the only hardware store in Silverwood and is run by Brock Jr., the son of the original owner. The store hasn't changed much over the years, the long aisles of wooden panels and hardware supplies are covered with a thick layer of sawdust that has probably been here since the store first opened.

Brock's B&B prides itself on being the town's one-stop-shop for all things construction, so every few feet there's a bin of miscellaneous power tools that you may or may not need to complete your home renovation.

A loud laugh hits my ears when I pull open the door to the back office, Mila's signature cackle bouncing off the bare walls of the tiny room. I slow to a stop when I see who triggered the reaction.

"Hey, Sky." Vector grins at me while Mila bends over, trying to catch her breath. Her dark hair creates a curtain over her face, the outline of her shoulders shaking with laughter.

I don't acknowledge him before turning to my co-worker, "We need to place another order for shiplap. Make a note to call Vipco tomorrow morning."

"Sure thing." Still wheezing, Mila pushes herself back up to standing and gives Vector a beaming smile, "Fuck, you're a riot. You should come around here more often."

He glances at me and smirks, "Maybe."

My shoulders tense as he walks towards me, the height difference giving me the choice to either stare at his chest or tilt my head back to make eye contact.

I choose his chest.

"Why are you here?"

"Always so hostile. Remember when you used to like to see me?"

"Remember when you used to be a good person?"

Mila snorts and a ghost of a smile crosses Vector's face.

"One of these days, little brother, you're going to be grateful for who I turned out to be."

I tilt my head back, finally making eye contact, "Will that be before or after you wind up in jail?"

His lip twitches and I look away. We've both had to make sacrifices over the years but it doesn't seem to weigh him down the way it does me. While my brother seems to cruise through the shit storm that brought us here, it feels as though I've been dropped with the anchor and pretty soon I'm going to run out of air.

Letting out a sigh, I drop my gaze back down to his wide chest.

"Why are you here, Vector?"

"To give you this." Reaching over the desk chair, he grabs a plain plastic bag and passes it to me. I take it without a word and Vector shakes his head.

"That's my cue to leave. My good deed is done for the day."

Mila chortles, coming round the desk to give my brother a hug goodbye. She has to stand on her tiptoes to wrap her arms around his neck, the orange reflection vest hanging loosely over her strapless crop top.

The dress code at Brock's B&B was pretty casual before she started working here, but now it's practically non-existent.

"Don't go soft on us now, Vec. Come back soon, yeah?"

"Just for you, Mila."

Vector takes his leave, letting the door slam shut behind him. My co-worker turns to me with a grin, "He's so hot."

I stare at her, taking in the easy smile, smooth brown skin, and long dark hair. We got together a few months after Mila started working here but it didn't last long. She had her heart set on falling in love with a tragic hero and I fell short.

I had the tragic part down but not the hero.

"You know that's my brother, right?"

She juts out a hip, the skin-tight blue jeans outlining the curve of her waist.

"That doesn't make him any less hot."

"He's a bully."

"He's a hot bully. That makes a difference." Mila flashes me another grin, "I've always loved a good villain."

Guess I wasn't much of a villain either.

"Whatever you say."

I shake my head and wander over to the desk that has definitely been here since the store opened. The bulky wooden frame makes it impossible to move, so we've had to adjust the rest of the room accordingly.

Running my eyes over the stacked papers, I pick up the time sheet that tracks all the employee hours.

"Let me put it to you this way: a hero would charge into battle to save his girl, but a villain would destroy anyone who touches her. Now, which one sounds more romantic to you?"

"Neither. They both sound violent." Flipping the pages until I find my name, I snag a pen from the desk and fill in my allotted time.

Mila flaps her hands, "Wrong answer. Everyone wants a guy who will burn down a kingdom for his true love."

I lift my head, "I didn't realize arson was the new romance standard."

"It's not about the arson, it's about the act itself. Wouldn't you want someone willing to throw away their morals to save you?"

My teeth clamp together, silencing my response.

Even if Mila hadn't been disappointed with my lack of heroic acts, we never would have worked out. She's too idealistic to realize that sometimes the cost of being saved is too high. Sometimes the morals you trade and the secrets you keep don't make you the hero or the villain.

It makes you the monster.

Mila sighs, "Learn to lighten up and have some fun, Sky. It's not good for you to be quiet and moody all the time."

"I'll keep that in mind." Turning on my heel, I leave the room and walk back to my spot by the till.

The plastic bag Vector gave me bumps against my leg as I slide back into the booth. Reaching into the bag, my heart stops as the crisp edges of a brand-new sketchbook greets me.

He bought me a new one.

Just like he promised.

Frowning against the lump in my throat, I flip through the pristine pages, thinking about what my next project is going to be. Normally, I do a collection of drawings related to an overarching theme, one that typically results in gruesome images of unleashed anger and cruel violence. The kind I grew up witnessing.

But I want this one to be different. I want this one to be a step towards a better future. The start of a better me.

And I know exactly what the theme is going to be.

Chapter 3

Lacey

"No more kissing! It's time to leave."

Grabbing my brother's shirt, I have to physically drag him out the door when he tries to go back and give Trip another kiss goodbye. I swear, the amount of PDA these two perform on each other is enough to make a nun nauseous.

Wesley laughs, finally following me out the door, "Pop a chill pill, Lace. Your session doesn't start for another hour."

"You know I like to be there early."

He clasps his hands together in prayer, "Thou shall not miss the companionship of thou garden."

"Whatever, Shakespeare."

Holding back a laugh, I follow him out of the residence building and towards the parking lot. To make sure I have time to read and write a response to Skylar, I always make sure my therapy ride gets me there fifteen minutes early. Given my natural obsession with flora, it wasn't hard to convince Wesley that every week I needed the extra time to admire Karen's flower garden.

I'm not sure why I haven't told anyone about the sunshine tissues Skylar leaves me. Starting a friendship with another therapy patient is nothing to be ashamed of, and a part of me is proud of the progress I've made since our correspondence began. Skylar makes it so easy to open up that it finally feels like these therapy sessions are working.

I guess a part of me wants to keep Skylar to myself for a little while longer. This is the first friend I've made without Wesley or Nico's help, and I don't want to do anything that puts our newfound friendship in jeopardy.

"Lola, you sexy beast! It's been too long."

Wesley purrs as we approach the godawful car my brother inherited on his sixteenth birthday. The old Ford's bumper is hanging on by zip ties and there's duct tape holding most of the ceiling together, but that has never impaired Wesley's love for the vehicle.

Personally, I think Lola's a bitch. The few times I borrowed her, she did everything she could to make my life miserable. She even went as far as to release the parking brake the one time I decided to park on a hill.

After that panic-filled day, I stopped asking to drive my brother's rust bucket.

"She's uglier than the last time I saw her."

Wesley gasps, "Don't listen to her, Lola. You're just as beau-tiful as the day I got you."

Using his sneaker to kick the door seal, he yanks the door handle until Lola pries herself open. I wince at the metallic screech, the rust flying off the door making me wish I was brave enough to ride the bus.

Wesley runs a loving hand over the dented roof, "Lola just needs some tough love to get going, that's all."

"Uh huh."

I wait for my brother to get in and kick open my passenger door from the inside. The handle nearly comes off in my hands when the door finally creaks open. I climb in with a smile.

"Don't say it." Wesley looks at me with pleading eyes, "What-ever you do, don't say it."

"Okay."

He sighs, "Thank you."

"Did you know they make cars that have working doors? Sometimes they even have keys that can lock the car from the outside."

Wesley groans and knocks his head against the steering wheel, "Every. Time."

I widen my eyes innocently, "Apparently there's even cars that start before you even get inside! Can you imagine?"

"Nope. I cannot imagine."

My brother winces as he turns the ignition and the car shud-ders beneath us. Nothing happens for a good ten seconds before the ancient beast roars to life and he jerks the gear stick into drive.

I can't help opening my mouth one more time as Lola groans her way out of the parking lot, "I heard there's even cars that can parallel park by themselves."

"I'm tuning you out now."

My heart is pounding with anticipation by the time we pull up to the nondescript building in Silverwood.

"Thanks for the ride. Love you, bye!"

I go racing out of the car the second we pull to a stop. My feet propel me along the gravel path towards the vibrant bellflowers running alongside Karen's front entrance.

Veering off the trail, I slow my vigorous pace and scan the beautiful garden for the unmistakable flash of yellow. Karen does a lovely job with her front garden, the bright flowers add a splash of colour to an otherwise bland backdrop, but I don't pay the flora any attention as I hunt for the sunshine tissue.

The usual hiding spot turns up empty and my heart starts to sink. Maybe this will be the week Skylar doesn't respond.

No. She wouldn't do that to me.

Refusing to give up, I drop to my knees and start pushing aside roots and fallen leaves, looking for another crack in the flower bed where Skylar always hides the tissues.

It has to be here.

It has to be.

Panic starts to replace my determination as my hands grow muddy and the damp grass starts to seep through my jeans. Tears start to build up and I desperately blink them away, refusing to believe that another person would let me down.

"Lacey? Are you alright?"

A warm hand touches my shoulder and I jerk away. The first tear that hits my cheek feels like a sign of defeat and it doesn't take long for more to follow.

"Lacey, what's wrong?" Karen peers at me, her concerned gaze bouncing from me to the mess I made of her garden, "Did you lose something?"

A hiccup escapes me as I hunch over, trying to protect myself from the outside world as the broken organ inside my chest starts to weep.

"Come on, dear. Let's get you inside and cleaned up."

I let Karen pull me to my feet and guide me towards the entrance. We walk through the small office that doubles as Karen's workstation and the cozy living room, but I don't register any of it as she gets me settled on the couch pushed up against the far wall.

Skylar abandoned me.

My only friend abandoned me.

Pressing my lips together to keep them from trembling, I cast a watery gaze over the living room that takes up one hour of my week, every week. The same grandfather clock chimes in the righthand corner and the same glass table separates the couch from the chair directly across from me. The box of sunshine tissues sits proudly on the table and my shoulders start to shake.

I'm just about to start sobbing when a yellow square catches my eye.

"What's that?"

I point towards the sunshine tissue that's lying on the side table next to Karen's chair. Adjusting her long, flowing skirt before sitting down, Karen gives me a light laugh.

"Oh, I found this tucked in my flower bed. I think someone must have lost it on the way out."

My heart stops as I register her words. Blinking until my vision clears, I clear my throat and try to keep my hopes from soaring.

"Can I have it?"

Karen blinks, "You want a used tissue? My dear, I don't think that's sanitary."

"I won't use it. I just want the message on it."

"Oh." Blinking a few more times, Karen shakes her head and gives me a warm smile, "Well, of course! We all need a little inspiration sometimes, don't we?"

I nod, "A special message can go a long way."

My damp jeans creak when I stand up and walk around to the side table. The quote of the day screams back at me in bold writing.

Every moment is a fresh beginning.

Holding my breath, I carefully lift it up and turn it around.

I'm not a pretty person, Lacey. I come from a family of angry men and as much as I wish I could say it skipped a generation, I can't. That's the real reason I'm here every Friday, talking to Karen.

A new onslaught of tears hit me as relief floods my veins. Clutching the tissue to my chest, my cheeks grow damp as I return to my spot on the couch.

"Thank you." I whisper the words and Karen looks at me in alarm.

"You can take as many tissues as you want, Lacey. There's no need to only take one."

I shake my head, feeling the ache in my chest slowly begin to fade.

"This is the one I want. Thank you."

Skylar

Something's missing.

I study the sketch in front of me, the sharp edges of the purple flowers drawing my attention to the garden that sits outside Karen's building. The overcast sky casts a shadow over the figure crouching in front of the garden.

Lightly running my pencil over the scene, I shade in the drizzle of rain to darken the sky.

"Are you still alive?" A sharp knock hits my door before Vector pokes his head inside, "Dinner is ready. Oh, and you're coming to my party tomorrow."

"I'll be down in a second."

Tilting my sketchbook, I try and look at it from another angle.

"So, you'll be at BEATS tomorrow night?" Pushing his way inside, Vector comes up behind me, "New project?"

"No to the first question, yes to the second."

He sighs and drops onto my bed, "Stop being a buzzkill, Sky. Come out with the team tomorrow."

"I can't be a buzzkill if I don't go out."

Vector shoots me a glare, "You're an antagonistic bastard, you know that, right?"

Choosing not to answer, I return to the paper in front of me. My bed squeaks as Vector hauls himself back up and wanders over to annoy me.

"Come out with us tomorrow and I'll tell you what's missing."

I narrow my eyes at him, "How can you tell something's missing?"

Vector flashes his teeth, "Because I'm brilliant. Now, what are you going to do tomorrow?"

He's bluffing. I'm sure of it.

But if he's not...

"Fine. I'll go out with you tomorrow." My shoulders slump with defeat and Vector claps me on the back.

"That's what I like to hear." He points at my sketchbook, "It needs more colour. Add some more flowers but make them blue or something. Maybe yellow."

Yellow. That's it.

Reaching for my colour pencils, the rest of the world fades away as I add the simple blot of yellow that's become my favourite part of each week. The addition is so small and yet the boldness of the colour makes the whole piece come together.

Just like what Lacey does to me.

"Not what I was suggesting but I guess it works." Vector's voice jolts me out of my thoughts and I quickly put the sketchbook down.

"What time are we going out tomorrow?"

He raises a brow, "Look who's getting excited to go out like a normal person."

"More like I need time to prepare myself."

"Well, review how to socialize with people." He gives me a harsh look, "Don't do your usual sulking in the corner, Sky. It's embarrassing."

I shrug, "Now you know how I feel."

"You're fucking impossible." A glimmer of anger flashes through his eyes but it burns out before it can spark, "Find yourself a bitch to take home tomorrow and maybe it will snap you out of this funk."

I stare back at him, watching the tension roll through his body. My attention snags on the muscles straining against his t-shirt, making me think back to a time when life was darker but so much simpler.

"Don't talk about women like that." Standing up, I brush past him on my way to the door, "Mom's waiting. Let's go eat."

"Can you miss someone you've never met?"

I voice the question as I pass the clean dish to my mother. By the time we finished dinner, Vector had snuck off to hang out with his lacrosse buddies and left me to clean up his mess once again.

Amber tilts her head, "Is this a theoretical question or is there someone special you've been talking to?"

"Forget I asked."

"No! I love these types of questions. Makes me feel like a young person again." She winks and takes the plate from my hands, "I just love being nosy as well."

I glance over and take in the kind eyes sparkling back at me. My brother inherited her pale blue eyes, I got her cheekbones, but neither of us got her dark hair.

Sometimes I wonder whether it hurts, knowing that both her children took after the abusive man she married.

She gives me a gentle nudge on the shoulder, "I think everything depends on circumstances, but yes, I do believe it's possible to miss someone you've never met. Sometimes the most powerful connections come from strangers we meet once and never see again."

The thought puts a frown on my face.

"But that would mean I'll never stop missing her."

"Aha! I knew there was someone special." My mother grins, "Anyone I know? A girl from school, maybe?"

"No." I plunge my hands back into the soapy water, "And no more questions or I'm abandoning dish duty."

"You wouldn't hurt your mother like that."

She's teasing but the words are like a punch in the gut. Dropping my gaze to the dishes floating in the sink, I don't have to look at her smiling face to know what I'll see.

The bump on her nose from when my father broke it.

The scar on her upper lip from when he backhanded her.

The lines of scar tissue on her forearm from when she fell on broken glass.

And those are only the ones I've seen. Who knows how many scars my father left on her body over their ten-year marriage.

"Can I at least get a name?" Amber taps her scarred lip in thought, "How long have you been talking?"

"Mom. I said no more questions."

She laughs and throws her arms around me, "Okay, I'll stop for now. But if things get serious, promise you'll bring her home to meet me?"

I sigh, letting her pull me in for a hug, "Her name is Lacey. And I'll think about."

"Ooh, what a pretty name."

It is a pretty name. One that I haven't been able to stop thinking about since she told me. I don't know anything about this girl besides the tidbit she shared on the tissues, but there's something special about her. Something different.

I just hope that when the time comes, she won't be disappointed with who I turn out to be.

Not a hero or a villain, but me.

Chapter 4

Lacey

"Should we invite your roommate?"

"Why the hell would we do that?"

"It seems rude *not* to invite her."

"I'm sure she's busy. Plus, she hates going out. I hear her complain to her annoying friend every time he drags her out to any sort of event."

The voices drift from the living room and my cheeks flush with embarrassment. Do they not know I can hear every word they're saying?

Cecelia's gruff voice drifts through my walls, "Whatever. Let's invite her and be done with it."

"Wait. Is this the virgin?"

"Well, she doesn't bring any boys home, so..." Snickers fill the air and I bite down on my lip to keep from shouting a response.

My roommate has never been the nicest person, but I didn't think she would talk shit about me to her friends.

I guess I can't blame her. I've put in little to no effort to get to know her, so it's only natural for a person to make assumptions.

Even with my rationale, my cheeks are still flushed with embarrassment when I answer the knock on my bedroom door. Cecelia greets me with a scowl that hasn't gotten any friendlier since the first day I moved in.

"My friends and I are going to a party tonight. Do you want to come?" She hooks a thumb over her shoulder, "Ava has agreed to DD, so the ride part is covered."

"Thanks for the offer but I've got some reading to do."

"I figured as much." Rolling her eyes, Cecelia turns and looks at the girl lounging on our dorm couch.

"See? I told you she wouldn't come."

The redhead gives me a wave, her pale skin and mass of freckles surprisingly cute, "I'm Maren. Nice to meet you."

On the couch opposite her, the girl with bleached dreadlocks doesn't bother lifting her gaze from her phone, "Ava."

"Uh, hi. I'm Lacey." I give Maren a small smile before turning back to my roommate who's busy lacing up her combat boots.

"I hope you have a good time tonight."

Maren pipes up from the couch, "Oh, we will. BEATS is supposed to be a million times better than the club here in Taber."

"BEATS?"

"It's Silverwood's hotspot." Ava looks up from her phone, "The lacrosse team is throwing a party tonight."

Pausing my trek back to the safety of my bedroom, I look at the girls, "You're going to Silverwood tonight?"

"That's right. We're heading into enemy territory." Maren lets out a hoot and Ava rolls her eyes.

"The rivalry between our schools is so dumb. Who watches sports anyway?"

Cecelia snorts, "Everyone except you, dumbass."

Ava flips her off and Maren lets out a laugh. Heart pounding in my ears, I go ahead and open my mouth.

"I'll come."

The room falls silent as they all turn to look at me. Clearing my throat, I try again, "If the invitation is still open, I would love to go out with you tonight."

Maren claps her hands, "Hell yeah! Welcome to the wild side, Lacey."

Ava nods her approval while Cecelia eyes me suspiciously.

"What changed your mind?"

Wiping my suddenly sweaty palms on my jeans, I give her a nonchalant shrug, "I've got a friend in Silverwood. Maybe she'll be there."

"Fine. But you better go change. We can't have your nun appearance chasing the guys away."

Ava snickers and I feel my cheeks heat up again. Walking back into my bedroom, I close the door and lean against it. Taking a moment to summon my courage, I shake the insecurities away and walk over to my little library. I pull out the hidden envelope and steal the sunshine tissue from inside.

It's time to make my wish a reality.

Clutching the tissue to my chest, I blow out a breath before walking over to my closest and picking out an outfit that won't send the guys running.

Not that I'm going to Silverwood to find a guy.

I'm going to find my friend Skylar.

"I call dibs on the Vin brothers." Cecelia lets out a drunken cackle from the passenger seat and Maren groans beside me.

"You can't have both!"

"Hell yeah, I can. Take your pick from the rest of the litter."

Ava snaps her fingers from the driver's seat, "She called dibs but if the Vin boys aren't in the mood for Cecelia's spunk then it's fair game."

My roommate thinks it over for a moment before nodding. "Deal."

I stare out the window, watching the prairie fields fly by. The sun has started to set, creating a gorgeous backdrop against the Rocky Mountains in the distance.

"Who are the Vin brothers?"

Maren's jaw drops while Cecelia shifts in her seat to look at me.

"You haven't heard of Vector Vin? The guy who put our captain in the hospital last year?"

I pause, thinking about Wesley's first lacrosse tournament. Cody had ended up in the hospital, but I hadn't paid much attention to who was responsible.

Actually, that's a lie. I think I remember Stella ranting about Silverwood's infamous bully.

Ava shakes her head, "I heard they grew up in an abusive household. Apparently, Vector had to kill the father so they could get out."

Maren sighs, "I love a tragic backstory."

I stare at her in horror, "Domestic abuse is not a romance trope. These are real people you're talking about."

Cecelia rolls her eyes, "Don't be so high and mighty, roomie. Mare was just joking."

"No, she's right." Maren looks at me with glazed eyes, the three drinks she had back at the dorm well underway, "I'm sorry, I shouldn't have said that. Do you forgive me?"

I give her a tight smile, "Nothing to forgive."

"The white hair is kind of hot, though." Maren giggles and lets out a hiccup, "Reminds me of President Snow."

"Fuck the white hair, what about the muscles on Vector?" Cecelia lets out a whistle, "That man can fuck me seven ways to Sunday."

Ava snickers and I go back to staring out the window. Reaching into my coat pocket, I trace the edges of the soft material with my fingertips.

Even if Skylar isn't there tonight, I'll find a way to meet her. "WE'RE HERE!"

Leaning away from the drunk banshee, I look out the windshield and watch the overflowing parking come into view. The place is so crowded already that people are parking on the empty plots of land nearby. Following their lead, Ava pulls off the main street and drives along the bumpy dirt road until an empty space comes up.

"I'm so excited I might pee myself." Maren gives me a toothy grin, "Do you have toilet paper by any chance?"

"If you piss in my car, you're paying to have it detailed." Ava shifts the car into park and turns around to look at us, "Time for some ground rules, ladies."

Cecelia rolls her eyes, "Here we go."

"Shut it. We have a newbie here who doesn't know the DDD."

I blink, "Is that a new term for designated driver?"

Ava flicks a bleached dreadlock over her shoulder, "It stands for Designated Driver Discipline. Meaning, if you don't follow my rules, I'll kick your ass."

Maren reaches over and pats my hand, "She's only had to do that once, and the girl had it coming. You'll be just fine."

I gulp and turn my attention back to the driver.

"There's only three rules you have to remember. First, if you're going home with a guy, I don't want to know about it. Second, under no circumstances will I be driving a guy home for you."

Cecelia nods in agreement, "Don't burden a hoe with a bro. I'll make sure to text the group chat."

"And third, if you need a ride home, meet back at this car by 1 AM. I don't plan on making my morning class tomorrow but driving after 2 AM gives me the creeps."

Maren draws a cross on her chest, "So creepy."

Feeling more than a little overwhelmed, I awkwardly raise my hand. It bumps against the car's low ceiling and I quickly pull it back down.

"What happens if we need a ride and its past 1 AM?"

Ava grins, "You're on your own, bitch."

Good to know.

"Enough chitchat, let's hunt down those varsity players!"

Cecelia hoots and hurls herself from the car.

The rest of us hop out and follow the swarm of university students heading towards the only establishment open at this time of night. The small, square building doesn't look like much from the outside, but the glowing BEATS sign and bass pumping from the open doors is enough to convince me we're in the right place.

The late fall air bites my skin as we race across the street, the thin material of my camisole and short skirt doing nothing to help my cause. The line moves swiftly and pretty soon we're handing over our IDs to the bouncer who gives each of us an appraising glance.

"You ladies are far from home tonight."

The burly man tilts his head towards the Taber University lanyard hanging from Ava's keys.

Cecelia throws him a wink, "Thought we'd see what the other side has to offer."

A faint smile crosses his face before he steps aside and lets us pass. I shiver as a blast of heat hits us, the humid scent of sweat-soaked bodies hitting me immediately. Squinting against the dim lighting, a sea of unfamiliar faces stare back at me and another shiver goes through me.

We're definitely not in Taber anymore.

Skylar

"All you gotta do is follow my example, Baby Vin, and you'll be just fine."

Walsh, one of my brother's teammates, gives me a sleazy smile and I lean away. Out of all the Saber players, he isn't the worst, but the guy has a seriously bad habit of harassing women. Especially when he's drunk.

"I'm fine, thanks."

He grins, shooting me with his finger, "You already got the first step down. Confidence is key especially when the bitch doesn't know she wants to go home with you yet."

I stare at him, deadpan, "Maybe you should find someone who wants to go home with you in the first place."

My brother shoots me a warning look from his spot at the bar. The night has just begun, but there's already a lacrosse bunny in his lap, running her painted claws through his hair while two more linger nearby. If I had to guess their names, I'd choose the ones ending in "i."

"You're kind of funny, Baby Vin. But you need to learn how to smile more." Walsh frowns at me, his glazed eyes bouncing from me to the girls nearby, "Nobody likes a moody bitch."

I shrug, "It's better than being a bitch who pressures drunk girls into sex."

"Skylar." Vector snaps his teeth and the girl in his lap nearly falls off, "Enough."

The lacrosse players around us snicker until my brother levels them with a glare. I sigh, turning away from the group and scanning the crowded room. The vaulted ceiling helps to make the place seem a lot bigger than it actually is, but that doesn't stop the owners from pumping as many university students in here as possible.

My eyes sweep along the room, taking in the couples groping each other on the dance floor while old men leer from nearby tables. It's disgusting, looking at this place from a sober point of view, but I guess this is how some people escape reality for a little while.

"Hey, Vec. There's word going around some Taber Tigers just showed up." A freshman steps forward with a grin, his rookie status placing him as the low man on the totem pole, "And it's a group of girls."

Murmurs go around the group and a flash of interest lights up my brother's face.

"Some cubs came to play, did they?" He smiles, "Let's give them a warm welcoming."

The girl sitting on his lap lets out a cry of protest when he stands up, forcing her to stumble back onto her own two feet. The freshman snickers and offers Vector another grin.

"No need to go chasing, Vin. They're coming this way."

He points to a group of four girls idling around the bar.

The small redhead seems to be the drunkest of them all, her flushed face and flailing arms giving away an intoxication level that probably shouldn't have been reached tonight. A girl with blonde dreadlocks is standing nearby, typing on her phone, while the one with green hair stares directly in our direction. I fight back a flinch when her predatory gaze lands on me.

Walsh lets out a whistle, "Check out the legs on Miss Skirt. I've always wanted to fuck a model."

I turn my attention to the tallest member of the group. The girl's midnight curls cascade down her back, bringing out the lavender colour of her top and the creamy shade of her skin. I can't determine the colour of her eyes from here, but I can tell from the way she keeps scanning the crowd that she's looking for someone.

I blow out a breath I hadn't realized I was holding. All the girls in the group are attractive, but this one is another level.

She's exquisite.

I'm not the only one who thinks so based on the looks she keeps getting from the guys lingering around the bar. Even if rumour hadn't gotten out these girls were from Taber, everyone would have known they don't belong.

She's got the kind of face you don't forget.

"Game face, fellas. Let's make sure our rivals get the authentic Silverwood experience."

The varsity team lets out a cheer and Vector sits back on his barstool, pulling the two remaining lacrosse bunnies closer. They respond accordingly, giggling and leaning into his embrace to help paint the picture of who holds the power in this town.

Dropping my gaze, I turn and walk away, refusing to condemn the throne my brother sits on.

I slip into the crowd, the rowdy chatter of the lacrosse team just beginning to fade when the girl with green hair steps out in front of me.

"Skylar, right?"

She smiles, drawing my attention to her harsh features, "I'm a big fan."

"You've got the wrong brother. The lacrosse player is that way." Jerking my thumb over my shoulder, I'm about to walk away when she grabs my arm.

"Actually, it was you I was hoping to get to know better." She runs a finger up my arm, causing my body to tense, "Your eyes are really something."

"You've got the wrong idea. I don't do one-night stands."

"If you perform well maybe we can make it more than one night."

She grins and I can only stare at her. She wants to fuck someone who doesn't even know her name.

"Sorry. Not interested." Pulling my arm from her grasp, I give her a shrug, "Maybe lead with your name next time."

The girl rolls her eyes, "Whatever dude. You should hit up my roommate so you two can lose your virginity together."

"Cecelia, be nice!" The redhead appears and gives me an apologetic smile, "I'm so sorry! She's not normally this mean, she's just in a mood tonight."

She gives me an obvious once-over and my shoulders stiffen.

"You're really cute, though. Just thought you should know."

I stare back, seeing the kindness in her face that Cecelia lacked. Most guys love a girl who isn't interested in emotional attachment but I find those encounters makes me feel used.

Unseen.

"Have a good night." I duck my head, trying to disappear into the crowd as quickly as possible.

Laughter and flirty banter echoes around me as I hunt for a quiet place to catch my breath. The club's small dance floor is already packed with sweaty bodies grinding against each other while a deafening rap song pumps through the speakers overhead.

I duck past the side exit that doubles as the smoke pit and find a small corner tucked away in the shadows.

Leaning against the wall, I breathe in a moment of peace and watch the Silverwood students mingle around me. A girl shrieks with laughter when her partner picks her up and swings her around, and the careless joy on her face puts an unexpected ache in my chest.

There's only one girl I want to see tonight and I don't even know what she looks like.

Chapter 5

Lacey

This was my worst idea ever.

For all I know, Skylar could be a middle-aged woman with two kids and a barn cat. I have no clue what she looks like or whether she's even a university student. My chances of finding her at this overcrowded bar are slim to none.

Not to mention, it's insane in here. BEATS must not have a limited capacity because the place has been packed for the last hour and people just keep pouring through the doors. I lost my girl group about twenty minutes in, so now I look like the bumbling idiot who decided to roll up to the rival's club alone.

Off to a great start, Lacey.

Taking a deep breath, I approach a group of girls chatting amongst themselves at the tabletop bar. I paste a smile on my face and tap the shoulder of the blonde sitting closest to me.

"Sorry to interrupt, but I was wondering if you could help me find my friend. Her name is-

"Aren't you a little far from home?"

I hesitate, trying not to be intimidated by the menace in her gaze.

"Well, yes, but you see-

"Maybe you should go back to Taber." A dark-skinned girl sitting nearby shifts in her chair to sneer, "We don't like cubs here in Silverwood."

I laugh awkwardly, clutching my purse like it's a lifeline.

"Oh, I'm not here to stay. I'll be gone in a couple of hours."

"Can you make it sooner?" The blonde tilts her head, "Everyone would really appreciate it. Your friend included, I'm sure."

I stumble back like she hit me. Blinking fast, I'm scrambling to come up with a dignified response when a smooth voice flows over me.

"Ladies. That's not how we treat special guests, now is it?"

A dark-haired guy steps forward and flashes me a smile, "What's your name, Beautiful?"

"Uh, Lacey." The blonde narrows her eyes at me and I quickly turn on my heel, "Thank you for your help but I need to go."

"Woah! Where are you running off to? We were just getting to know each other."

The guy goes to grab my arm but I jump out of reach. Full blown panic hits my system as I scan the crowd, desperately hoping Cecelia and her friends are somewhere nearby.

I can't be alone with a guy like this.

Not again.

"I think we got off on the wrong foot. I'm Walsh." The guy smiles and takes another step towards me. I take another step back.

"Nice to meet you. Now, I really must be going-

"Who are you looking for?" His eyes bore into mine and I clutch my purse tighter. The sunshine tissue is probably crushed beyond repair by this point, but there's nothing I can do about that now.

"You said you were looking for a friend. I can help you find them." Walsh tilts his head, his gaze dropping from my face to my legs, "I would really love to help you."

"I don't need any help. Please go away." My voice comes out muffled, the warning bells blaring through my head creating a sound barrier.

He grins and takes another step closer. I go to take another step back but the edge of the bar stops me. My lungs stop working as the realization hits me.

I'm trapped.

"Is your friend as pretty as you? Maybe we could all have fun together." Walsh leans in and I freeze, paralyzed by the memories breaking through my conscious.

"Stop." I whisper, trapped in the past that broke me the first time, "Please stop."

"But we haven't done anything yet."

He's so close I can smell the alcohol on his breath.

"Walsh, baby, I thought we were hooking up tonight."

The sultry voice steals his attention and the moment he turns his head, I feel the spell break. Holding my purse as tightly as I can, I bring up my knee. Hard.

"What the fu-

Walsh keels over in pain and I shove past him, sprinting for the closest exit sign. I push through the line of Saber students still waiting to get inside and don't stop running until I reach the parking lot.

Come on, Lacey. You either love me or you don't. It's that simple.

I do love you I just don't think I'm ready. Not yet.

I guess that's an answer in itself.

"STOP!" I scream into the night and collapse on the ground. Nausea rises up in my throat as my shoulders start to shake and the memories pull me back into the darkness.

That's not fair. I do want to do this with you, but can't we wait just a little while longer?

This whole time I've been waiting for you, Lacey. Can't you see how unfair it is to ask me to wait even more?

But it's only been six months. I turned sixteen a couple of months ago.

So now you're guilting me? I see how it is.

No, that's not what I meant-

Look, I'm going to make this simple. Either show me how much you love me or I'm gone.

Can't we just talk about this?

I'm tired of talking. All we do is talk. At this point we're basically friends. You make me feel pathetic.

That's not what I want.

Then show me what you want, Lacey. Show me how much you want me.

I curl up in a ball, right there on the uneven concrete, and cry. I cry until there's no tears left and then I cry some more. My skin starts to itch from the salty residue but my body keeps going. Even when my soul is broken, my body has always kept going.

My breathing starts to come in short bursts, the telltale sign I'm hyperventilating my way to a panic attack, but I don't care. I don't belong here.

I don't belong anywhere.

My purse tumbles to the ground beside me, the contents spilling out in front of my face. The bright yellow tissue hits my blurry gaze and I reach for it, grabbing on to the one thing that keeps me going.

The one person who makes me feel less alone.

Sucking down chunks of air, I start to reign myself back in using Skylar's calligraphy as a focus point. Gradually, my shoulders stop shaking and the tears run dry. I rub my cheeks to stop the itching and start collecting my things from the ground.

A bitter laugh slips out when I see the colourful romance novel lying on the dirty concrete. I pick it up and make my way back to Ava's parked car. The reflection of the darkened windows tells me all I need to know about my makeup's survival, so I do my best to clean up the mess. Giving my semi-decent reflection a sad smile, I make myself comfortable on the ground and open my book.

It might be fictional but at least in this world there are no broken girls.

Skylar

"What happened to you?"

I watch in amusement as Walsh limps his way past the dance floor. His usual charisma is gone and his boyish good looks seem to have vanished along with it.

"The model fucking bagged me." He snaps his teeth, an un-flattering scowl crossing his face, "That bitch lured me in then cock shot me."

"The only person who lures around here is you."

"Fuck you, Skylar. Can't you see I'm in agony here?" Walsh groans and cups his package over his jeans, "I think she broke my dick."

I shrug, "If you learned how to respect women maybe you'd be walking right now."

"Would it kill you to be more sympathetic?" He groans again and hunches over, "Shit. I think I need to go to the hospital."

"The fuck is your problem, Walsh?" A blonde rookie walks by and claps him on the back, "You're gonna need a mirror if you're trying to see your asshole."

Walsh flips off the freshman before looking at me, "I think I need the ER."

Ignoring his pleas for help, I turn and look back over the crowded bar. It's getting close to midnight and the students are getting drunker and sloppier by the hour.

"Baby Vin, I'm serious. You need to take me to the ER."

I flick my eyes back to his pained expression.

"Consider this to be your first lesson of consent."

He bares his teeth, "If Lacey hadn't fucked up my body, I would fucking break you. I wouldn't even care that your brother would come for me. Seeing your pathetic head snap back would be worth it."

My vision darkens as I turn and press a hand against his chest.

"What did you just say?

He laughs, "I said I'd fucking break your weak ass."

"No. Before that." My breathing grows shallow, "What did you say her name was?"

"Huh? Oh, Lacey but that's not the point-

I'm already gone by the time he finishes the threat. Heart pounding out of my chest, I start running through the crowd, searching for the dark-haired girl I saw earlier. *Lacey.*

My mystery girl.

I push my way onto the dance floor, scoping out the faces in search of the one I want. The longer I search, the stronger my anxiety grows.

I can't let her slip through my fingers.

Not when we were this close.

"Have you seen a girl in a purple top?" I grab the closest person to me, a familiar face from a couple of my art classes.

The guy blinks, shock written all over his face, "Since when do you talk to me?"

"That's not important. Have you seen her?"

"Don't think so."

I turn away, already moving on to the next person of inquiry. My question is met by blank stare after blank stare, but I keep going, pushing past the silence that has kept me safe all these years to find the one person who means everything.

The flower that brings colour to my darkness.

"Have you seen the dark-haired Taber girl? Tall, wearing a purple top?"

"No, I heard she was hot though. Let me know if you find her."

A headache starts to form as I work my way around the bar. Socializing with strangers is at the bottom of my shit list, and with every disappointing answer, my nonexistent social battery drops a little lower.

I'm almost completely burnt out when green hair catches my eye. I pivot and almost crash into the perpetrator herself.

"Watch where you're going." Cecelia bares her teeth and I take a cautionary step back.

"I'm looking for Lacey. Have you seen her?"

She narrows her eyes, "What do you want with her?"

I open my mouth to respond, but she cuts me off, "Actually, I don't care. Just don't drop her back home crying. God knows she does enough of that already."

"Don't talk about her that way." My teeth snap together as a thread of anger weaves through me, "She's your roommate and my friend. Show some respect."

Cecelia's eyes widen and she takes a step back. Shame quickly replaces the anger when I see the fear in her eyes.

"I didn't mean to snap at you. Please, can you tell me where she is?"

She sighs, "I have no idea where she is, but if I had to guess, she probably escaped to go read somewhere. That girl always has a book in her hand."

"Thank you."

I watch her disappear into the crowd, my mind racing to think of a quiet spot Lacey could have found. One immediately springs to mind and I go running for the side door.

A brisk breeze slaps my face, the refreshing break from the bar's humidity ruined by the cigarette smoke filling the air. Holding back a cough, I start walking around the small smoke pit, the flickering overhead lights making it look like a scene from a horror movie. I blink through the haze, peering at every face I pass by.

The adrenalin starts to fade when I reach the end of the section and look at the couple making out in the corner.

"Have you seen a girl in a purple top? Long dark hair? Might have been holding a book?"

The guy breaks away from his partner and gives me a smile.

"Sounds like a special one."

I blow out a breath, "Can you answer the question?"

"Nah, we haven't seen her, have we babe?"

The girl tilts her head, mulling it over, "Is she the one from Taber University?"

I nod, feeling my spirits skyrocket.

She grins, "I heard she shoved Walsh's balls back up where they belong."

"He had it coming."

"Definitely. That man has been a creep since freshman year." She pulls a cigarette out of her flannel pocket and fiddles with it, "But to answer your question, no, I haven't seen her. If you find her, be sure to pass my thanks along."

The last bit of hope drains from my body. Numbness washes over me as I turn and walk back towards the doors.

I lost her.

My mystery girl was here in Silverwood and I fucking lost her.

Stumbling past the chain smokers, I'm about to slip back inside when a firm hand grips my shoulder.

"Stamp, please." The bouncer flicks his eyes to my wrist, "You need a stamp to get back inside."

My gaze drops to my bare wrist. *Shit.*

In my rush to find Lacey, I forgot to get a re-entry stamp.

"I don't have one."

"Then you'll have to get back in line."

He points to the front entrance where students are lined up around the block. There's only an hour or so left until closing, so there's no way I'm getting back inside before it shuts down.

The burly man rolls his shoulders and subtly shifts into defensive position. I stare at him, wondering how many fights have broken out because of a missing stamp.

Probably too many.

"Okay." I take my leave before he can respond.

The echo of my shoes slapping the pavement gradually gets louder the farther I get from the club. I stare at the ground the entire walk to the parking lot, the weight of what I lost pressing down on me.

Pulling out my keys, I'm about to unlock my car when a sudden movement catches my eye. I jerk to the side, expecting one of my brother's goons to jump out at me, but no one does.

I wait five seconds, ten seconds, but nothing happens. Trying to calm my racing heart, I peer around the side of my car and squint into the darkness. The shift happens again, but this time I can see its someone sitting on the ground.

Curiosity drives my feet forward until I'm close enough to see the person using their phone flashlight to look at something. The light moves again and suddenly I get a clear shot of the person's lavender tank top.

My throat goes dry as my heart stops.

It's her.

Chapter 6

Lacey

"Lacey?"

I glance up from my book and find a guy standing a few feet away. Shining my flashlight in his direction, I catch a glimpse of loose jeans and a blue button-down shirt.

There's probably a cautionary tale about a girl reading alone in a parking lot somewhere, but for some reason, I don't feel afraid.

Maybe it's his voice. This guy's got a really nice voice.

"Do I know you?"

I wince, knowing with absolute certainty that's the question that gets you featured on a true crime podcast.

"Sorry, that came off as rude." Closing my book, I hug my knees closer into my chest, "It's been a long night."

He goes to take a step forward then pauses.

"Is it okay if I come closer?"

My skin is dry and irritated from my earlier tears and yet this one simple question puts a warm glow back in my heart.

"Go ahead."

He takes three steps then stops. There's still five feet of space between us, but he doesn't make a move to come any closer. My shoulders drop in relief.

"I don't really know how to say this." He shuffles his feet, never taking his eyes off my face, "But I think you might be the person I've been writing to for the last few weeks."

I blink and he gives me a shy smile.

"I'm Skylar."

My mouth opens and closes but no words come out. Skylar shoves his hands into his pockets and drops his gaze.

"I know I'm probably not what you were expecting."

The disappointment in his voice has me sitting upright.

"No, it's just... you're a guy?" Stating the obvious like the idiot I am, I can't stop the rest from falling out, "I thought you were a middle-aged woman with a barn cat."

He tilts his head, "Did I give off lonely cat vibes in my letters?"

Laughter bubbles up and slips past my lips, "I think we were both giving depressing cat vibes."

"Not wrong." Skylar gestures towards the spot across from me, "May I?"

I wave my hand like I'm not sitting in a dirty parking lot, "Make yourself at home."

Watching him like a creeper, my heart starts to race as I register the two facts I grossly overlooked.

Skylar is a boy.

Skylar is a very cute boy.

My cheeks flush when I think about all the secrets I shared. Skylar made it so easy to open up that I just assumed he was a girl. It was a biased assumption but that doesn't change the fact that Skylar is my friend.

Even if he is really pretty.

Skylar settles himself down on the dirt across from me and I can't help but stare. The white-blonde colour of his hair brings out the high cheekbones and mesmerizing colour of his eyes.

One blue. One brown.

Equally beautiful in their own right, the combination of them together takes my breath away. He's not handsome but he's striking. Different.

The most beautiful human being I've ever seen.

I should feel bad for staring, but I don't. Skylar is doing the same thing, staring at my face as if I might disappear at any moment.

Silence falls between us until he clears his throat.

"Are you okay?"

For a moment, I think he's questioning my inability to look away from his face, but then he continues, "I heard Walsh went after you."

The night's events filter through my mind and I start blinking rapidly, "Oh, that."

He doesn't say anything as a tear hits my cheek, just watches my expression carefully. Most people would push for an answer, needing to hear the false confirmation of being okay, but not Skylar. Just like in his letters, he lets me not be okay.

"It just... it brought back some painful memories, that's all." I swallow, letting the darkness of the night sky give me courage, "I have a bad habit of freezing. When things go sideways."

He doesn't push for more, just waits patiently.

"I froze again tonight and that makes me angry. A girl nearby ended up distracting Walsh long enough for me to get away, but if she hadn't?" I blow out a breath, "Then I'm no better than where I was two years ago."

"It's okay to be angry sometimes. If you don't let it out, it will find a way to control you." Skylar clears his throat, "But the fact you recognize the problem shows you are better than where you used to be."

I smile, "You're even smarter in person."

He shrugs, "Not really. I just go to therapy."

Laughter takes a hold of me and soon my tears become positive ones. Wiping them away with a smile, I find Skylar studying me.

"What?"

"You keep laughing."

I laugh again, "That's because you're funny."

He blinks, "Most people don't get my sense of humour."

A smile breaks across my face, "Most people don't appreciate deadpan humour. I love it."

Skylar's eyes light up and I feel it all the way to my toes. A lot of people have a tough time interpreting deadpan humour because they don't look beyond the surface. Skylar might not joke with his smile, but his eyes tell a different story.

My eyes dance between the blue and brown irises, soaking in the warmth radiating through them. There's something precious about him, something that makes me think there's a minefield of gems hiding beneath the quiet exterior.

"I actually drew something for you." He shifts uncomfortably, "I don't have it with me, but you were the inspiration behind it."

"It's not a cat lady, is it?"

"I'm saving that for the next one."

I throw my head back and laugh, nearly giving myself a concussion against the hard exterior of Ava's car. Skylar watches me with bright eyes and I feel myself start to blush.

"You'll soon find out I'm not the most coordinated. Or graceful."

He shrugs, "Coordination is overrated. I was always picked last for sport teams."

"Me too! God, I hated gym class." I laugh, feeling my embarrassment ebb, "There's always that one person who sucks at everything. That was me."

"I'm sure you didn't suck at everything."

"Oh, no. I was the worst. You know the king's court? When you move up a level every time you win?" I shake my head, "I was a permanent resident of the toilet bowl."

Skylar pauses, thinking it over.

"Okay. Maybe you did suck at everything."

I laugh, "That's what I'm saying!"

He huffs out a chuckle, a rusty baritone that sounds like it hasn't been used in a while. I stare at him, feeling my heart swell with the knowledge that I did that.

I made Skylar laugh.

The edge of my purse brushes my hand and I glance down to see the sunshine tissue peeking out from the silver clutch. Skylar follows my gaze and stills, his eyes locked on the bright piece of material.

"Is that...?"

"Your last message." I quickly grab the tissue and offer it to him, "Karen stole it from the flowerbed, so I kept it. I hope you don't mind."

He leans forward and gently takes it from my hands. Our fingers brush and I pull away, suddenly feeling shy.

"My response is on the back."

Skylar doesn't say anything as he turns it over and reads it. I hold my breath, thinking about the words I had written, the ugly truth I left there for him. If he was ever going to turn and run, now would be the time.

Skylar slowly lifts his eyes back to mine and I wait for it. The hounding questions, the look of pity, the awkward change of subject. It happens every time.

"Do you want to go somewhere?"

His question catches me off-guard, and it takes me a moment to realize that Skylar is the exception. He isn't going to interrogate me and make sure I'm okay like everyone else. He just accepts me for who I am.

Broken pieces and all.

"Yes." I breathe out the word, knowing this is the pivotal moment I will always look back on.

The night I finally found my friend.

The night I found Skylar.

Skylar

She's so beautiful it hurts.

I can't help but sneak glances at her as we walk through the parking lot. Up close, her features are immaculate, the big green eyes framed by thick eyelashes and a smile ready to be released at any moment. I knew she was resilient from her messages, but I hadn't expected the driving force of her personality.

Even if we hadn't exchanged notes via therapy, there's no doubt in my mind that I would have been drawn to her. There's a darkness that lurks just beneath the surface, the achingly fragile strength of a survivor.

I saw the way she shied away from my touch. The fear in her eyes when she thought I might get too close.

It's just like my mother.

"Is it okay if I grab something from my car?" I glance over and wait for a nod of confirmation.

"Of course."

Lacey gives me another smile, and for a moment, I forget how to breathe. She has a way of looking at me that makes me feel like the hero I will never be.

And she thinks I'm funny.

Warmth seeps through my chest as I think about her confident response. Nobody likes deadpan humour and yet this girl insists that she does.

No. She said she *loves* it.

Punching the button on my keys, I quickly pop the trunk and grab the Saber sweater I'd stashed away earlier. Doing my best not to look awkward, I offer it to her with a shrug.

"Thought you might be getting cold."

She blinks, a look of pleasant surprise crossing her face, "That's so thoughtful."

Gently taking it from my hands, I try not to stare as Lacey pulls my favourite hoodie over her head. I'm not that tall for a guy, and with her impressive height, we're about the same size. By the time she tugs it down past her waist, it almost fits her perfectly.

"Thank you, Skylar."

She hugs the material tighter, the smile taking over her face making me wish I had a hundred more to give her. I sneak a glance at her bare legs, the short skirt making them seem impossibly long.

"I didn't think to pack extra pants. Will you be alright?"

"I'm good."

We fall in step beside each other as I lead us down Silverwood's main strip. The mom-and-pop shops have all closed up for the night, but the dim glow of the streetlights helps to give the town an ethereal feel.

"I've always wanted to explore Silverwood more." Lacey studies each boutique we pass, "It's got the small-town charm Taber lacks."

"People are going to think you're a Saber with those fighting words."

She laughs and I quickly glance her way to capture it.

"Oh, I'll always be a Tiger but that doesn't mean I can't appreciate what the other side has to offer." She gasps, pointing towards the end of the street, "You have a bookstore here?"

I nod, "Betty's Books and Nooks. The same family has run the store since the 80s."

"I'm so jealous. The closest thing Taber has to a bookstore is the university library." She blushes and shoots me a glance, "Sorry. That's super nerdy."

"I don't think being passionate about something makes you a nerd." I pause, choosing my next words carefully, "If you ever want to visit Silverwood, I'd be happy to give you a tour. In the daylight, I mean."

Lacey beams, "I would love that."

"Consider it done."

We branch off at the end of the street, taking a sharp right that leads to the university's residential buildings. Built to match the rest of town, the student apartment buildings are long and wide with old-fashioned trimming along the side.

"Wait. That's the university?" Disbelief fills Lacey's voice as the glistening structure comes into view.

I sigh, "Ruins the aesthetic, doesn't it?"

"It looks like a spaceship." She scrunches her nose, "Why is it so... metal?"

"Wish I could tell you."

Silverwood University rises above us like a great metallic wave. Sitting right in the centre of a clearing, the imposing structure does resemble a spaceship that crash landed among the quaint small town.

The ultra-modern structure was built only a decade ago, and while the monstrous school looks completely out of place in Silverwood, it offers advanced geothermal technology that helps to draw in students from around the country.

As much as I hate to admit it, our town needs the revenue university students provide eight months of the year.

"Is it a good school at least?" Lacey glances at me, "Do you like it here?"

I shrug, "All the auditoriums and classrooms are brand new so I can't complain."

"But do you like it?"

Her green eyes scan my face, hunting for an honest answer. There must be something in the air tonight because for the first time in my life, I don't feel like brushing it off with a nonchalant answer.

"Not really." I meet her gaze, "The facilities are nice, but I don't love the people. They're either from a big, glamorous city or we went to preschool together. Either way, it feels suffocating."

She nods, "I get that. I followed my brother to Taber so I wouldn't have to see the same people anymore."

Lacey ducks her head but not before I see the pained expression on her face. My mind flashes back to her last message and I feel my stomach clench.

A looming structure rises in the distance, the unmistakable outline of Silverwood's one and only football stadium piercing through the night sky.

"Oh my gosh, is that the stadium?" She whips her head around, "We have to go."

"You want to visit an empty stadium?"

Lacey grins, "Pretty please? This is the only chance I'll get to be a varsity athlete."

I stare at her, taking in the raw excitement spreading across her face. Even if I was the strongest man in the world, I wouldn't be able to say no to this girl.

"Does this mean you're competing as a Saber?"

"Obviously." She points to my sweater with a smile, "I've got the merch now."

My eyes drop to the university logo plastered across the grey material. It's resting on the shoulders of a rival and I don't think it has ever looked better.

"Let's go find an empty stadium."

Chapter 7

Lacey

Football stadiums are so romantic.

Sweeping my eyes along the painted turf, I let out a sigh as I picture the famous scene of Austin Ames running off the field to find his Cinderella. The wooden bleachers stand tall and proud along the edge, the massive scoreboard lying dormant under the dark sky.

Over the years, I've been to many stadiums to watch Wesley and Nico's lacrosse tournaments, but I've never had the chance to touch the field before.

"Is it everything you'd hoped it would be?"

The low pitch of Skylar's voice sends a shiver through me. I hug his sweater closer, trying to play off my body's response.

"Absolutely."

I sneak a glance in his direction and find both eyes trained on my face. The blue iris is easier to see in the dark, but the dark one draws me in more. His face is completely expressionless, but I can see the curiosity shining in his eyes.

"Remember when I said I was competing as a Saber? I lied." Hunching my shoulders, I pretend to prowl towards him, "I'm a tiger in disguise."

I leap forward and tag him before sprinting in the opposite direction.

"YOU'RE IT!"

Stealing a glance over my shoulder, I find Skylar staring after me as if he's not quite sure what to do. I throw my head back and laugh, feeling freer than I have in a long time.

"Come on, Skylar! Don't let the rival win."

He hesitates, looking around as if to see if I'd be playing with anyone else. I slow down, suddenly aware he might not know the rules of tag, when he breaks into a run. I wait until he's close enough to reach me before dodging and racing for the closest goal post. I'm just about to reach it when a gentle tap hits my shoulder.

"Too slow, Flower."

I whip around, trying to grab him but he jumps out of reach. Skylar turns, sprinting in the opposite direction and I go charging after him.

This man must have been lying about his sports history because he can run. My lungs are screaming by the time I make it halfway down the field and I have to hold up a hand in defeat.

"Time out!" Gasping for air, I bend over and brace my hands on my knees. Skylar jogs over, looking anything but winded.

"Had enough of the varsity status?"

I gulp down a breath and shake my head, "Not what it's cracked up to be."

Skylar huffs out a quiet laugh and I use the moment to my advantage. Lunging forward, I lean over and tap his leg. I pivot, about to make my great escape when my toe gets caught on the turf and I go crashing down.

Right on my face.

"Ow." I grumble the words into the fake grass and roll onto my back.

"Are you hurt?"

"Yes." Skylar steps into my line of sight and I pull a face, "My dignity is completely gone."

He tilts his head, "Your dignity is still intact, but this did confirm your coordination sucks."

I sigh, "Guess I won't be making the lacrosse team anytime soon."

Leaning my head back against the ground, I let my eyes drift up to the sky. Hundreds of stars shine back at me, their tiny dots a white splash against the dark blanket of the night.

"Wow."

Skylar clears his throat, "Is it okay if I join you?"

"Of course."

I move over and Skylar settles himself down beside me. He leaves enough space so that our shoulders aren't touching, but I can still feel the presence of his body. My heart starts to race and I can't tell if it's from fear or excitement.

"Tell me a secret."

He turns to look at me, our faces a couple of feet apart, "What do you want to know?"

I shrug, "Anything."

Skylar falls silent, his eyes tracing my face. He doesn't leer like most of the guys I know, he just looks at me. Studies me in a way that makes me feel seen.

Wanted.

The thought has a blush heating my cheeks. I haven't been with anyone since the incident, and honestly, I haven't felt the need to. My lips and body have been untouched for two years now and I didn't think that would ever change.

But now I'm starting to wonder what Skylar's lips feel like.

"I read your messages every night." He swallows and drops his gaze, "Since the first day you left me a response, I've read them every night."

My heart stills.

"You kept them all?"

He nods, "I like seeing your handwriting. Makes it feel more real."

A strand of white hair falls across his forehead, and without thinking, I reach out and brush it back.

We both freeze when my fingers touch his skin and I quickly snatch my hand away. I open my mouth to apologize, but Skylar breaks the silence first.

"Your turn."

My breathing turns shallow, the possibilities running through my mind. There are so many things I want to tell him that I don't know where to start.

Skylar tilts his head back to study the stars twinkling above us, giving me the time to think it through. He does it casually, as if my prolonged silence is nothing unusual.

And suddenly I know my answer.

"You make me feel normal." I whisper, feeling a lump rising in my throat, "Even on my worst days, you make me feel like I'm not another broken anomaly."

Skylar turns and stares at me, silence falling between us once more. I can see countless emotions flickering through his eyes, the steady rise and fall of his chest.

"You make me feel normal too."

His face breaks into a smile and my world stops.

Lips tilted up at the corners, Skylar's face transforms in front of my eyes. His stoic features soften into a boyish grin, his mismatched eyes crinkling at the corners. The sharp definition of his cheekbones somehow become more prominent while the white hair falling in his eyes gives him an angelic glow.

In the blink of an eye, my new friend went from beautiful to devastating, and my heart is having a hard time comprehending.

I swallow, trying to tear my gaze away from the radiant boy beside me. I almost succeed when my eyes decide to do something stupid.

Stop and stare at his lips.

There's a shift in the air, or maybe I'm the one who shifted, because suddenly there's a lot less space between us then there was before. The warmth of Skylar's body is close enough to touch and the space between our faces has shrunk down to mere inches.

He sucks in a breath and it's drawn straight from my chest. Excitement and fear charge through my system, the heady combination of adrenalin and Skylar's proximity making my heart slam against my ribcage.

"Tell me another secret."

The tip of our noses brush and my stomach goes into a free fall.

The world falls away until all I can hear is the erratic beat of my heart. He shifts closer, nudging his nose against my own. My core clenches at the simple movement, a single trail of heat making its way down between my legs.

"I, uh..." My eyes dart between the two beautiful colours in front of me. One iris shines through the night while the other welcomes me in the dark.

"Flower?"

The weight of Skylar's stare caresses my cheek, his warm breath painting my lips. The nickname enfolds me like a blanket and it's all I can do not to burst into tears.

"You're more perfect than I could have possibly imagined." I breathe out the words and Skylar breathes them in, "In every way."

I watch his eyes flutter down, the delicate lashes brushing his pale skin. Raising my hand, I stroke his cheek and whisper the rest of my secret.

"And I'd really like it if you would kiss me now."

Skylar

She thinks I'm perfect.

My chest feels hollow as I bring my eyes back to her face. The broken organ that should be beating inside is gone, stolen right in front of my eyes.

I come from a family of monsters and she thinks I'm perfect.

Before the doubt can start to creep in, I lean forward and press my lips against hers. Lacey lets out a gasp at the first contact, but it doesn't take long for her to welcome me home.

Tracing the seam of her lips with my tongue, she parts them eagerly, threading her fingers through my hair while I explore her mouth. She strokes my face as I kiss her, the gentle press of her fingers against my skin leaving me breathless.

My hands itch to slide over her warm body and discover every curve and dimple she has to offer, but I hold back. There's too many unknown variables about her past to let my hormones take over.

Lacey's fingernails glide down my neck and I shiver, fighting the urge to roll over and press into her. A breathless moan slips past her lips and I swallow it whole, drowning in the one person who helps me remember what it feels like to be alive.

Pressing my lips against hers for one last time, I leave a silent promise behind. No matter what happens after tonight, I will always take care of my flower.

Even if her future doesn't include me.

Opening my eyes, all I can see is Lacey's smiling face. Swollen lips, sparkling green eyes, and rosy cheeks stare back at me in the most beautiful combination of broken pieces.

"Maybe you were right about empty football stadiums." Slowly easing away, I give her a hesitant smile, "They're kind of awesome."

Lacey beams, her face lighting up like a Christmas tree, "I told you."

She sits up and pieces of artificial grass fall from her rumpled hair. I swallow, letting my eyes roam down the Saber sweater and the black skirt barely covering her thighs.

She looks like a dream, and for a moment, I want to fall back to sleep.

Her skirt rides up as she climbs to her feet and I quickly look away, not wanting to make her feel uncomfortable with my wandering eyes.

Clearing my throat, I risk a glance over my shoulder, "Can I give you a ride home?"

"That would be lovely."

Lacey gives me another wide smile and my chest cracks wide open. She's so transparent with her emotions, so honest and trusting with every smile. It makes me wonder what happened in the days that led to her trying to take her own life.

What kind of monster tried to dull my flower's shine.

Rage, sharper than any knife, cuts through me so quickly my body starts to shake. My hands clench as violent thoughts flash through my mind, each one more horrible than the last. I grind my teeth, trying to tamper the fury exploding through my system.

I want to fucking kill him.

The person who did this to her. The person who almost stole her from me.

"I was wondering if maybe you'd want to exchange numbers or something." Lacey blushes, tucking a strand of hair behind her ear, "So we could talk more often. Maybe hangout again."

The haze in my eyes is so thick I can barely see, the anger choking me until I can't breathe. My muscles tremble as I fight to keep the beast inside, the need to release the pressure over-powering me.

"Do you have a pen?" I choke out the words and Lacey nods.

"I think so... one second." She rummages in her purse, and I focus on bringing my heart rate down like Karen taught me.

"Here you go." Her smile slips into a frown, "Skylar, what's wrong?"

"I-I need to draw." I gulp down a breath, looking anywhere but her face. All night we've been trading secrets, but here I am, struggling to keep the biggest one at bay.

Dropping my gaze to the ground, I feel my shoulders hunch as I try to shield myself from Lacey's kind eyes.

I don't deserve her kindness.

I don't deserve her.

"Skylar, look at me." She lifts my chin until I have no choice but to look at her. Lacey stares at me, seeing the ugly side for the first time, but she doesn't turn away.

"You're safe here." She presses the pen into my hands, "I don't have any paper, but you can draw on me."

I freeze, my fingers clenching the pen painfully, "I can't draw on you."

"Yes, you can." She smiles, shrugging out of my sweater, "It will only take a shower or two to wash off."

I stare at her, thinking about the hideous pieces I have spent my life drawing. The kind of violence no one wants their children to see, let alone have traced onto their skin. If Lacey had any idea of the kind of art I create, she would run away screaming.

"Stop overthinking." Lacey holds out her bare arm with a fake pout, "I'm not leaving this stadium until you draw me something."

I swallow, reaching out to touch the soft texture of her skin. Goosebumps break out and Lacey bites her lip. My fingers tremble as I push aside the thin strap of her tank top and press the tip of the pen down.

"Ooh, that tickles." Lacey starts to giggle and the sound puts a dent in my rage.

Taking a deep breath, I trail the pen down over her shoulder, letting the steady glide of the ink lead the way. Losing myself in the artistic process, I let every stroke and dip of the pen loosen the clutches of my anger until I can slip away.

Feeling my control lock back in place, I blow out a breath and continue drawing, not wanting to leave Lacey with an unfinished piece.

"You're doing so good, Flower. Just a little longer." I murmur quietly, carefully rotating her hand so I can finish the last section.

"Don't forget to add your number."

She squirms slightly when I reach the sensitive underside of her wrist. I pause, leaning down to press a kiss against her skin.

"Okay. All done."

Stepping back, I hold my breath as she holds out her arm for assessment. It wouldn't take more than a good scrub to wash the ink off, but that doesn't change the fact I want her to like it.

"Are these bellflowers?"

She rotates her arm slowly, her eyes glistening as they soak in the consequence of my temper. I managed to keep the blood out of this one, but it's not a dainty piece by any means.

The flowers that grow along Karen's front garden now creep along Lacey's arm in a tornado of paper fragments and flowers, the twisted vines wrapping around her wrist while wilted petals float down from her shoulder.

I clear my throat with a nod, "It seemed like the most fitting."

"I love it." She looks at me with glassy eyes, "Thank you, Skylar"

Shame heats my cheeks and I drop my gaze to the ground.

"I'm sorry you had to see that."

"What are you sorry for? You got to draw, and I got a beautiful memento." She tilts her head, "Have you ever thought about being a tattoo artist? You're really good."

"You don't think it's too dark?"

She shakes her head, "No way. The darkness helps make it seem real."

Warmth washes through me. Instead of being afraid of my darkness, Lacey matches it in every way possible.

Pulling out the sunshine tissue from my back pocket, I let the note unfold in front of me. My eyes skim the last couple of messages, pausing to reread our last exchange one more time.

I'm not a pretty person, Lacey. I come from a family of angry men and as much as I wish I could say it skipped a generation, I can't. That's the real reason I'm here every Friday, talking to Karen.

So, you're here for anger management and I'm here because of a suicide attempt. I guess we're both just a couple of ugly people.

Using the same pen I used on her arm, I jot down my phone number and a response.

If being ugly means I get to talk to you, then I don't ever want to be pretty.

Chapter 8

Lacey

"I kissed a boy."

The words slip out and there's no stopping the smile taking over my face. Wesley's jaw hits the ground and Nico leans over to give me a high five.

"With tongue?"

"Dude." My brother snaps his mouth shut with a groan, "Why do you always have to take it too far?"

"What? I didn't ask if she dropped to her knees and gave him a blowjob."

I hold up my hand, "I'm right here. And yes, there was tongue."

Nico beams, "That's my girl."

Wesley shudders and refocuses his attention on setting up the dorm's ancient television. Sunday movie nights used to be a tradition growing up, and out of nowhere, Wesley declared it was finally time to reintroduce the tradition. Trip decided to sit the first one out, and as much as I love her company, I am grateful to have some quality time with my brother and my closest friend.

Grabbing the pile of mismatched blankets from the couch, I drop them onto the floor. Nico steals the closest one and wraps it around me with a grin.

"I need more details about this kiss. Name, number, location. Go."

I laugh, "His name is Skylar, his number is in my phone, and it happened in an empty football stadium."

Wesley whips his head in my direction, "What were you doing alone in an empty stadium?"

Nico rolls his eyes, "She was hunting for the most romantic make out setting possible. Need I remind you who followed an innocent freshman into a courtyard first-year?"

"That was different."

"Ignore him." Nico wraps his arms around me and picks me up with a shriek, "What's important is our girl is back out playing the field!"

"Pun intended." Wesley blows out a breath, "Was he a gentleman at least?"

I bury my face into Nico's neck and smile, "He was perfectly respectable. Didn't make a move until I asked him too."

Nico pulls a face, "He didn't make the first move?"

My brother shakes his head, "Lacey needs someone with a lot of patience. Someone who won't expect anything right away."

The truth of his words slap me in the face, the sting leaving my cheeks flushed pink.

"You don't have to make me sound like a freak." I swallow the lump rising in my throat, "Not everyone has sex on the first date, you know. Or the third date for that matter."

Guilt filters through Wesley's face, his green eyes apologizing to me even before I extract myself from Nico's arms and walk into the bathroom. I lock the door and lean against it, feeling my chest start to cave in.

A gentle knock hits the door.

"I wasn't calling you a freak, Lace." My brother's voice drifts through the door, "I just meant you need someone who isn't just trying to get into your pants. You're special, Garden Girl, and you deserve someone who appreciates that about you."

I hang my head, refusing to acknowledge the broken girl in the mirror, "I am a freak, Wesley. What kind of eighteen-year-old doesn't want to have sex?"

"Speaking from a brotherly point of view, knowing that my baby sister doesn't want to have sex is the best news I've heard all day."

I choke out a laugh and he continues, "But that doesn't make you a freak, Lace. It makes you an intelligent woman who knows her limits."

"But what kind of guy would be willing to wait?"

What kind of guy would be willing to wait for me?

Wesley sighs, "A decent one. And by the sounds of it, you may have already found him."

Wrapping my arms around myself, I hunch over, wishing that Skylar was here. Not because he's the boy I kissed but because he's my friend.

A broken sound escapes me and the bathroom door starts to rattle.

"Lacey? I need you to open this door."

I freeze, hearing the panic flood his voice. The handle continues to rattle and I hear Nico let out a stream of curses on the other side.

"Mi amor? Come on out so we can talk this through. Don't lock us out again."

Again.

The girl in the mirror widens her eyes and I stare at her. It's the same face I saw the night I took my mother's sleeping pills, but this time I turn and unlock the door.

My brother rushes in and crushes me into a hug.

"I didn't mean to scare you." I squeeze him back, guilt washing over me.

"You can hide in your room or another building, but no more bathrooms okay?" Wesley pulls back and gives me a weak smile, "I fucking hate bathrooms."

Nico shoves him aside and scoops me up, "I've got the perfect remedy for this evening. Three words, one football stadium."

"*A Cinderella Story*?"

"You got it, babe." Nico carries me over to the blankets covering the ground and plops me down right beside him. Throwing a blanket over my legs, he turns me into a burrito before making himself comfortable.

"It's time to see if the real life version matches the charm of Chad Michael Murray." Nico grins and tosses my brother the remote, "Do you have your earmuffs ready?"

Wesley flips him off before snatching a blanket and joining us on the ground. I lean against his shoulder and he pulls me close.

"I'm sorry for upsetting you, I just..." His voice breaks and I clutch him tighter, "I just don't think I can stand seeing you hurt again."

The stitches holding my heart together start to rip as the consequence of my actions fall apart beside me. Wesley's shoulders shake as he holds me, the splash of his tears on my cheeks making my own start to fall.

"I'm not going to leave you."

My voice is barely above a whisper, the pain of my past radiating through the person I love the most. When my ex-boyfriend hurt me, I didn't even try to hurt him back. Instead, I did something so much worse.

I turned the pain onto myself and tried to leave everyone I loved behind.

Wesley squeezes me tightly, "You better not. I can't be stuck with Nico for the rest of my life."

Nico sniffs indignantly, "You would be blessed to spend the rest of your life in my presence."

I laugh, wiping away my brother's tears before my own. There's been so many mornings when I've wanted to give up and let the darkness take me, but seeing the impact it had on my family made me realize that sometimes you don't live for yourself.

Sometimes you have to do it for someone else.

"Are you ready for a cinematic masterpiece, mon frère?" Pulling out the rustiest French accent I can manage, I give Wesley my best impersonation of a car salesman.

He grins, popping out a couple of dimples, "Mais oui. Nico, press le button."

Nico groans, "Both of you, put the horrific French accents away. You're giving me PTSD from our last code red." He gives Wesley the stink eye, "When you ignored my pleas to stop."

I smile, "Sounds like the perfect wingman to me."

"I was phenomenal. Do you know how hard it is to get down on your knees when your assistant coach is waiting, buck-ass naked, in your doorway?" Wesley shakes his head, bringing up a hand to protect his heart, "That's the real trauma right there."

Nico smirks, "If you're blessed to be in my presence, you were fucking baptized when you saw Mo's fine ass. My man is hung like a horse."

Wesley frowns, "I'm pretty sure I've seen bigger."

I stare at him, "Why are you checking out naked men? You're in a relationship."

"Don't be so judgmental. I'm a curious guy, that's all."

Nico snorts, "He likes to know where he falls on the size scale."

My brother nods in agreement, "I like to confirm I'm above average. It's good for the morale."

Grimacing, I lean over and snatch the remote out of Nico's hands.

"It's time to end this conversation. Are you guys ready for the movie?"

"Let's do it."

Skylar

I tap my eraser against my desk, trying to calm my nerves.

The number on the clock mocks me, it's digits slowly getting closer to midnight. I blow out a breath and reach for my phone.

She's probably asleep by now. Chances are it'll go to voicemail anyways.

I hesitate, my finger hovering over Lacey's number. It's only been 12 hours since I dropped her off but I want to talk to her again. I want to hear her voice, make her laugh, and maybe learn another secret.

It's only been 12 hours and my heart hasn't been the same since.

Blowing out a breath, I think through all the reasons this is a terrible idea. I mean, do people even call each other anymore?

Fuck it.

Pressing the call button, my heart rattles in my ribcage as I wait for the line to connect. I hold my breath, continuing through the list of why this is a horrible idea when Lacey picks up.

"Skylar?"

At the sound of her voice, I almost drop my phone. Gulping down a breath, I glance over my shoulder to make sure my bedroom door is safely shut.

"Hey, Flower." I clear my throat, "Sorry I know it's late..."

"No, this is great. I was hoping you would call." She pauses and I find myself pressing the phone tighter against my ear, "This might sound weird, but I was thinking about you today."

An ache hits my cheeks as my lips tug up.

"I was thinking about you too."

There's silence on the other end and I can't help but wish we were in person so I could see what type of smile is spreading across her face right now.

"Would you want to hang out again? My schedule is pretty free this week." She hesitates, "There's no pressure, of course."

"How does tomorrow sound? I could pick you up and take you to the little bookshop."

Lacey lets out a gasp, "I would love that! My little library hasn't grown in so long."

"You have a library?"

She sighs, "Not really. I have a small collection of romance novels precariously stacked between my textbooks and mound of plants."

"A library and a greenhouse? I'm starting to wonder where you sleep."

Laughter echoes down the line and warmth seeps through me. Pushing back from my desk, I wander over to my bed and lie down. The popcorn ceiling has seen better days, but the white canvas makes it easier to picture Lacey's smiling face.

"It's a tight fit but I make it work. Taber University has the world's smallest dorm rooms, so we only get a single bed and a desk that sits two feet away."

"Sounds cozy."

"It is, actually. I've put in enough effort to make the room feel like my own." She lets out an awkward laugh, "Sorry, this isn't really interesting. Just tell me to stop when you get bored."

I frown, "Boring is not a word I associate with you."

"That might change after you see me in the bookstore tomorrow."

"How could it? I'll get to be with you."

She sucks in a breath and I clutch my phone tighter.

"I didn't mean for that to sound cheesy." I run a nervous hand through my hair, "I'm just looking forward to seeing you again."

Silence falls between us. Staring up at the ceiling, I start tracing invisible bellflowers in my head, wondering if Lacey has washed off the piece I drew for her yet.

"Can I tell you a secret?"

"Always."

She pauses and my breathing follows suit.

"You might be the most romantic person I've ever met."

A quiet laugh escapes me, "I'm just being honest."

"Well, you should keep doing it. I like it."

I can hear the smile in her voice and there's no amount of money I wouldn't give to be able to see it right now.

"I'll keep that in mind."

Lacey makes a satisfied sound, "Good. Now, tell me about you."

There's movement on the other end of the line and I picture Lacey shuffling around a tiny dorm room overflowing with colourful books and blossoming plants. The image has my lips pulling upwards.

"What do you want to know?"

"Everything."

Everything.

The air disappears from my chest.

Most people write me off as the sullen younger brother of the town's bully, the guy with the weird eyes and a sketchbook under one arm. But Lacey isn't asking about the reputation that has stained the family name.

She's asking about me.

I swallow, sweeping my eyes around my room. I can't remember the last time someone genuinely wanted to know me, so I have no idea where to begin.

My sketchbook catches my eye and I decide to go with the obvious.

"Well, I like to draw."

Lacey laughs, "I already know that. Tell me something else."

My cheeks grow warm as embarrassment hits me.

"I don't know what to say. I'm not that interesting."

"That's not true. You're creative, funny, thoughtful, and played tag with me in an empty stadium last night. If that doesn't scream interesting, then I don't know what does."

The crack in my chest grows wider with every kind word that floats down the line.

"Okay, I have an idea." Excitement leaks into Lacey's voice, "We'll do five minutes of speed dating. I had to do this as an icebreaker in my management class and it was actually pretty fun."

"What do I have to do?"

"It's easy. I'll ask you a series of questions and you just have to answer."

Nerves hit me and I grip my phone tighter. It's a silly game but I don't want to disappoint her.

"Okay."

"Are you ready?"

I've never been less ready for anything in my life.

Shaking my head at the wall, I gulp down a breath, "I think so."

"Okay! Here we go. What's your favourite colour?"

"Purple." I hesitate, wondering if two answers are allowed, "But green has recently became a favourite as well."

"Ooh, I love purple. Light or dark?"

"Dark."

My mind flashes to the violent bruises that used to cover my mother's body. The black and blue skin would swirl together in the most beautiful way, and I always wondered why such beauty came at such a high cost.

Lacey clucks her tongue, "Very nice. Favourite hobby that isn't drawing?"

"I like to run."

She gasps, "I knew it! You made running that football stadium look easy."

"Wasn't it?"

"No, Skylar. It was not." Laughter escapes her, "I thought I was going to have an asthma attack last night. You're lucky my coordination took me down before I lost a lung."

My eyes widen in alarm, "Do you have asthma?"

"No. I'm just that out of shape." She blows a raspberry and redirects the conversation back to the questions.

The five minute mark slips by but we keep playing the game, taking turns asking each other superficial questions while the night slowly creeps by.

"Favourite flower?"

"I don't have one."

Lacey heaves a sigh, "Everyone has a favourite flower, Skylar. You just haven't acknowledged it yet."

"I apologize for the ignorance."

She laughs, "You're forgiven. Now, answer the question."

Shaking my head, I smile up at the ceiling, "I need a moment to think about this. What's your favourite flower?"

"Azaleas."

"I'm going to have to Google that one."

Laughter echoes down the line and my smile grows wider.

"It's a flowery shrub with bright, delicate flowers. They're very pretty but surprisingly fragile if you don't take care of them properly." She hesitates, "You have to drain the soil properly so it doesn't drown, but not everyone takes the time to understand that."

There's a vulnerability in her voice that wasn't there before. I fall silent, knowing we aren't talking about azaleas anymore.

Lacey sighs, "It's getting late. We should probably turn in."

I chew my lip, debating my next move. She hasn't brought up the suicide attempt or the situation with her ex-boyfriend, so I don't want to push.

"I think the most beautiful things in life take the most effort." I speak slowly, trying not to overstep, "Even if it does take a little longer to help it grow."

Her breathing goes shallow, "But what if it doesn't turn out the way you want it to?"

"If someone's heart is set on a single outcome, then there's only one solution."

"What's that?"

"You buy a fake plant."

Lacey bursts out laughing, "That's one way to put it."

I shrug even though she can't see me, "Having something turn out exactly the way you imagined it sounds a lot more boring than discovering new features along the way."

"Maybe you're right." The smile shines through her voice, "Thank you."

"Nothing to thank me for. I'll see you in a few hours, okay?"

"Okay. Goodnight, Skylar."

"Goodnight, Flower."

Ending the call, I set my phone down and pull off my shirt. I crawl under the covers, glancing at the clock one last time to count down the number of hours until I get to see Lacey again.

A smile breaks across my face as a rare thought crosses my mind.

Tomorrow is going to be a good day.

Chapter 9

Lacey

"So. You and Skylar."

My roommate crosses her arms and stares me down. I fidget, sneaking a glance at my phone to see if Skylar is here yet.

"Uh, yeah. We're friends."

She raises an eyebrow, "I didn't realize friends talk to each other until 3 AM."

A flush stains my cheeks, the guilt of keeping her up all night washing over me.

"I'm really sorry. I didn't realize I was being that loud."

"Well, now you know." She sniffs, looking me up and down, "I should have known you'd get one of the Vin brothers."

"What do you mean?"

"Look at you." Cecelia waves a hand in my direction and I glance down at the oversized fleece and leggings I'm wearing,

"A long-legged Bambi waiting for a man to take away her innocence. Guys love that shit."

I flinch as her words penetrate my skin. Jerrell said something similar that night, the accusation that my stature and physical features were the reason I ended up in the backseat of his car.

Swallowing the nausea rising up in my throat, I force my shoulders back and remember one of the first things my therapist taught me.

"How people behave has nothing to do with what I look like."

You're not to blame for what happened, Lacey. You asked him to stop and he decided not to listen. That was his choice, not yours.

Cecelia smirks, "Uh huh. Have you told Skylar you're a virgin yet?"

"I'm not a virgin."

Her eyes narrow just as my phone pings with a text. Walking past her to put on my shoes, my hands are shaking as I tie up the purple laces. Memories threaten to bubble up, but I shove them down, refusing to acknowledge the darkness when Skylar is outside waiting for me.

Pasting a smile on my face, I stand up and give her a nod.

"Have a good day, Cecelia."

Her glare burns a hole in my back all the way through the residence building and I don't take a breath until I finally make it outside. The faded blue paint of Skylar's car catches my eye and the lingering tension fades away.

Skylar climbs out of the car and I break into a run, throwing my arms around him before he has a chance to say anything.

"Thanks for picking me up."

I pull back and give him a smile. His eyes drop to track the movement and my heart starts to beat faster.

"No problem." He clears his throat and gently pulls away, "Hopefully you can find the book you're looking for."

"Oh, I'm not too worried. There's never been an occasion when I haven't found a book I want."

I follow Skylar around the car, watching the way the sun catches the pale strands of his hair.

He catches me staring and I quickly duck my head and climb inside the car. Trying to keep my cheeks from flaming, I stare out the windshield and wring my hands together. Skylar climbs in after me and I wait for the ignition to start.

But nothing happens.

A full minute goes by until I finally turn and look at him. He's watching me with bright eyes, a playful sparkle reflecting back at me.

"Are you having engine problems?" I ask politely, trying not to notice the way his flannel shirt brings out the flecks of gold in his dark iris.

"Not that I know of."

I wait for the rest of the sentence but he falls silent, just staring at me.

"Why aren't we moving then?"

"Because I want to look at you." A smile lights up his eyes, "And I want you to know that you're allowed to look at me too."

A blush hits my cheeks, "I didn't mean to check you out."

He goes quiet for a moment, silently searching my face for questions that haven't been asked yet.

"Do you want to know a secret?"

At my nod, Skylar's face breaks into a wide smile.

"I like it when you look at me."

I swallow, squeezing my legs together.

The matter-of-fact way Skylar communicates leaves no room for interpretation and no room for doubts. He's completely transparent and it's probably the hottest thing I have ever experienced.

"I like it when you look at me too."

The confession slips out and I bite my lip, staring at the honest boy sitting next to me. Skylar tilts his head, looking at me as if he can see the damaged layers hiding underneath.

"That's okay too."

The lack of expectation in his voice has my shoulders dropping with relief. He leans forward and turns the ignition, casting one last glance in my direction.

"Ready to go book shopping, Flower?"

I close my eyes, soaking in the sound of my nickname on Skylar's lips. When I open them, he's still watching me and I can't fight the smile that takes over my face.

"Absolutely."

"I'm transferring schools."

Awe drips into my voice when we step inside the most adorable bookshop in Southern Alberta. Betty's Books & Nooks isn't just designed for book shoppers, but readers as well.

The tiny shop is split into different sections based on genres, with each closet-sized room set up to look like a personalized library. Worn love seats are strategically placed in each section to encourage visitors to have a seat and start their next favourite book.

It's cozy and simple and I think I've just fallen in love.

"Oh my God. Is that a romance section?!"

I grab Skylar's arm and drag him towards the sign hanging above the second closet. The wooden sign has pink hearts painted along it and I have to stop to snap a picture.

"Good to know your loyalty lies with whoever holds the most romance novels."

Amusement dances through Skylar's gaze as he looks around the room. I quickly snap a photo of him as well before tucking my phone away.

It seems silly to want proof this boy exists, but a part of me doesn't believe it myself.

"Happy ever afters are my secret addiction."

I shoot him a smile before turning my attention to the colourful spines lining the shelves around us, "There's something reassuring about knowing everything is going to work out in the end."

Skylar wanders over and pulls a book from the shelf. The half-naked model takes up the entire cover, the engorged muscles big enough to see from where I'm standing.

He holds it up with raised eyebrows. "I can see the appeal."

I laugh, "Not all of them look like that. You're looking at the erotica shelf so those books are going to be more intense."

"Erotica?"

"You know. Books that are more focused on physical attraction than plot."

He tilts his head, "That doesn't sound intense to me."

Biting back a smile, I walk over and take the book from him. I flip open the cover to the trigger warnings and pass it back. Skylar reads them silently, his cheeks growing pinker with every BDSM act listed on there.

"I take it back. This is very intense."

Giggling, I take his hand and lead him over to the contemporary shelf, where the cheerful cartoon covers lie in wait.

"There's a lot of sub-genres in romance. You have dark romance, sports romance, queer..." I point to the different shelves around the room before bringing his attention back to the one in front of us.

"This is the romance I like. Not too dark but angsty enough to feel real." Reaching over, I grab a familiar cover, "This is the one I was reading in the parking lot."

Skylar takes it and flips it over, reading the synopsis. Trying not to obsess over his reaction, I scope out the rest of the options lining the shelves. The owner did a good job organizing, making sure series and authors stayed relatively in order.

"It sounds fun." He doesn't make a move to put it back and a thrill goes through me.

"Are you going to get it?"

"Yeah." He gives me a shrug, "I could use a happy ever after too."

The brutal honesty tugs at my heart. There was a reason I felt drawn to my mystery pen pal all those weeks ago, and it wasn't because we both believed in fairytales.

It was because we both needed one.

The love seat pressed against the wall catches my eye and suddenly an idea sparks.

"Here, let me pick out a book and we can read together." I point towards the oversized chair, "Would you be comfortable sharing that?"

Skylar blinks in surprise and nerves hit me unexpectedly. I don't want this day to end, so here I am, making another ridiculous suggestion in the hope that we can spend more time together.

I blow out a breath, "Never mind. That was a silly idea-

"Okay." Skylar nods slowly, flicking his gaze from me to the small couch, "Let's do it."

"Really?"

"Yeah." He walks over to the ancient furniture and analyzes it, "We'll fit better if we each take a side. Our legs might overlap though."

"That's okay." The words slip out much too quickly and Skylar glances at me with bright eyes.

"Did you pick out a book yet?"

"Uh... yes." Grabbing the one with an adorable purple cover, I press it against my chest and creep closer. Skylar holds out a hand and I stare at it, suddenly feeling nervous.

"Can I see it?"

I blink, realizing the hand is for my book and not me. Passing it over with a blush staining my cheeks, I'm about to suggest we abandon this idea when Skylar turns and walks out of the room.

Skylar

"Skylar Vin! Aren't you a sight for sore eyes."

Betty croons at me as I approach the checkout desk, her octogenarian status shining through the thin tuff of grey hair and countless wrinkles lining her face.

"Good to see you, Betty. Can I purchase these please?"

She grins, "How's your mama holding up? It's been too long since she came to visit me."

"I'll let her know she needs to come by."

"I'm just playing you." She cackles, showing off the few remaining teeth, "The lovely Amber was in to see me just last week. Now, you and your brother on the other hand..."

She shakes her head, "You've both been denying me a proper visit. An old bitty like me needs to see some handsome youth or else I'll shrivel up and die, you hear me?"

"I'll keep that in mind."

She barks out a laugh before ringing in my order, "That sneaky humour of yours is going to get you into trouble one day. Don't tell your brother this, but you've always been my favourite of Amber's children."

"I'm sure you tell Vector the exact same thing." Passing over some cash, I slide the two books back into my arms, "Take care, Betty."

"I always do."

I duck back into the romance section and find Lacey browsing the shelves again. Her fleece sweater rides up when she reaches for a book on the far shelf, exposing a sliver of skin. My eyes follow the smooth line of her stomach, down the curve of her ass, and over the endless length of her legs.

Even though she said she likes it when I look at her, I try not to do it too much. She's skittish and a little unsure at times, so I've been doing my best not to scare her.

It's hard though. I've never met a more beautiful person in my life.

"Did you find something else?"

Lacey jumps and I scold myself for not making my presence known.

"No, I was just looking." Her eyes drop to the receipt in my hand and she gasps, "You didn't have to do that!"

My shoulder lifts in a shrug, "I wanted to."

"Well, thank you." She blows out a breath before giving me a tentative smile, "Are we doing this?"

Glancing at the aging couch, it looks a lot smaller than it did a few minutes earlier. I had said our legs would overlap but I'm starting to think we might be a lot closer than I'd originally anticipated.

My eyes flick to hers and I find her watching me closely. I can't tell if she wants me to back out or go through with this, so I decide to take the leap.

"Yeah."

She nods, murmuring something to herself before walking over and sitting tentatively on the far side of the couch. I follow suit, taking the other side, and the worn material dips with my weight. My heart is in my throat when I pass Lacey her book, watching as she shifts around to make herself comfortable.

I must not have been thinking clearly because this love seat is clearly not big enough for two people. Especially when one of them has legs that go on for days.

A pink tinge hits Lacey's cheeks when her long legs brush against mine, her earlier bravado completely disappearing when I shift and straddle them with my own. Praying that my body won't react to her proximity, I meet her wide green eyes with a hesitant smile.

"Is this okay?"

She swallows, "Uh, yeah. It's okay."

I tear my gaze away from her blushing face and look down at the colourful book in my lap. There's no way I'm going to be able to focus with Lacey's legs wrapped around me, but I pick it up anyways.

It doesn't take long for my suspicions to be confirmed. I stare at the words on the page as the minutes tick by, unable to think about anything except the weight of Lacey's limbs pressing against mine.

Sneaking a glance in her direction, I find her completely engrossed in the book in front of her.

The pastel colour of the cover looks dainty in her hands, the bursts of yellow flowers on the front making me think of our sunshine tissues. I watch as she turns the page, her chipped nail polish a lighter purple than that of the cover, and marvel at the way she's slipped away from reality right in front of my eyes.

Watching Lacey read reminds me of what it feels like to draw. The way the rest of the world fades away until all you can see is the ink on the page.

Laughter slips past her lips and I can only stare as she turns yet another page, completely oblivious to my presence. I wish I had my sketchbook with me so I could try and replicate the joy radiating from this moment.

"Oh my God. Skylar, you have to read this." Giggling, she waves me over, "I would try and read it to you but it wouldn't do it justice. Get over here."

I drop my gaze, trying not to look like I just spent the last ten minutes staring at her. Swinging my legs off the couch, I take a step over to where Lacey is sitting. She pushes herself upright and pats the space beside her.

I slowly sit down but the dip in the cushion causes Lacey to fall against me. Her shoulders dig into my chest as she tilts sideways but the sharp impact isn't the problem.

I freeze, feeling her hand land on my upper thigh as she catches herself, her fingertips grazing the edge of my crotch. I let out a sharp exhale and Lacey quickly turns her head.

"I'm so sorry, did I hurt you?"

Not trusting myself to speak, I shake my head. Big green eyes stare at me, the few inches between us not helping the situation below.

"Skylar? Why aren't you saying anything?"

I blow out a breath, "Can you move your hand?"

"Huh?"

"Your hand." Gritting my teeth, I squeeze my eyes shut, "I need you to move it."

Finally, the teasing pressure leaves my body and I breathe a sigh of relief. Muffled giggles float towards me and I peel one eye open to see Lacey covering her mouth with her hand.

"Having fun, are you?"

She giggles, "I'm sorry, I'm trying not to laugh."

"You're doing a marvellous job of it."

Laughter spills from her mouth and she leans into me, shoulders shaking as humour takes control of her. I shake my head, feeling a smile hit the corner of my mouth.

"What scene did you want to show me?"

"Never mind. It was nowhere near as funny as that was." She wheezes, trying to pull herself together, "Just to clarify, I'm not making fun of you."

"Of course not."

"It's just..." Laughter takes hold of her again and soon she's wiping away the tears streaming down her face, "That has never happened to me before."

"You've never gotten a boner in a bookstore before?" I shake my head, soaking in the smiling face next to me, "You're missing out."

"No, I mean I've never caused a guy to..." She gestures towards my jeans which thankfully are not tented, "Struggle to keep things under control."

I frown, unable to comprehend how any guy would be able to stay in control around her. From her lack of coordination to the way she laughs out loud when she reads, Lacey reminds me of everything good in this world.

"His loss."

She smiles and a wayward curl falls across her face. I gently brush it aside, hearing the sharp intake of her breath as I lean forward.

"You must be Lacey!"

I jerk back, snatching my hand away from Lacey's face. Her eyes go wide, looking over my shoulder to the newcomer beaming at her from the doorway.

"Do I know her?" She whispers and I smother a groan.

"I can't believe this is happening."

The woman limps into the romance section and gives us a bright smile. I close my eyes, wishing I was anywhere but here, and turn to face the intruder.

"Hey, mom."

Chapter 10

Lacey

Skylar's mom is adorable.

After awkward introductions were made, she immediately wrapped me in a hug and insisted I join them for dinner.

"I'm making Shepherd's Pie tonight, Skylar's favourite." Amber Vin looks at me with a mischievous glint in her pale blue eyes, "He would be so disappointed if you didn't join us, isn't that right, honey?"

Skylar, who hasn't stopped glaring at his mom since she stepped into the room, finally looks over at me. His cheeks are stained pink and there's an embarrassed glow in his eyes.

"You're welcome to join. Don't feel like you have too, though."

I smile, "I would love to join you for dinner."

Placing my hand on his arm, I give him a reassuring squeeze. Amber tilts her head, tracking the movement and I quickly drop my hand.

"That's settled then. Once you two finish up here, come on over and we'll have a proper catch up." She beams, "I'm so glad I decided to visit Betty today!"

Skylar narrows his eyes, "I'm sure that's exactly what happened."

"Oh, hush. You know that woman loves to socialize." Amber tugs at the grey cardigan draped over her shoulders, "I'll see you two in a little bit, okay?"

"See you soon!"

Giving her a parting wave, I watch Skylar's mom disappear from the romance section. The moment she's out of sight, I turn to Skylar with a smile, "Your mom is awesome."

"She's a busybody." He sighs, "But yeah, she's pretty awesome."

"And very pretty. I can see where you get it from."

He blinks, "You think I'm pretty?"

Panic trickles through me as I press my book tight against my chest. I made the mistake of saying something similar to Jerrell once, complementing his pretty boy features, but it didn't have the effect I intended.

"I-I didn't mean to say that." I swallow, feeling heat rise onto my cheeks, "Please don't be mad."

First you don't put out and now you're calling me pretty. Jesus, Lacey. Why the fuck do I put up with you?

"Flower." Mismatched irises peer at me, pulling me back to the present, "You just complimented me. Why would I be mad at you?"

I clutch my book tighter, using it as a protective shield, "Because it's not something you're supposed to say to a guy. I didn't mean to offend you, I promise."

"I'm not offended. I'm flattered."

My eyes widen as I bring them back to Skylar's face, the sincerity in his tone matching the warmth in his gaze.

"Oh."

Skylar tilts his head, the fluorescent lighting casting a shadow over the definition of his cheekbones. I meant what I said, the sharp edges of his face give him a delicate silhouette that is as unusual as it is beautiful.

"Someone asked me if I was an albino the other day. Being called pretty is probably the best compliment I've gotten all year."

A laugh escapes me, "I don't think you like an albino."

Skylar shrugs, "It doesn't matter if I do. The point is you can say anything you want around me, Flower. I will never judge you for speaking your mind."

Letting the book fall from my chest, I feel my walls start to crumble.

It took me a long time to realize my past relationship was toxic in many ways, but one of the worst parts was the easy way Jerrell could manipulate me. With a couple of cruel words, he could twist any situation so I came out looking like the bad guy.

There was so much guilt for so long that I got into the habit of apologizing before I even knew what I had done wrong. It seems silly now, looking back, but at the time it was the easiest way to appease Jerrell and keep the hurtful words to a minimum.

I open my mouth to thank him, but Skylar cuts me off with a shake of his head.

"I will always be honest with you, and you're welcome to return the favour, but you never have to thank me. Okay?"

I nod, trying to keep the tears at bay. Skylar leans over to grab his romance novel lying on the love seat before gently taking my hand.

"I think it's time we got some dinner. Apparently it's my favourite tonight."

He delivers the line with a straight face, but the teasing glint in his eyes gives him away. I laugh, tears forgotten, as our fingers intertwine and Skylar leads us out of the bookstore.

"And here's Skylar as a baby."

Amber passes me the photograph with a wide grin and I bite back a laugh. Skylar declared himself in charge of clean-up the moment his mom insisted on showing me the family photo albums. I'm not sure if his mom is purposefully trying to embarrass him or just trying to welcome me into the family.

Either way, it's working.

"He's so cute." I smile, looking at baby Skylar beaming into the camera. His chubby face is full of expression, so unlike the boy I've gotten to know over the last few days.

"He was such a happy kid. Never stopped smiling." Glancing over her shoulder conspicuously, Amber drops her voice to a whisper, "Don't tell him I told you, but Skylar has the most beautiful smile. It doesn't come out very often, but when it does, look out."

"Oh, I know. The first time I saw it, I nearly had a heart attack."

I'm expecting her to laugh, but instead, Amber sits up and grabs my arm. I jump in surprise, her small hands gripping me with a surprising amount of strength.

"When did you see him smile?"

"Uh..." I trail off, trying to remember, "He smiled when we were talking in his car earlier today. Maybe in the bookstore as well."

Amber's eyes well up with tears, "You made my boy smile."

"Well, I wouldn't say that-

"Thank you." She grabs my hand and squeezes it tightly, "Thank you, Lacey."

Unsure of what to do, I glance over the back of the couch and peek into the kitchen. Skylar's back is to us, his flannel shirt rolled up to his elbows as he silently washes the dishes from dinner.

The Vin household's main floor is split into a kitchen and a living room that overflows into the staircase leading upstairs.

Like the rest of Silverwood, the house is small but quaint, its open concept leaving room for natural light to filter through the paned windows. The walls are a soft yellow and the kitchen cupboards are a pristine white that look as though they've been replaced within the last few years.

Clearing her throat, Amber releases my hand with a sad laugh, "Don't mind me, I have a tendency of being overly emotional. Let's try and find some older pictures of our boy."

Our boy.

My heart swells at the simple distinction. Dropping my gaze back down to the photo album, I watch Amber flip through the pages until she reaches middle school.

"Oh, this is such a good one! Here he is at a cross country meet." She slides the picture out of its slot and passes it to me.

"Has he always been a runner?"

Bringing the picture closer, I study the two boys in the shot. Their arms are thrown around each other, the grey jerseys screaming out the school logo.

"Skylar? Oh, no. He used to hate running. His older brother made him join the team just to get him out of the house." Amber smiles wistfully, "They used to be so close."

I squint at the photo, trying to pick out Skylar. Both of the boys in the photograph are short and lean, their white-blond hair identical except for length.

"They look like twins."

Amber laughs, "They sure did. Until Vector hit his growth spurt, we didn't think either of them would ever grow taller than 6'0. The Vin brothers were known for being small and quick until puberty hit."

"Thank God it did."

The raspy voice hits my ear and I startle, turning around to see a massive man towering over us. My eyes widen as I take in the grey t-shirt stretched tight across his muscular frame, his biceps bulging from beneath sweat-stained sleeves.

Amber shifts on the couch to face him, "Hi, honey. I thought you were staying over at a friend's house tonight."

The guy grins, "I was until I heard Skylar brought a girl home. Thought I'd pop over and introduce myself."

Those pale blue eyes do a quick sweep of my body and I feel myself stiffen. Amber reaches over and pats my hand, offering some unexpected reassurance.

"Lacey, right?" He tilts his head, a sly smile spreading across his face, "It's nice to meet you."

"I'm sorry, I don't know your name."

"No? Skylar has been holding out on you." He clicks his tongue, "I'm Vector, the older and better looking Vin brother."

"*You* are Skylar's brother?"

I look back down at the photograph in disbelief. Assuming Vector kept his hair the same length, that would make him the guy standing on the right. Besides the unusual hair colour, the scrawny figure smiling at the camera looks nothing like the guy standing above me.

Vector sighs, "I know. I stole all the good genes in the family. My poor brother took after our mother's side of the family."

"Is that what happened?"

Skylar steps forward with a dish towel slung over one shoulder. Standing next to each other, the two brothers look like night and day.

Only coming up to his brother's shoulder, Skylar's narrow chest is less than half the size. But the differences don't end there. Where Skylar is made up of delicate skin and sharp angles, Vector's face is like a square, his jaw bulky and uneven while his skin is spotted with faint traces of acne.

Throwing me a wink, Vector turns to his brother with a grin, "I also took the time to learn a little thing called weight lifting. Sky always preferred more... neutral settings."

Skylar takes the jab without a word and I frown at him. Vector is trying to put on a power play, knocking his little brother down in front of a stranger, and I don't like it one bit.

"I've always thought art takes a lot more skill than weight lifting." I shrug, meeting Skylar's eyes, "Anyone can hit the gym, but not everyone can draw something worth looking at."

Silence descends upon the living room, but I don't feel bothered by it. A warm glow has filled Skylar's eyes, and the knowledge that I put it there spreads the warmth all the way to my heart.

"I like her."

Vector breaks the silence with a laugh, giving his brother a pat on the back, "Try not to fuck this one up."

"Language." Amber shifts to give her son a stern glare, "Don't make me wash your mouth out with soap, young man. You know I'll do it."

"Cruel woman."

Vector grins and bends down to plant a kiss on his mom's cheek. She laughs, swatting him away, and the motion sends the cardigan sliding off her shoulder.

Warped skin becomes exposed as the grey material slinks past her forearm, displaying crisscrossed lines of scar tissue dancing its way up Amber's body.

A gasp escapes my mouth and the room falls silent once more.

Skylar

"Amber, what happened to your arm?"

Lacey puts a hand over her mouth, as if that might erase the scars decorating my mother's body. Vector stiffens next to me and I drop my gaze to the floor.

"Oh, these are old scars." Amber laughs as if she can't feel the tension in the room, "My ex-husband knocked over a vase and I was silly enough to fall into the mess."

Vector clenches his hands, the anger visible from the bulging tendons running down his thick arms. My own frustration pricks at me, but I shut it down quickly, refusing to let it ignite.

"That's horrible." Lacey bites her lip, "Does it still hurt?"

"Not at all. When you're as clumsy as I am, you get used to having a few bumps and bruises."

The lie slides out of her mouth as easily as it did back when she was wearing long sleeves to cover up the bruises my father would leave behind.

Even after all these years, she still makes excuses for him.

"Jesus Christ." Shaking his head in disgust, Vector turns and storms from the living room. Amber watches him go, her brows knitting together when she hears the front door slam shut.

"I better go talk to him." She sighs, "Skylar, why don't you show Lacey the rest of the house? I'm sure she would love to see some of your artwork."

Ignoring the sting in my chest, I step forward to help her get off the couch, but she stubbornly shakes her head. Lacey and I both watch as she struggles to push herself up off the cushions, the painful wince when she lands on her feet impossible to miss.

"Behave and I'll let you keep your bedroom door closed." Amber cracks the joke, giving me a quick hug as she shuffles past, "Just remember to be responsible. I'm too young to have grandchildren."

"Mom."

"I'm just saying, use your head to think and your heart to feel. Don't let your other anatomy take control."

Her laughter echoes down the hall and I turn back to my blushing flower.

"Humour is her defence mechanism when things get uncomfortable." I clear my throat, trying to keep the pain from spiralling out of control, "You get used to it after a while."

"It's okay. Nico does the same thing."

"Nico?"

"He's my closest friend." Tucking a strand of hair behind her ear, she looks at me shyly, "Besides you, that is."

I stare at her, feeling a balloon inflate inside my chest.

The few relationships I've had over the years never worked out because no one could see past the tortured soul who needed saving. The broken boy with the messy family.

The problem was, I wasn't looking to be fixed.

I was looking for a friend.

Lacey bites her lip, shifting her gaze from me to the staircase, "Do you want to show me your room?"

"Do you want to see it?"

She hesitates, "Yeah, I think I do."

I swallow, trying to calm my sudden nerves, "Follow me."

Pushing herself off the couch, Lacey follows me up the stairs and down the narrow hall to my bedroom. I hold my breath as I push the door open, hoping I didn't leave any underwear on the floor this morning.

"Here it is."

Lacey gingerly walks by me, her dark curls brushing my arm as she slips through the door. I trail after her slowly, watching for her reaction.

For such a small house, my room is surprisingly big. The queen size bed pushed back against the wall leaves enough space for a decent-sized desk to sit in front of my window. Looking out over the backyard, the four panes of glass provides me with enough natural light to draw and a sense of freedom that lets my art run wild.

"It's cleaner than I was expecting." Lacey muses, walking over to the small closet and taking a peep inside. I don't have many clothes, but the boxes piled along the floor are full of the sketchbooks I've filled over time.

I shrug, "Most of my life is messy. I try not to add to it."

She wanders over to my desk where my current sketchbook sits, waiting. Lacey picks it up with a smile.

"Am I allowed to peek behind the cover?"

"Sure."

Instead of flipping it open, Lacey walks over and sits down on my bed. I stare at her, unsure of what to do when she gestures to the spot beside her.

"Promise I won't fall over this time."

I huff out a laugh and take a seat beside her. To my surprise, she immediately passes over my sketchbook.

"Will you show me?"

I swallow, giving her a shaky nod. Our knees aren't even touching but this feels like the most intimate experience of my life.

Taking a deep breath, I turn to the first page. Lacey gasps and leans closer, her reaction and proximity making my heart kick into overdrive.

"Is that Karen's garden?"

She runs a finger over my drawing and I freeze, watching her touch a piece of my soul with a chipped fingernail.

"Yeah."

I can barely breathe as I watch her trace the figure kneeling in front of the flowerbed. Her fingers dance lightly over my pencil marks and the corresponding tug in my chest makes me think this is what it feels like to be seen.

She sighs, "It's stunning, Skylar."

"It's for you."

Her eyes widen, "You drew this for me?"

My head drops in a nod, "This is the one I was talking about the first night we met. When I said you were the inspiration behind it."

Lacey was the inspiration behind this entire collection, but I keep that to myself.

"I don't know what to say."

"That's okay."

Carefully tearing the page out of my sketchbook, I pass it over to her. Her teeth flash as a giant smile spreads across her face. I watch in awe as the skin around her eyes shrinks to accommodate the joy radiating through her.

She's so pure. So unrestrained with her emotions.

My gaze flicks from the luminous girl beside me to the dusty boxes piled along my closet floor. Each one contains hundreds of pages that reflect the person I truly am.

Angry. Broken. *Violent.*

The repulsive thought pushes me off the bed and away from the one bright light untouched by my family's history. Nausea climbs in my throat as I think about the memories stashed away in those boxes, the evidence of the unfiltered rage running from my bloodline to the ink staining the page.

I used to think the monster living under my bed was the one I had to fear. As I got older, I realized the real monster wasn't the one lurking in the shadows of my bedroom. It wasn't even the man who beat my mother every night.

It was the one hiding under my skin.

"You should go." Looking anywhere but Lacey's direction, I feel my body start to shake, "This is wrong."

"What are you talking about?"

I squeeze my eyes shut, "You shouldn't be here, Flower. Look at this place. Look at *me*."

My bed squeaks as she climbs off it.

"I am looking at you, Skylar. And there's nothing I don't want to see."

Frustration burns through me. She's standing two feet away, watching me with unsuspecting eyes.

"Do you want to know what really happened that night? Do you want to know how my mother got her scars?"

I shake my head, feeling wildly out of control. The thundering beat of my heart feels like it might explode at any moment.

"Let me tell you a secret, Flower. My father despised his job, said every minute he spent working was a minute wasted. So, every night he would come home in a mood. Most people would bitch or complain to their significant other, but not Vincent Vin."

A tear hits my cheek as a hysterical laugh leaks out, "He had triggers. Sometimes you knew what they were, other times you didn't. My mom was the detonator. She would say or do something that would set him off and suddenly she had a new bruise or cut that needed to be covered up."

I want to stop the words from falling out of my mouth, but I can't. Like a coke bottle that's been shaken too many times, the horrifying truth bubbles up and spills past my lips.

"My mom made his favourite meal that night. He'd had a rough week and we were all walking on eggshells, waiting for the next eruption. She forgot to set an alarm and when the food came out burnt, he grabbed the closest thing he could find and threw it at her."

Lacey's arms wrap around me as she pulls me close. I don't realize I'm crying until the light colour of her sweater starts to darken with my tears.

"She tripped and fell on the broken glass. I tried to call the ambulance but she wouldn't let me. There was so much blood, Flower. There was so much blood."

I fall apart in her arms, crying into her neck like it might expunge the past that has never stopped haunting me. Lacey holds me tightly, not saying a word as I drench her skin with my tears.

"You don't want to be a part of this family." I pull back, blinking at her blurry outline, "We're no good. *I'm* no good."

She shakes her head, gripping my face with her hands.

"Don't say that."

"It's true, though."

Another tear leaks out, dripping from my nose to my lips, "You don't want me, Flower. I'm damaged goods."

Silence falls between us as my tears continue to fall. Lacey hasn't let go of me, her hands clutching my face like it's the only thing holding me together.

"Maybe you're right." She swallows, brushing away the damp streaks on my cheeks, "Maybe you are damaged."

I stare at her, tracing every inch of her face with an invisible brush to commit it to memory. There's an ache in my body that wasn't there before, but I shove it aside.

At the end of the day, my flower deserves someone who doesn't have the darkness of abuse tailing alongside them. Someone whose family isn't held together by misguided lies and misshapen scars.

She deserves a hero and that is the one thing I will never be.

Lacey leans forward and presses her sweet lips to mine. I freeze, tasting the salty residue of my tears, and wait for her to say goodbye.

She pulls back and gives me a sad smile, "But you're perfectly damaged for me."

Chapter 11

I used to think being the broken girl meant I was destined to be alone.

Being made of pieces instead of a whole means that when it comes to love, I no longer have a heart to give. Only fragments, sharp edges of the decisions I've made and the regrets I will always carry.

But now, holding Skylar in my arms, I realize that you don't need to be complete to love someone. You just need enough pieces to fill the empty spaces between the ones they are missing.

Skylar closes his eyes and slumps against me, the wind knocked out of his sails. I gently comb my nails through his hair, feeling the delicate strands part for my fingers.

"You have really soft hair." I murmur the words in his ear, hoping for a huff of laughter. He stays silent, but thankfully his ragged breathing starts to slow.

I play with his hair some more, not because I think it's helping, but because it's too pretty not to play with. Skylar shivers
when my fingers graze the back of his neck and I can't stop the
jolt of lust that races through me. Our bodies are completely intertwined, and with every inhale, I can feel Skylar's chest pressed
tight against my mine.

On every exhale, the unbreakable clasp of his hands.

"I use conditioner." He whispers against my skin, sending
goosebumps in every direction. I clutch him tighter, the air
around us growing thick with a different kind of tension.

Skylar nuzzles my neck gently and I close my eyes as desire
washes over me. My nails dig into his shoulder when he presses
a kiss against my throat.

"I don't deserve you."

"Yes. You do."

He shakes his head before planting another kiss on my neck,
slowly creeping his way upward.

"If I was strong, I would drive you home and never look
back." He pauses to skim his lips along my jawline, "I would let
you run as far away from me as possible."

Heat pools between my legs and a whimper escapes my
mouth.

"Don't be strong then."

His tongue sneaks out to lick the sensitive skin beneath my
ear. I gasp, arching into him and he groans softly.

"I will never be your hero, Flower. I'm not ambitious and I'm
not brave."

He catches my earlobe between his teeth and tugs it gently.

"I'm not even cool enough to be a villain."

I grab his face and pull him up until those bloodshot eyes are on mine. His hair is wild and tangled, his eyes are swollen and puffy, and his flawless skin is tainted with red splotches running along his cheeks. He's a complete and utter disaster.

Yet so perfect for me.

"Why would I want a hero or a villain when I can have a boy who leaves me messages on sunshine tissues?"

Skylar stares at me with dilated pupils, his heavy breathing pushing against my chest. I cradle his face, rubbing off the last of the grainy residue.

"It's not even a competition because I choose you." Wrapping my arms around his neck, I breathe out the unfiltered truth, "I will always choose you, Skylar."

His mouth is on mine the moment his name leaves my lips. I stumble back, bumping into the edge of his bed, and we go tumbling on top of it. Our lips stay fused together as Skylar rolls over so we're side-by-side, carefully keeping his weight off of me.

My lips part and his tongue slips inside, drawing out soft moans with every stroke. Body burning with desire, my hands wander down the length of his back before sneaking under the edge of his shirt. He hisses out a breath when my fingers brush his bare skin.

"Is this okay?" I whisper the question and he responds by sitting up and pulling his shirt over his head.

Lying back on the bed, I soak in the sharp edges of his narrow chest, pale skin and lean muscles greeting me at every turn. My eyes drop to the skin stretched tight over his stomach and I let out a gasp.

"You said you weren't an athlete!"

Skylar blinks, his gaze unfocused as he glances from me to his exposed torso.

"I'm not."

"Liar." I point accusingly at the abdominal muscles obscuring my vision, "How do you explain those then?"

He shrugs, "Skinny boy abs. It's a thing."

"Nuh uh. Those are fit boy abs."

His face lights up with a smile, "I didn't realize there was a distinction. Do you want me to put my shirt back on?"

"Don't be ridiculous."

I pull him back down and relish in the quiet laughter flowing through his body. Amber was right, Skylar does have the most beautiful smile.

But nothing beats feeling it pressed against my own.

My palms press against his skin and he tenses, reaching up to grip the comforter above my head. Sliding my hands upward, I trace every bump and line as Skylar latches his lips back on mine. I'm memorizing every inch of his skin, feeling every shiver that goes through him, but it doesn't take long for me to realize something is wrong.

Breaking away, I glance at the white knuckles clenching the comforter.

"Skylar?"

"Yes, Flower?"

"Why aren't you touching me?"

He blinks, our proximity close enough that I can see the thought process flash through his eyes.

"I didn't want to make you uncomfortable."

A blush hits my cheeks and Skylar lets go of the comforter to stroke it.

"I didn't mean to embarrass you."

I bite my lip, tears threatening to make an appearance, "How did you know I would be uncomfortable?"

How did you know I wasn't normal?

Shifting to rest his head on the pillow, Skylar looks at me with swollen lips and flushed cheeks. There's no judgement in his gaze, but I find myself holding my breath all the same.

"The first night we met you shied away from my touch." He lifts a narrow shoulder, "For years my mom flinched when someone came too close, her body instinctively reacting from years of abuse. I figured it might be a similar situation for you."

My bottom lip starts to tremble, "Am I that obvious?"

"No. I just happen to know what to look for."

I close my eyes, fighting not to let a single tear slip out. Skylar presses his thumb against my bottom lip and his voice drops to a whisper.

"It's okay, Flower. Your secret is safe with me."

Losing the battle, I feel a tear run down my cheek. Here I am, wrapped up in the only person who understands me, and I can't let go of the past long enough to enjoy this moment.

I am so tired of being the broken girl.

Peeling my eyes open, I find Skylar studying me. His white hair seems to glow against the dark pillowcase, a polar opposite to the dark strands covering my own. A flicker of desire sneaks its way down my body as I stare at the beautiful boy beside me.

I don't want to be broken anymore.

Not with Skylar.

"Can you touch me?" The blush returns with a vengeance but I don't break eye contact, "Please?"

For a terrifying moment, I think he's going to say no. Dropping my gaze to prolong the mortification, I watch Skylar's chest collapse on an exhale.

"You never have to say please." He clears his throat, the gravel in it making my heartbeat quicken, "Not when you're with me."

I open my mouth to apologize then quickly close it. Skylar smiles in approval.

"How do you want to do this?" He pauses, "I mean, where do you want me to touch you?"

"Everywhere."

My immediate response has Skylar muttering a curse. He closes his eyes, his lips silently moving as if he's giving himself a pep talk. A giggle slips out of my mouth and the sound has Skylar glancing at me with bright eyes.

"Okay. I'm ready."

He doesn't ask if I'm ready, we both know I'm not. Fear races through my system as I shift over and lie back, struggling to breathe as the memories flood back in.

Jerrell, stop. You're hurting me.

Shh, it'll feel better in a moment.

No, please. Just stop.

It'll get better, baby. Just push through for me, okay?

"Flower?"

Skylar's soft voice breaks through the darkness. Gulping down a breath, I focus on the patience and understanding shining through his mismatched eyes.

This won't be like last time.

Skylar won't hurt me.

Repeating the mantra over and over, I reach for my last shred of courage and give him a nod.

"Go ahead."

Skylar

I want his name and social security number.

Seeing the fear fill Lacey's eyes when she lay back on my bed was enough to make me want to break something. Even now, I can feel the rage curdling my blood as I look at her, fidgeting nervously while she waits for me to touch her.

My flower thinks I'm going to hurt her.

The thought puts a lump in my throat and I have to flex my fingers against the comforter to keep them from reaching for a pen. The pressure in my chest is uncomfortable, but not unbearable, so I force the anger aside and focus my attention on the petrified girl lying next to me.

A part of me wants to call this whole thing off and drive Lacey home so she can think about what she wants, but the other part of me is dying to touch her. Having her legs wrapped around me in the bookstore earlier today filled my head with too many ideas, graphic ideas that no respectable man should have.

My hands twitch again, but this time it's not for a need to draw.

I want to trace every inch of her body. No amount of artistic talent would ever do her justice, but I want to try. I want to study every divot and dimple, discover every freckle and mole and paint them with my lips. I want to find out what makes her shudder and what makes her scream. And then I want to do it all again and capture it through ink on a page.

But more than that, I want to see Lacey comfortable around me. See her let down her guard until I can strip off her insecurities and help her forget her past for a little while.

Swallowing the lustful thoughts racing through my head, I slowly reach out and touch her shoulder. She flinches but doesn't move away.

I fucking hate the guy who did this to her.

It's hard to focus when I can see Lacey watching me with fearful eyes. I can tell she's fighting the urge to run away from the restless way her eyes keep dancing around my bedroom.

"Flower." I wait until her eyes land back on mine, "You can tell me to stop anytime. We won't do anything you're uncomfortable with, okay?"

She starts blinking rapidly and the sight has my heart breaking.

"Okay."

I lean forward and kiss her, if only to have an excuse not to see her cry. I don't mind when she sheds tears talking about her past, but seeing her eyes well up at the most basic display of kindness just about destroys me.

Lacey kisses me back softly, her hands coming up to stroke my face. I breathe her in, letting the kiss ease the tension from her body before I trail my hand down her arm. Wrapping my fingers around her own, I give her an anchor to hold on to as my other hand brushes her collarbone.

She lets out a gasp and I break away so we can watch my fingers trace the delicate juts of skin before drifting lower. Her back arches when I reach her breasts, silently encouraging me to cop a feel.

The material of her fleece sweater is surprisingly thin as I run my fingers up over the pad of her bra and press down. A groan escapes me when I feel the sharp peak of her nipple, my dick thickening against the zipper of my jeans.

"Are you okay?" Lacey starts to giggle.

"Shouldn't I be asking you that?"

She laughs for real this time, throwing her head back and exposing her throat.

"I think you have *harder* things to worry about."

I shake my head with a smile, "You're a menace."

"Maybe." Lacey's emerald eyes sparkle at me, and all I can do is stare back, trying in vain to capture this moment.

"Are you doing okay?"

She nods, "It was scary at first but now it's not so bad."

Easy for her to say.

I'm about to ask her something else when she takes my hand and moves it lower. My eyes go wide when she presses it against her pussy.

"I want you to touch me right here." She pushes my hand hard against her core, the material of her leggings doing a poor job of hiding her heat.

A strangled sound escapes me when I feel the dampness leaking through the material, suggesting her panties are either completely soaked or she's not wearing any at all.

I lied when I said I was ready for this.

Lacey bites her lip, her cheeks flushed when she looks at me from beneath her lashes, "Do you think you could do that for me?"

I'm having a hard time thinking between the blood rushing to my dick and the barely covered wet pussy pressing against my hand. My other hand is still intertwined with hers, and the amount of pressure she's using to squeeze my fingers tells me just how nervous she is.

"Yeah." I swallow, "I can do that for you."

Pressing my middle finger down, I slide it up until I hit the swollen bump of her clit. It's hard to tell through the leggings, but the gasp Lacey lets out helps to confirm I found it. Rubbing it gently, I slowly piece together what my flower likes from the sound of her moans and the flex of her legs.

"More pressure, Skylar."

Bucking against my hand, she uses her own hand to grind my fingers harder into her. Our current position makes the angle too awkward to properly press into her, so I quickly extract my hand.

A frustrated yelp escapes her, "What are you doing?"

Rolling onto my side, I grab her hips and pull her flush against me. My right hand is completely trapped under Lacey's body, but it leaves my left one free to slide between her legs.

I've always been ambidextrous, but I've never considered it to be a life skill until this moment.

"*Oh.*"

Her legs spread wider as I start the friction back up, pressing and rubbing her clit until Lacey's head falls back against my shoulder. Her ass grinds back against me on every stroke, and it takes every ounce of will power not to grind against her.

"You're doing so good, Flower." I murmur the words into her ear before increasing the pace. Lacey lets out a quiet moan, and my will power breaks in half.

Thrusting forward, my tented jeans meet the backward momentum of her ass, and she freezes against me.

Oh fuck.

I'm about to throw myself off the bed when she grabs my hand, "Do that again."

My hips follow her command before I can even process what she said. I press into her, using my fingers to stroke her clit while I grind against her from behind.

It doesn't take long for my slow pace to speed up, the friction of Lacey's pussy against my hand and her ass against my dick pushing me close to the edge.

"Tell me what you need." Gritting my teeth, I'm trying to fight back the fast approaching release. Lacey's breathing is fast and uneven, her hips bucking against mine.

"Can you say it?"

I groan when her ass cheeks push hard against my dick.

"What am I saying?"

A flush creeps up Lacey's neck and I don't think before I lean forward and lick it. She gasps, pressing against me harder still and grabbing my hand.

"My name. The one you call me."

Looming orgasm momentarily forgotten, a giant smile spreads across my face when I realize what she's asking for.

"Anything for you, Flower."

The nickname sends her over the edge and the frantic bounce of her hips has me coming not far behind. Our heavy breathing fills the room as Lacey falls limp beside me. I pull her close, ignoring the fact I just came in my pants like a pubescent teen.

Lacey rolls over to face me and her flushed cheeks and tired eyes has my heart expanding three times its normal size. I'm waiting for her to make a joke about my stained pants, but instead she gives me a hesitant smile.

"You didn't try and take my clothes off."

Her eyes scan my face, the statement coming off more as a question. The rage from earlier resurfaces as I catch a glimpse of the cracks someone else left behind.

"You didn't ask me to."

Lacey closes her eyes and I quickly press a hand to her lips before she can try and thank me.

"Get some rest, Flower. I'll drive you home when you're ready."

Chapter 12

Lacey

"Where have you been?"

Nico crosses his arms, the pink polo shirt he's wearing tight enough to show off the lean lines of his chest.

"Your roommate nearly killed me when I woke her up this morning." He sniffs, "She has no appreciation for morning routines."

I bite back a laugh and swipe my access card to the residence building. With a flash of green, the door unlocks and I wave for him to follow me inside.

"Sorry, I should have texted. I stayed over at a friend's place last night."

Nico draws to a halt, right in the middle of the hallway.

"Was this friend male by any chance?"

"Uh...."

"I KNEW IT!" Letting out a shriek, Nico charges towards me and scoops me up, "My girl is back on the band wagon! Taber University better look out cause this sexy lady is on the prowl."

I laugh, "Put me down, you ridiculous man. You're gonna get housing services called on us."

"Hell, yeah I am. Tell me *everything*."

Nico grins and bops my nose, "Actually, wait until we're back at your dorm so you can pull out a ruler and I can see what we're working with."

I shake my head with a smile, "Does your mind always jump to sex?"

"Is that a rhetorical question?"

Setting me back on the ground, Nico doesn't give me a chance to walk away before he grabs my hand and twirls me around.

"I am so proud of you, mi amor. You're finally putting yourself out there again."

"I'm trying."

He grins, "That's all you can do. Come on, let's go get that ruler."

A student walking by shoots us a concerned look, but I'm too busy laughing to notice.

"He's a little... skinny."

Nico zooms in on the picture I took of Skylar at the bookshop, "The white hair is adorable though. And I don't hate the emo vibe he's got going on."

I reach over and take back my phone.

"He's a very talented artist. You should see the flowers he drew for me the other night."

"So, he's good with his hands."

I blush, remembering the way Skylar touched me last night. Nico immediately notices and lets out a hoot.

"You *did* have a good time last night."

We're sitting on my bed, backs against the wall and legs dangling over the edge. Being around Nico is safe and comfortable, but I hadn't realized how much I missed the intoxicating excitement of being around someone you're attracted to until I met Skylar.

"It was incredible, Nico." Pulling my knees closer, I squeeze them into my chest, "He made me feel alive."

Dark eyes study me intently, the teasing smirk softening into a genuine smile.

"You deserve to feel alive every damn day, Lace. And if this skinny kid does it for you, well, there's nothing left to say except I'm happy for you."

"Thank you."

He throws his arm around me and I lean into him. Breathing in Nico's cologne, I let the scent envelope me and smile, thinking about how far we've come.

"You were the first boy I ever loved, you know." I let out a rueful laugh, "I used to wish on every birthday candle that one day you would wake up and realize you were attracted to girls instead of boys. It was so selfish, but I couldn't tell the difference between love and friendship."

"It's not ridiculous. I used to do the same thing."

Nico shakes his head, "When I went to visit you at the hospital, I remember thinking it was my fault. If my sexuality hadn't gotten in the way, none of this would have happened."

I frown, "I made my own decisions. You had nothing to do with it."

"But you wouldn't have had to make those decisions if I'd been able to love you back."

His eyes start to glisten, "I had the whole thing planned out. We would have been best friends through elementary, pretended to hate each other during junior high, and finally given in to our feelings in high school. I would have taught you the unbearable talents of my tongue, and by the time we graduated, we would have been engaged to be married."

Nico's voice breaks and so does another piece of my heart.

"We would have lived happily ever after, mi amor. That's how it was supposed to be."

I close my eyes as a wave of grief washes over me. The story Nico painted is the same one I used to imagine for myself, the young girl who wanted to fall in love with her childhood best friend, the boy who understood all my quirks and didn't question my idiosyncrasies. All I wanted was a love story, complete with a happy ever after.

Instead, I got reality.

"Do you know why my birthday wishes never came true?" I choke out a laugh, wiping the tears from his cheeks, "Because we weren't wishing for something real."

"But it could have been."

"No, Nico. Life doesn't end with marriage proposals and babies wrapped up in bows. Life is hard and ugly and sometimes people and relationships get damaged and lost along the way."

I press a kiss to his cheek, "We are exactly where we are meant to be. You've found someone who scowls as much as he smiles and I've found someone who smiles with his heart. Neither might work out but at least we know there are good men out there who treat us how we deserve."

"Maybe you're right." Nico slumps with defeat, "I just wish you didn't have to go through that to get to where we are now."

"I know."

Nudging his shoulder gently, I try to lighten the mood with a smile, "It never would have worked out between us. I don't have nearly enough muscle mass for you."

Nico snorts, wiping his eyes with the cuffs of his sleeves, "Apparently I have too much muscle for you. Seriously, babe, maybe we should put that kid on a cycle. He looks like he's one strong breeze from falling over."

"Skylar is perfect." I smile, thinking about the boy whose broken pieces align seamlessly with mine, "And he's got very talented fingers."

"I bet he does."

Nico cracks up and it doesn't take long for me to join. Even though I missed out on the fairytale, there's no one I would rather have in my corner than Nico. He's the friend I always needed, the one person I could always turn to until my life spiralled into darkness.

I almost gave up our friendship with a bottle of pills, but just like our ill-fated love story, it wasn't meant to be the end. The doctors who pumped my stomach gave me a second chance and this time I won't lose sight of what's important.

"Wait. Does this mean I get to meet him?"

Nico sits up, making me fall over on the bed, "Oh my God, he should come to our next movie night! Wes will be so excited to meet him."

Pushing myself upright, I huff out a laugh, "Inviting Skylar over to watch a movie with my older brother and his closest friend sounds like a terrible time. No offence."

"Babe, we both know I'm your closest friend, but I see your point." He pursues his lips, thinking it over, "What about inviting him to our next lacrosse game? Then you could chill in the bleachers and we could do the casual bro hug at the end."

"Do you even know what a bro hug is?"

He scoffs, "Of course, I do. I'm just too sophisticated to swoop to that level of childish masculinity."

"Uh huh."

"Don't get cheeky with me, Miss Sleeping Over at a Boy's House. I'm not above blackmail."

I laugh, "Pretty sure I have more blackmail on you than you do on me."

"Touché." He grins, taking my hand and giving it a squeeze, "Just make sure I get to meet Skylar first. I can't have Wes holding that over my head for the rest of my life."

"I'll do my best."

Skylar

"Blue or green?"

Lacey hums, thinking over her answer. We've talked on the phone every night since that first call, and every time it lifts some of the weight off my chest. There's something about hearing her voice that makes me feel like I can breathe without my past bleeding through the layers.

"I'm going to say green. I love the aesthetic of thick, heathy leaves."

I bite back a smile, "So, your ideal phone background would be a pile of fertile leaves."

She laughs, "If you saw my succulent collection, you would understand. My plant babies have some of the prettiest shades of green. My favourite is probably this little cactus that's a dark green colour, almost like a tainted emerald."

"Like your eyes?"

The question stuns her into silence and I clamp my mouth shut.

I would have to be blind not to notice Lacey's devastating features, but I do my best not to draw attention to them. Her long legs and sparkling green eyes are such a small part of my attraction to her that it feels shallow to complement the outer layers when there's an even more enticing beauty underneath.

At the end of the day, my flower is so much more than the petals on her stem.

"You've noticed the colour of my eyes?"

"I've noticed a lot of things about you, Flower. I know the way your eyes change shape when you smile. The way your cheeks darken when I catch you looking at me. The sound you make when you're reading a funny book. The weightlessness that fills my chest whenever you're nearby."

Swallowing thickly, I whisper the rest of my confession, "I know that you're the only person who makes me feel like more than just Skylar."

Silence falls on the other end of the line. I lay my head back and study the chipped state of my ceiling. My pillow still smells like Lacey's shampoo from the night she spent here, a flowery scent that has helped to chase away the demons on more than one occasion.

I don't know if I will ever deserve her, but I do know she felt perfect coming apart in my arms.

"I think it's my turn to tell you a secret." Lacey blows out a breath, "I used to think you smile with your eyes but recently I discovered that wasn't true. You smile with your heart and it's easily the most beautiful thing I have ever seen."

I freeze, feeling the air vacate my lungs.

"Your blue iris catches the most attention, but the brown one is my favourite. It speaks to the darker parts of your soul and it gives my own a safe place to land. You don't waste words with dishonesty and you have the most unexpected yet brilliant sense of humour."

She pauses, "But most of all, you help me remember what it's like to want to live again. Not for my family, but for myself."

I try to suck in a breath but there doesn't seem to be enough oxygen in the room.

"You might be the only person who sees me." I can barely choke out the words, "Nobody else looks past the outer layers."

She falls silent and I fall back on the age-old breathing technique my therapist taught me. It doesn't help the burning hole in my heart, but it does ease the pressure in my diaphragm.

"I've always seen you, Skylar. Even when I didn't know what you looked like."

"You aren't disappointed I didn't turn out to be a middle aged woman with a barn cat?"

She blows a raspberry, "I'm not sure that vision could have gotten me off the other night, but you never know."

Laughter, loud and unrestrained, explodes out of my mouth. The boisterous sound takes me by complete surprise, echoing off the walls of my bedroom as my stomach muscles clench against the foreign sensation. I hunch over as laughter takes over my body, the shake in my shoulders from mirth rather than tears.

Lacey's corresponding giggles float down the line and it sets me off again. By the time I catch my breath, it's impossible to keep the smile from stretching across my face.

"I wasn't expecting that."

"Thought I'd take a page from your book and go for honesty."

"Now I see why you like it so much."

She laughs, and the sound only makes my smile grow wider. It feels like my face is about to splinter right down the middle, the elation bubbling through my bloodstream.

"You're something special, Skylar. You just need to start believing it."

"I'll work on it."

She clicks her tongue, "Promise?"

"I promise."

"Good." She sighs, "I don't want to say goodbye but I really need to go to bed. I have a midterm tomorrow morning."

Sneaking a glance at my clock, I'm shocked to see the midnight hour staring back at me.

"That's okay. I'll talk to you tomorrow."

"I'm looking forward to it. Goodnight, Skylar."

"Sweet dreams, Flower."

Ending the call, I roll out of bed to brush my teeth. There's still a smile staining my face when I swing open my bedroom door, but it quickly disappears when I see the hulking figure leaning against my doorway.

"How long were you standing there?"

Vector tilts his head, studying me in the dark hallway between our two rooms. The glow from my desk lamp is just strong enough to illuminate the shadows under my brother's eyes, the gaunt features hidden beneath the endless pounds of brawn.

"Not long." His gaze flicks over my face, "It's been a while since I've heard you laugh like that."

Carefully tucking my emotions back under my skin, I feel my stoic expression lock back in place.

"There hasn't been much to laugh about."

"Don't do that." He clenches his jaw, the volatile temper simmering just beneath the surface, "Don't make it sound like it's my fault."

"I didn't say it was your fault."

"Like hell you didn't." Vector shakes his head, "I'm not the villain you paint me out to be. I did what needed to be done."

"I know you did. But why are you still hurting people now?"

I stare at him, feeling my earlier joy slink away. My brother's actions have always been a source of tension between us, but that's because he doesn't understand. He doesn't understand that every sprained ankle, every broken bone he's left in his wake have all landed on my conscience. That every person he's hurt has snipped away at the tattered edges of my soul.

Vector rolls his eyes, "You make it sound like I go around assaulting people. The only people I've hurt are the ones who deserved it."

"Did Cody Ellsworth deserve it?" I fire back the question, frustration cutting through me, "Did any of the players you put in the hospital deserve it?"

"Lacrosse is a contact sport, Sky. It's supposed to be aggressive."

"But *you* don't have to be aggressive." My teeth snap together, "Haven't we seen enough violence?"

The tension in the air ignites the fire in his eyes.

"You're blowing it out of proportion."

"Am I? Tell me, when was the last time mom went to see one of your lacrosse games?" I give him a bitter smile, "That's right. She stopped attending your tournaments after that goalie had to get emergency surgery. All because you couldn't control your temper."

"You're one to talk."

He bares his teeth, bending down so we're eye-to-eye, "You think I don't know about the box of crayons you keep hidden under your bed? I know exactly how many pencils you've broken drawing scenes that would make grown men cry. I've seen the evidence, Sky. You might act like you're better than me, but deep down we're the same."

"No."

I shake my head, taking a step back from the monster living inside me, "I'm not better than you. I just choose to express my anger in ways that don't impact other people."

"Not all of us get that choice."

"There's always a choice." I breathe out a sigh, "You just have to be strong enough to make it."

He glares at me, the fury in his gaze identical to the one we used to see every night before our mother would start to cry.

"For fifteen years I had to stand by and watch mom take beating after beating because I was too weak to do anything." Vector shakes his head, his pale blue eyes darkening, "I would rather die than watch someone else lay a finger on her ever again. The same goes for you. If someone messes with either of you, I'll fucking destroy them."

I stare at him, seeing the stains and shattered pieces even my brother isn't strong enough to hide.

"Then that's your choice. Just don't drag me down with you."

Chapter 13

Lacey

"Let me get this straight: you invited your new boyfriend and school rival to come support our lacrosse game today?"

Wesley blinks, his face breaking into a dimpled smile, "That's fucking sick."

Trip rolls her eyes, "A lot of people come to the season opener. Just because we aren't competing against Silverwood doesn't mean their students can't show up here."

My brother leans over and tugs the lacrosse jersey his girlfriend is wearing. Trip's jersey is identical to mine except for Wesley's player number engraved along the back. The school's trademark tiger roars from the bright orange material, and as cheesy as it sounds, it really does add to the excitement of game day.

"But think about the implications of this monumental event. Two rival schools coming together over one couple." Wesley pretends to wipe away a tear, "Billy would be so proud."

Trip wrinkles her nose, "Billy?"

"Shakespeare, of course."

I laugh and Trip shakes her head with an exasperated sigh. She looks very pretty today, her wavy hair falling loose over her shoulders instead of pulled back in her standard style of ponytail. The makeup sparkling around her eyes helps to draw out the unique grey colour, and if I had to guess, I would say her roommate probably helped her out with that.

Trip is many things, but makeup inclined is not one of them.

"Always so dramatic." She scrunches her eyes in a fake scowl, one that never fails to put a grin on my brother's face.

"You love it." Wesley plants a kiss on her frown line before giving me a quick hug, "I've got to go help Nico set up, but I'll see your gorgeous faces later."

I smile, "We'll be cheering from the bleachers."

"With the rival." Wesley wiggles his eyebrows, "If anything goes wrong today, I'm blaming him. Feel free to quote me on that."

Trip rolls her eyes, "Skylar doesn't even play lacrosse."

"Doesn't matter. I blame the rival either way." He blows her a kiss and pivots, disappearing into the crowd to rejoin his teammates. Trip watches him go with a smile, and I have to bite back one of my own.

When Wesley brought her home to meet the family over winter break, it took less than twenty minutes for her sarcasm and awkward social interactions to win over my parents.

He needs someone who helps ground the outgoing social persona he loves to show off, and that person just so happens to be the lovely girl beside me.

"Ignore your brother. Everyone is excited to meet Skylar." Trip gives me a shy smile, "It will be nice to meet someone from another school. Taber can be a bit suffocating sometimes."

"It sure can."

There's an excited buzz in the air as students flutter past, the bright orange and black merchandise showcasing a school spirit that is admirable for a university this small. Lacrosse is one of the more popular teams here, but it still amazes me that so many people would willingly give up their weekend to go watch strangers chase after a ball on a field.

"How are you feeling?" Trip swivels her head, searching the crowd for Skylar even though she doesn't know what he looks like.

"Nervous." Raking my gaze over the Taber students around us, I feel butterflies take flight in my stomach, "I'm worried he's not going to like it here."

After experiencing the hostility of Silverwood students that night at the bar, I'm scared that Skylar will arrive with a bad impression already ingrained in his mind. My brother jokes about his rival status, but at the end of the day, Silverwood is Taber's biggest rival. And like it or not, our schools have competed for the top spot in lacrosse for years.

"I don't think that's something you have to worry about. From what I've heard, Skylar sounds like a thoughtful young man."

I laugh softly, "He is very thoughtful. Kind, too."

"Can't ask for more than that." Trip gives me an understanding smile and a question bubbles up on my tongue.

"How did you know when you were ready? For your first time, I mean."

Her eyes widen, "Like sex?"

My head drops in a nod, "If you don't mind me asking."

"Well..." Trip hesitates, a pink flush creeping up her neck, "Wes is the only person I've slept with."

Oh God.

I grimace, trying to erase the mental picture, "Sorry, that was a really personal question, you don't have to-

"No. It's okay." Trip tucks a piece of hair behind her ear, "It's kind of weird because it's your brother, but basically we had a conversation about trust and what he could do to make sure I felt safe and comfortable. As for how I knew I was ready for sex, I guess I didn't really, it just kind of happened."

"Did you feel comfortable?"

"With Wes? Always." Trip smiles, "He kept stopping to ask if I wanted to keep going and I started to hit him."

"That's... cute."

I shudder, wishing we weren't talking about my brother. Trip catches my reaction and laughs, "Maybe not from a sibling perspective, but it was cute."

"I'm glad it was a good experience."

"Me too. I hope you get the chance to have a good experience as well." Trip pulls a face, "Not with your brother, though. That would be sad for me and gross for you."

Smothering a gag, I shake my head, "I think it's time to change the topic."

"Agreed." Trip starts to giggle and it doesn't take long for me to join in.

"Did I miss something?"

I turn and see Skylar watching us with bright eyes. A wide smile breaks free as I throw my arms around his neck, pulling him close.

It seems silly to miss someone when you talk to them every night, but somehow my heart manages.

Skylar wraps his arms around my waist and presses a soft kiss against my neck. I close my eyes, finally feeling a little bit more complete.

Trip clears her throat, "You must be Skylar."

Gently pulling away from his embrace, I shoot her an apologetic smile, "Skylar, this is Trip, my brother's girlfriend. We were just talking about their sex life."

He glances at her, "That's unfortunate."

Trip laughs, "It really was. Nice to meet you, Skylar."

"Likewise."

He brushes white hair from his eyes and my gaze drops to the plain black t-shirt he's wearing. The material hangs loose off his slim frame, but my attention snags on the piece of paper pinned to the middle of it.

A delighted gasp escapes me, "Did you draw that?"

"I didn't want to show up without some show of support."

"I love it."

I lean in closer, admiring the fine lines of the tiger crawling along the paper. It's an exact replica of Taber's mascot, the predator's mouth open in a fierce roar that our lacrosse team is known for making before each game.

He shrugs, "You're welcome to have it after the game."

"I'm going to hold you to that."

A ping sounds and Trip quickly pulls out her phone, "It looks like my roommate has secured our seats. We should probably head over there before she scares away more students."

Skylar tilts his head, "Is your roommate scary?"

"Only when she wants to be." Trip blows out a breath, "Game day tends to bring out her competitive side. And *that* is terrifying."

I laugh, reaching over to take Skylar's hand as we start the trek to the stadium. He observes the mass of students cutting through the manicured lawns without a word, his grip on my hand tightening the closer we get to the stadium.

"Have you ever been to Taber before?" I ask the question as the massive bleachers rise up above us, the stream of students merging together to slip past the entrance.

"It's been a while."

We flash our student IDs and follow the sea of orange and black up the stairs to the bleachers. Trip leads us past the main stretch of wooden benches to the row closest to the field. Skylar's hand slips from mine as we walk towards the platinum blonde wearing tiger stripped face paint.

Stella lets out a shriek when she sees Trip. I laugh, watching the tiny ball of energy bounce from side-to-side. Cody leans forward in his seat to throw me a wave and I return it with a smile.

"Skylar, meet Stella and her boyfriend... Skylar?"

I whip my head around, searching for the boy who had been right behind me two minutes ago.

"What's Skylar Vin doing here?" Stella frowns, pointing over my shoulder to a figure heading in the opposite direction.

"He came with me."

I turn to go chase him down, but a small hand grabs my arm.

"Do you know who he is?" Stella looks at me with wide eyes, "The Vin family is bad news, Lacey. You do not want to be a part of that."

Trip frowns, "Do you mean Vin as in Vector Vin?"

"That's exactly who I mean." Stella shakes her head, "He's the guy who put our captain out of commission last year."

Cody pipes up from behind her, "All things considered, I think I did pretty well."

"You are not helping, Ellsworth."

He grins, "Just making sure you get the facts right."

Stella shoots her boyfriend a glare before turning back to me, "He doesn't belong here, Lacey. Let him go."

"No." I shake off her hold, refusing to let another person make snap judgements about the boy I love, "I know exactly who Skylar is."

Stella opens her mouth but I beat her to the punch.

"He's my friend."

And then I turn and run after him.

Skylar

He's here.

The one with a kind smile. The one who got trampled because my brother can't control his temper.

The fallen captain is here.

My feet propel me forward, desperately trying to get away from the people holding my last name accountable. The moment I saw Stella O'Brien, I knew it was all over. Lacey was finally going to discover the violent reputation my brother has thrown over the family name.

Nausea creeps up my throat when I think about the injuries Vector left on Taber's lacrosse captain this time last year. It took Cody six weeks to recover from the cracked ribs and the pictures of his broken cheekbone had me throwing my sketchbook across the room.

My brother is a fucking monster.

All the men in the Vin family are monsters.

The sharp sting of self-loathing fills every pore as I hurry away from the stadium. The last time I was here, Cody got carried out on a stretcher while my brother got slapped with a couple of anger management sessions.

It was wrong every way you looked at it.

"Skylar, wait!"

Lacey's voice rips through the crowd, and my steps falter. I can hear the distress in her voice and it makes me sick knowing I put it there.

I glance over my shoulder and find Lacey running towards me. Ducking my head, shame heats my cheeks as I back into the shadows of a nearby corner.

Lacey draws to a halt in front of me, her breathing heavy and uneven from the spurt of activity. Keeping my head down, I lower my gaze to the purple laces of her sneakers.

"There you are."

She reaches out to touch me, but I quickly pull away. Silence falls between us as I bore a hole into her shoes, the pressure in my chest building with each inhale.

"Skylar. Can you look at me?"

When I don't move she lets out a soft sigh, "Alright. Can you tell me why you won't look at me?"

I swallow, feeling the nausea return, "I don't want to see you look at me like everyone else does."

"How does everyone else look at you?"

"Like I'm the rival." I close my eyes, feeling the bitter truth penetrate my skin, "The bad apple from a line of rotten seeds. The black sheep from the other side of the tracks."

"Skylar." Lacey breathes out my name but I shake my head.

"They're right, Flower. I'm the son of an abusive man and the brother of a violent one. I just... I just wanted you to see me as just Skylar for a little bit longer."

All along I've been telling her I wasn't a hero. Just the broken toy people use as a cautionary tale. The little Vin brother who has to draw his way through anger management.

The sad fact of the matter is, people like me don't get a happy ending.

Lacey steps forward, her fingers reaching out to caress my face. I press my cheek into her hand, wishing I was strong enough to turn away.

"You've never been just Skylar."

She cradles my face, trying to get me to look at her, "You're the only person I've wanted to talk to since I found your first message. Every week, I would count down the days to my next therapy session just so I could see your writing."

Her words scrape the rough edges of my heart, but I don't raise my gaze from the ground. Being around Lacey has helped me not hate the person I see in the mirror every morning. She's helped me remember just how many parts of myself are still good.

But if she looks at me now, that will all change. Because there is no hiding from the irrefutable stain of the Vin last name. The violence my brother unleashed on Taber's lacrosse field last year.

All because of my silence.

Lacey clears her throat, recapturing my attention, "And then I met you and my world got so much brighter. Finally, I had found someone who wasn't afraid to linger in the darkness. Someone whose secrets were just as heavy as mine."

She runs her finger up my cheek and down my nose, gently tracing my face.

"You don't need to be afraid, Skylar. I don't blame you for what happened to Cody and I don't hold it against your brother either."

I shake my head, "Vector hurt him, Flower."

She sighs, "I know. But that doesn't change the way I see you. And it shouldn't change the way you see yourself either."

Slowly, I drag my eyes over her Tigers jersey and up to her face. Lacey stares right through me, her big green eyes filled with warmth and understanding.

But there's one aspect she doesn't understand.

I open my mouth to tell her the truth, the reason I've carried around so much guilt all these years, when she kisses me.

Pushing me back against the wall, Lacey presses her body against mine, stealing the breath straight from my lungs. Her nails scrape against the back of my neck and my hands instinctively latch on to her waist, pulling her flush against me.

My train of thought gets completely derailed when Lacey swivels her hips against me. Letting out a quiet groan, I scrape my teeth along her bottom lip as my hands trail down to feel the soft flesh of her ass. She grinds against me in response, her tongue tangling with mine as I gentle press into her.

Intertwining our fingers, I bring her arms up over my neck before running my hands down both sides of her torso. She shivers against my touch, and I break away to trail my lips along her jaw and down her throat.

"Skylar."

Lacey's nails dig into my shoulder and I freeze, suddenly afraid I pushed her too far.

"What's wrong?"

"Nothing." She smiles at me with flushed cheeks, "But the game is going to start any minute now."

I blink, struggling to process the information when I can still feel Lacey's soft body pressing against me.

She lifts her hand and strokes my face gently, "Do you re-member what you promised me last night, Skylar Vin?"

My last name flows out of her mouth like nothing I've ever heard before. There's no contempt, no fear, no hatred. There's just three letters and one syllable.

The lustful thoughts slip away as my body starts to ache for an entirely different reason.

"Yeah."

"What did you promise me?" Her fingers grip my chin, forc-ing me to look at her, "What you were going to start believing?"

The edges of Lacey's face begin to blur as tears burn my eyes. "That I'm something special."

A tear slips down my cheek but Lacey catches it before it can fall. Swiping her thumb under my eye, she wipes away the evidence without so much as a blink.

"Say it again."

"I'm something special."

Lacey shakes her head with a sad smile, "Now you just have to believe it."

I stare at her, feeling my chest collapse with the unconceivable notion that she would want anything to do with someone like me.

"If I'm not allowed to thank you then you're not allowed to look at me like that." She taps me on the nose, "Now, I've got to go watch the Tigers play but you don't have to join if you don't want to."

I hesitate, thinking about the demons waiting for me in the stands. Cody Ellsworth represents everything I've tried to escape this past year. Everything I've tried to forget through art and an endless number of therapy sessions.

But I promised my flower I would be there.

"I'll come." I blow out a breath and loosen my grip on her waist. Too many promises have been broken in my household to throw away another one.

A bright smile flashes my way, officially sealing my fate. Taking my hand, Lacey leads us back to the bleachers that nearly destroyed me the last time.

We fall in step beside each other, our fingers intertwined as I re-enter the rival's spectator arena. The sight of the painted lacrosse field has one last secret bubbling up inside me, but I shove it back down before it can leak out.

I need to tell her the truth, but not today.

I want today to be a good day.

Chapter 14

Lacey

My brother scores a goal and the crowd goes wild.

The players wearing orange and black jerseys go running for a celebratory huddle, jostling Wesley for tying up the game with a seventh goal in the last quarter. Nico pushes up his helmet and lets out a cheer from his position in the crease, the excitement on his face easy to see from our front row seats.

Even Mighty Mo, Taber's graduated lacrosse legend and Nico's partner, looks pleased from his assistant coach position on the sidelines.

The energy of the crowd washes over me, the excitement in the air palpable from every Taber supporter in the bleachers. Stella is jumping up and down beside Skylar, her enthusiasm rubbing off on nearby spectators. Cody is grinning beside her, shaking his head as the players break off and run back into their positions.

"I swear to God, half the shots Wes make are pure luck."

Stella snorts, "It's not luck, it's strategy. That man studies lacrosse videos in his spare time."

Trip laughs, "It's true. I caught him googling new training drills last week."

Skylar stays silent beside me, his fingers nervously tapping his thigh. Besides a quiet murmur of acknowledgement to Cody and Stella, he hasn't said a word since we sat down.

I lean over and nudge him gently, "What do you think?"

"Of the play?"

At my nod, Skylar lifts a shoulder, "Stella was right, it was a strategic move. He purposefully waited until the other forward made a breakaway so the defensemen would be preoccupied when he made his shot."

I'm stunned, speechless, and that's before Stella turns and gives him a nod of acknowledgement.

"I'm glad somebody else understands lacrosse."

Cody barks out a laugh, "Says the woman who has never stepped on a lacrosse field."

"Doesn't make it any less true."

Taber's old lacrosse captain shakes his head, "Next date, we're playing lacrosse. Then we will find out who knows more about the sport."

Stella smirks, flicking a braid over her shoulder, "Get ready to have your ass whooped, Ellsworth. Better start working on your losing skills now."

He grins, "Good thing I'm not the sore loser in this relationship."

The couple starts bickering and I shift closer to Skylar. Reaching into his lap, I take his hand to stop the nervous fidgeting. I stroke his thumb gently, silently offering some reassurance.

"You know a lot about lacrosse. Did you ever play?"

Skylar shakes his head, squeezing my fingers, "This was always my brother's territory. I just picked up some things from watching his games."

"Did you watch a lot of them?"

He flicks his eyes to mine, "I watched every single one."

I bite my lip, thinking about the number of players Vector has put in the hospital. Skylar does everything he can to avoid violence and yet his brother goes out of his way to inflict it.

After meeting Amber and seeing the scars she carries around, it makes me wonder how the two brothers could have chosen such different paths.

"That must have been tough."

"Some were." Skylar huffs out a quiet laugh, "But someone had to take responsibility."

Before I can question his response, the ref blows his whistle and the game resumes. Wrapping my hand more securely around Skylar's, together we watch the Tigers run around the field, the varsity athletes moving with accuracy and speed as they whip the ball across the field.

"What strategy are they doing now?" I whisper softly in his ear, noticing the shiver that runs through him.

"This offensive play is called an invert, it's pretty common among the university circuit."

Skylar points to different players lined up on the front line, casually explaining the formation and objective behind it. He does it in a way that is plain and simple, leaving no room for confusion or complexity.

It blows my mind how much of a patient person he is. From the hours he spends on his art to the way he lets me linger around a bookstore, Skylar's ability to wait is incomparable. I've never met someone who feels comfortable letting the silence grow if only so I can have more time with my thoughts.

He's cautious yet meticulous. Precise yet undemanding.

It makes me wonder what he'd be like as a lover.

The thought has discomfort spreading over my skin like a rash. I haven't been able to properly read a sex scene for the last two years, and now that Skylar is on the scene, it's starting to bother me. At this rate, I would be better off being the virgin my roommate paints me out to be.

I'm a freak and not in a good way.

Skylar shifts beside me, interrupting my spiralling thoughts, "Here he goes again. Any minute now, number twelve is going to fall back so six can swing left and pass it back…"

Just like the he predicted, Wesley drops back and sprints to the open position the other forward player helped to open up. With a flick of his wrist, the player passes the ball and my brother takes the shot. The goalie dives in the crease, stretching out his hand to make the save, but the ball drops right before he can make contact and rolls into the net.

The timer on the final quarter sounds and the crowd goes wild once more.

"Tequila coming in hot!"

Nico deposits the tray down on the table and Wesley lets out a groan.

"You are not allowed to buy the drinks anymore. I hate this shit."

Nico smirks, passing him a shot, "It's not my fault you have the tolerance of a fourteen year-old girl."

Trip laughs and snags one from the tray, "He's got you there."

Wesley reaches over and lifts his girlfriend from her chair onto his lap, "You're lucky I am so confident in my masculinity or I would be weeping right now."

She rolls her eyes, "You should try being less confident. Maybe your lacrosse helmet would fit better."

I laugh and Skylar glances at me with bright eyes. His anxiety has gone down a lot since the game ended and the group separated so Stella and Cody could partake in their own celebration.

I'm pretty sure that's code for sex, but I decided not to question it.

"God, I love it when you're mean to me." Popping out a couple of dimples, Wesley pulls her close and plants a kiss on her lips.

Nico pulls a face and claps his hands before things can get too messy. I love Trip to pieces, but she really does have the worst habit of encouraging my brother's love of PDA.

The Tigers won this afternoon, so the atmosphere is light and festive as students and parents chat amiably amongst themselves. The bar itself has a honky-tonk feel to it, with hunting trophies lining the wall behind the bar and a hockey game playing on the television.

It's easy to forget Taber is a conservative small town when I'm living on campus. The miles of corn fields and rusty pickup trucks seem like a different world compared to the manicured lawns of the university.

"So, Skylar." Tossing me a wink, Nico passes him a shot, "What are your intentions with our gorgeous girl over there?"

Oh my God.

Fighting the blush taking over my face, I cross my arms and glare at Nico's smirking one. My brother finally extracts his mouth from Trip's and shoots me a sympathetic glance.

"We drew straws on who got to be the bad cop."

Nico grins, "At least I was kind enough to buy tequila."

Skylar picks up the shot and throws it back. Carefully setting the glass down on the table, he makes eye contact with Nico.

"I'm going to need a few more of those."

Wesley laughs then stops, squinting at Skylar's straight face.

"I can't tell if he's joking."

Laughter bubbles up in my throat as Skylar glances at me, his mismatched irises sparkling past his stoic expression. The dim lighting of the bar makes his white hair and cheekbones stand out that much more, but Skylar's angelic features aren't what captures my attention.

It's the flicker of happiness hiding just beneath the surface.

Skylar

Lacey's brother is not what I was expecting.

Neither is her friend Nico, for that matter. Despite the earlier jokes, both of them seem more inclined on getting me to like them rather than conducting an interrogation.

Wes, Lacey's brother, reminds me of an overexcited puppy with a larger-than-life personality and a dimpled smile. It took less than a second for me to figure out who was Lacey's biological relation given the midnight curls and bright green eyes both siblings inherited.

Her brother might be the loudest member of the group, but Nico isn't far behind. Wearing a flashy dress shirt and a permanent smirk, the handsome Latino seems to spend most of his time using ridiculous innuendoes and sexual comments to trigger a reaction.

If I had to pick a favourite, Trip would probably be it. She's quieter than the two guys, her remarks dry and witty without being over-the-top. The unsuspecting humour aligns most closely with my own, and besides Lacey, she seems to be the only one not concerned about my lack of expression.

"...and now we fuck on the regular." Nico grins at me, completing his recount of the volatile relationship he has with the team's assistant coach.

I stare back at him, wondering if he normally shares such intimate details with strangers.

"Congratulations."

"Fuck. You're a hard nut to crack." Nico leans back in his chair, studying me from across the table, "Do you ever smile?"

"Skylar smiles all the time." Lacey reaches over and wraps her hand around mine, "You just have to be lucky enough to see it."

She squeezes my hand and I stare at it, feeling the weight of my shortcomings. Everyone has been going around the table sharing their favourite memories of university, and each one resulted in peals of laughter and bright smiles from everyone except me.

"Or, maybe Nico is just a bad storyteller." Wes uses the joke to break the awkward silence and Nico lets out a gasp.

"Take that back. Take that back right now or I'll call housing services the next time you two decide to get freaky in a study room."

"Don't be a hater. We were studying anatomy."

Nico smirks, "More like the outline of Trip's cervix."

Lacey wrinkles her face in disgust. My eyes drop to the mass of freckles lining her scrunched nose, the faded marks making me want to pull out a pen and connect them all.

Wes holds up his hands in surrender, "Hey, I was just making sure I would pass the class."

A couple of dimples pop out when he looks at his blushing girlfriend, the affection he holds for her evident from the way his hand keeps sneaking under her shirt.

"How did you two meet?" I direct the question at Trip, trying not to stare as her boyfriend gropes her under the table.

"Me and Wes?" At my nod, she glances at him, "Do you want to take the lead on this one?"

"Hell no. I love it when you take the lead."

Wes throws her a wink and I politely look away when he pulls her ass further onto his lap. The social butterfly and the sarcastic introvert seem like an odd pairing but they certainly have physical touch down.

Trip rolls her eyes before leaning back against his chest and giving me a smile.

"We met during move-in day our freshman year. Wes tried to help carry my boxes and we ended up flat on our backs with my underwear blowing across the front lawn."

Lacey laughs, "My brother always has the best intentions but they never seem to work out the way he plans."

Wes pauses the groping session to draw the cross on his chest, "The universe likes to keep me on my toes but she always delivers. Amen."

Trip rolls her eyes again, "As you can imagine, I had no interest in this clown until he started showing up everywhere, insisting we were friends."

Nico interrupts with a smirk, "He was pathetic but persistent."

She shrugs, meeting my curious gaze, "Eventually we started hanging out and here we are now."

"One year later and desperately in love is what Miss One Trip forgot to say." Shifting on the chair, Wes leans forward and kisses her.

Lacey lets out a soft sigh and it doesn't take long for me to spot the heartache swimming through her gaze. My chest tightens when I think about the romance novels she loves to read, the meet cutes and happy ever afters she keeps safely stored in her little dorm library.

After everything she's been through, it seems cruel that my flower has to watch her brother secure the storyline she always dreamed about.

Nico's phone rings and he snatches it from the table, "Sorry team, but I've got to split. I've got a charcuterie board stamped with the name Maurice O'Brien waiting for me."

Pushing back his chair, Nico walks over to give Lacey a hug, "You better head out before Wes and Trip get any nastier."

She huffs out a laugh, "Say hi to Mo for me."

"I will." Nico plants a kiss on her head before turning to me, "I said I was going to be cool and do a bro hug, but I can't bring myself to do it."

Without missing a beat, Nico saunters over and wraps his arms around me.

"It was nice meeting you, Expressionless Wonder. Ten bucks says I'll break a smile out of you next time."

I freeze as the warmth of his body envelopes me in a cloud of cologne and confidence. Lacey catches my eye over his shoulder and gives me a reassuring smile.

Blinking back the sudden surge of tears, I can't bring myself to speak as Silverwood's rival goalie gives me a glimpse of what it feels like to have a normal family.

Nico gives me one last squeeze before pulling away, "Alright. It's time for me to get my freak on. Go make terrible decisions for papa."

Blowing one last kiss to the couple making out across from us, Nico turns and makes his leave. Lacey lets out a light laugh before glancing over at me.

"Are you ready to get out of here?"

I stare at her, tracing the face that has become my safe haven these last few weeks. I thought she was exquisite the first night I saw her, but nothing could have prepared me for the compassionate soul sitting next to me.

"Absolutely."

Lacey's dorm is exactly what I was expecting.

Tiny but efficiently furnished, a large desk takes up most of the floor space between her single bed and the far wall. Her closet is tucked in behind the door and the remaining space is allocated to succulents of every shape and size imaginable.

"You weren't kidding about having a greenhouse."

I shuffle along the few feet of carpet, peering at the row of plants and romance books stacked precariously between her textbooks. As small as the room is, Lacey managed to make it completely her own with an explosion of colour on every surface available.

"I probably shouldn't have brought all my plant babies here, but I couldn't bear the thought of leaving them at home." She bends down and carefully extracts a dead leaf from one of her plants.

Trying not to stare at her bent over form, I turn my attention to the romance books lining the desk's top shelf. Each spine is cheerful and bright, identical to the ones we saw in the bookstore the other day. Reaching up, I grab the pastel pink one and study the polaroid pictures decorating the front cover.

"Is this your entire book collection as well?"

"Oh no. This isn't even a tenth of what I have back home."

My lips tug upward at the confession. Opening the book, I flip through the pages and catch a glimpse of sharp black smudges. I frown, flipping back through the pages until I find the intrusive mark.

Thick, black lines cut through the words, and my first thought is there must be some sort of a printing error. I lean in closer, trying to pinpoint the starting point when I notice the shaky and uneven curvature.

As if someone purposefully crossed them out.

Slowly setting the book down, I grab the next one on the shelf. The same markings reside in this one too, repeating continuously throughout the book. My heart starts to pound as I stare at the destroyed pages in front of me, the harsh slash of the permanent marker holding only one thing in common.

Each one was used to cross out a sex scene.

"Can I get you a drink or something? Sorry, I should have asked earlier..." Lacey's voice dies off when she sees the books lying open on the desk. Letting out a nervous laugh, she tucks a strand of hair behind her ear.

"Oh, you found my annotations. It's a silly habit I got into, but it's very popular with the romance community right now."

I turn and stare at her, "These aren't annotations, Flower."

She bites her lip, avoiding my gaze, "Some of them are."

I flick my eyes back to the words crossed out on the page in front of me. The jagged lines are thick and merciless, refusing to let a single letter bleed through.

The whole thing is so... *angry.*

Slowly raising my gaze to her guilt-stricken face, I can barely breathe as I take in the consequence of someone else's actions.

"What did he do to you?"

Chapter 15

Lacey

I've really done it now.

Wringing my hands, I do everything I can not to look in Skylar's direction. I should have known someone would stumble across the scenes I blacked out during my darker moments.

A hopeful part of me thought no one would ever look through my books, so it wasn't something I had to worry about. The other, more rational side assumed that if someone did find the marks, they wouldn't bother to look past the annotated surface.

"Flower?"

He's waiting for an answer, but I don't know if I can give him one. I've never told anyone the details of what happened that night, partly out of shame but mostly out of embarrassment.

"I, uh…" Heat creeps up my neck as I glance at him, "Sometimes it hurts reading things that aren't true. So, when the pain gets too much I just cross it out."

There's a sliver of hope that Skylar hasn't clued in to what parts of the book I try to erase, but that futile dream quickly gets blown away.

"You cross out the sex scenes."

I flinch like he ripped a splinter straight from my skin.

"Look, it's no big deal. I just had a bad experience and it makes me angry when authors create fictional worlds where sex is enjoyed by both parties."

Skylar's eyes widen and I hurry to fix the slip-up, "I mean, I know sex can be enjoyable for both parties. I hear my roommate have a fantastic time every weekend, so I know it's true."

The joke falls flat and silence fills the room. I shuffle over to the narrow edge of my bed and sit down, nervously picking at the polish on my fingernails.

After a beat, Skylar walks over and sits down next to me. Our shoulders aren't touching, but the distance does nothing to ease the tension from the room.

"Can you tell me a secret?" His voice is rough, like each word is causing him physical pain. I close my eyes, knowing exactly what he's asking for.

"It's not pretty, Skylar."

"That's okay."

When I open my eyes, he's looking at me, the broken pieces of his soul reflecting my own. I should have known Skylar would see through my weak efforts of normality. He always sees me, even when I don't want to be seen.

I turn away, feeling my bottom lip start to tremble.

"I started seeing this guy just before I turned sixteen. His name was Jerrell Thompson. He was new to town and came from a wealthy family."

Skylar stays silent but I can feel the weight of his stare on the side of my face.

"He took me on these extravagant dates, just like what you see in the movies. He liked to buy me things, liked taking me to fancy restaurants. I got caught up in the romance, I guess."

A bitter laugh leaks out, "Jerrell was the most charismatic guy I had ever met, he could turn on the charm at any time and win anyone over. But he could also turn the charm off."

Pulling my knees up to my chest, I hug them close, "He could be so cruel. He would say these things, simple things that would cut straight through me."

"What did he say?"

"The usual stuff. Questioning why I didn't feel the need to dress up or put on makeup. Why I would rather stay home and hangout then go out with his friends. Why I always made him feel unwanted."

Skylar hisses out a breath and the sound puts an ache in my chest.

"He had this idea that we weren't a real couple if we didn't have sex. We'd done some other stuff, but every time he pushed for more, I would say no."

I bite my lip, staring at my fingernails as the humiliating truth presses against my chest.

"After a few months, he gave me an ultimatum. Have sex or the relationship was over."

"Did you want to have sex with him?"

I shake my head, letting the pathetic truth slip past my lips, "No. I just didn't want to lose him."

Silence falls between us until Skylar reaches over and takes my hand.

"What happened next?"

I swallow, wishing my story had a different ending.

"We were in the backseat of his car, so there wasn't a lot of room. He started kissing me and taking off my clothes. I got scared and asked him to slow down."

I squeeze my legs together as the memory resurfaces.

"He kept telling me it was going to be okay. That I just had to make it through the first part and it would get better. But he didn't get me ready, so when he pushed himself inside me, it hurt. It hurt so bad."

My voice breaks on a sob, "I kept asking him to stop but he kept going. The pain got so bad that I started to cry. I didn't understand why he kept hurting me. Why he was enjoying hurting me."

Skylar's fingers clench around mine but I keep going. I know that if I stop now, I won't be able to start again.

"I wanted to die. Just to make the pain go away. Then it finally ended and the pain got so much worse. He pulled up his pants and told me it hadn't been worth the wait. That I hadn't been worth the wait."

I hunch over, sobs wrecking through my body. Skylar pulls me back on the bed, wrapping his arms tightly around me as I cry out the rest of my love story.

"The next day, he told everyone at school I was a bad lay. I was so embarrassed. The rumours going around made it so my friends didn't want to hang out with me anymore. My heart was in pieces and I felt so alone. I didn't see a way out."

"I found my mom's prescription pills five days later. My brother found me unconscious in the bathroom and rushed me to the hospital. When I woke up, I was so disappointed. I didn't want to be in this life anymore. But then I saw Wesley's face, I saw the devastation in his eyes, and the disappointment turned into guilt."

A strangled laugh escapes me, "Turns out, the only thing worse than having your innocence stolen is waking up to see your brother's face after you try to commit suicide."

Skylar doesn't say anything as I break down and cry, my body curled up against his. My fists dig into his shirt, clenching the soft material like it's my lifeline. Skylar presses his lips against my neck, softly stroking my hair as he waits for my tears to run out.

My hiccups break the silence of the room, echoing off the walls of my dorm. It takes a while for my ragged breathing to calm down, but once it does, Skylar shifts back to look at me.

"You have really soft hair. Do you use conditioner too?"

I choke out a laugh, remembering the last time I used that line. Our roles were reversed, but just like before, it helps to diffuse the thick waves of grief clouding the room.

"Maybe."

Skylar stares at me, seeing every uncovered shard I have to offer. I'm fully dressed and yet I feel completely naked, stripped down to the raw edges of my being.

"What did you mean when you said he didn't get you ready?"

I blink, surprised by his question.

"Uh, well, he didn't touch me."

Skylar's brows furrow and I start to blush, "Like foreplay. It doesn't take much to turn me on but he just went straight to sex. So, I wasn't... wet."

I grimace at the crude word, dropping my gaze to Skylar's chest. I watch his breathing grow still as tension bleeds through his body.

"He fucked you dry?"

Glancing at his face, the breath gets knocked from my lungs. A fire lights up his mismatched eyes, the blue one glinting dangerously while the brown one darkens into a bottomless pit. I can see the fury coming to life inside him, the rage he tries so hard to hide fighting to break through the surface.

"Yeah, but it was my first time. I'm sure he thought the blood would help-

"Don't make excuses for him." Skylar snaps his teeth together, "There are plenty of other options to make the experience more enjoyable for women."

His body trembles against me, his fingers twitching restlessly against the duvet. I stare at him with wide eyes, trying to think of a way to relieve the tension.

"It's okay, Skylar. I'm okay now."

"No." His head jerks to the side, "It's not okay. Nothing about that situation was okay. He raped you."

I press a hand against his chest, "No, he didn't. I gave my consent when I agreed in the first place."

He lurches away from me, "Consent can be taken away at any time, Flower. It's not a one and done deal."

Skylar scrambles off the bed, his eyes feral as they sweep around my room. It takes me a moment to realize what he's looking for.

"Pens are in the top drawer."

Propping myself up on the bed, I watch as he rips the drawer open and grabs the first pen he can find. The tendons in his forearm bulge from the pressure he's using to hold it.

"My notepads are next to my bookshelf."

Skylar grabs one from the pile, his eyes dancing over the crossed out sex scenes lying open on my desk. He closes his eyes, his breathing heavy and uneven as he clutches the pen and paper in his hands.

I slowly climb to my feet, eliminating the distance between us.

"Start to draw, Skylar. It's going to be okay."

His eyes flick open, meeting mine in a storm of rage.

"I'm sorry, Flower. I have to go."

I take a step forward, "You can draw here. I don't mind."

"No." Skylar stumbles back, trying to increase the space between us, "You aren't going to want to see this one."

I bite my lip, wishing he felt comfortable enough to stay. I want to apologize for getting him in this state, but I know that will only make it worse.

"Okay." Stepping to the side, I open my bedroom door. Skylar brushes past me but pauses before he makes it out the door.

"Thank you for telling me. I'll call you tomorrow?"

I give him a small smile, "Call me tonight after you've calmed down. Thanks for supporting the rival today, Skylar."

He stares at me, the ferocious gleam in his eyes dimming the slightest bit.

"You've never been my rival, Flower. I'll talk to you soon."

Skylar

Four boxes of crayons later and I feel just as angry as I did two hours ago.

The broken pieces stare back at me, the sheets of paper thrown around my bedroom floor like a science experiment gone wrong. My body feels like a ticking bomb, the itch in my skin counting down the minutes until I explode.

I can't see anything except the pain I want to inflict on Jerrell fucking Thompson.

My hands shake as I reach for another piece of paper.

I have to fight it. I have to fight-

"Who got your panties in a twist?"

Vector peeks his head through my doorway, and it takes all my self-control not to hurl the closest crayon at his head.

I want to smash in someone's skull and I don't care whose it is.

"Get out."

"In a mood today, are we?" Vector pushes his way inside and I squeeze my eyes shut, trying to remember the tricks my therapist taught me.

Find a focus point and use it as an anchor. Deep inhale and exhale. Do it again.

"Oh, shit. Are these intestines?"

My eyes flick open to see Vector studying one of the many drawings I spent the last two hours creating. The level of detail on each one is gruesome to an extreme degree and it makes me hate myself that much more.

"I told you to leave." I snarl at him, torn between ripping up the murderous drawings and stabbing out his eyes. I would use my sharpened pencil to pluck out each one before shoving them down his throat.

The anger isn't what controls you, Skylar. It's the fear of the anger. Find something that helps ease the pressure and hold on to it.

My brother laughs, oblivious to the horrifying picture I just painted in my mind, "Clearly this isn't working. Put your weapon down and let's go burn off some steam."

I clench the pencil tighter, "I don't want to go anywhere with you."

"Too bad. Mom wants us to spend more quality time together, so I'm paying my dues. Throw on your running shoes and meet me outside in five."

"No."

"You have five minutes to get outside or I will carry your ass out of this house." Vector tilts his head, a smirk staining his features, "Tick tock, Sky."

He turns and leaves before I can say anything else. Picking up the closest drawing, I tear it to shreds before stomping over and grabbing my running shoes.

I fucking hate him.

I fucking *despise* him.

The thought fuels my rage right up until I see Vector stretching by the tree in our front yard. His hair is pulled back in a low ponytail, the shoulder-length strands just as long as they were back in middle school. We used to meet out here every morning to train for our cross-country meets, and I didn't think I would ever call anyone else my best friend.

My eyes drop to the leg muscles bulging from his gym shorts, the same muscles that fuelled the ego and the violence that led to our distancing.

"Twenty seconds to spare. I'm almost disappointed." He flashes me a grin, "Let's see if you can still run the loop in under an hour."

I don't say anything as I turn and start to run, the punishing pound of the pavement echoing in time with my heartbeat.

Vector falls in step beside me, his giant frame showing no signs of lag as he keeps up with me.

With every block we pass, I push the pace faster, trying to outrun the monster snarling inside. My lungs feel like they've been doused with gasoline and set on fire, but I don't slow down. Every step, every ragged breath feels like a punishment and I gladly take each one.

Vector stays by my side the entire time, refusing to let me get one step ahead. I used to get annoyed he was always trying to prove who was stronger, but now I'm grateful for it. His presence helps drive me faster, pushing my pathetic athletic abilities over the edge of comfort.

Sweat stings my eyes as we round the last corner, the shakiness in my limbs making me think they might give out at any second. The tree in our front yard marks the end of our loop, and the moment I see it, I break into a sprint.

Every morning, Vector would win the unofficial race and there's no doubt in my mind that today will be the same.

He's always been the faster one. The stronger one.

Despite the inevitable outcome, I pump my arms and drive my legs as hard as possible. The tree flies by my line of sight as I hit the finish line, and I wait for Vector's celebratory shout to hit me.

The heavy fall of footsteps echo behind me and I whip my head around. Vector slows to a jog, offering a modest shrug when he catches me staring.

"You looked like you needed the win today."

My face crumples at the same time my body does and I collapse to the ground. Lungs seizing with the need for air, I gasp and choke as my muscles scold me for the extreme exertion.

"If you hit the gym on a regular basis, this wouldn't be so embarrassing."

Vector steps into my line of sight and I can't even lift my hand to flip him off.

"Fuck...you." I wheeze out the words, refusing to acknowledge the truth in his words. He barks out a laugh before offering me his hand.

"You better get up before the neighbours start talking about your lack of stamina."

"Just go. I'm going to be here a while."

Vector heaves a sigh before plopping down beside me. Stretching out a long leg, he starts doing cool down stretches while I struggle to remember how to breathe.

"You didn't have to do that." I gasp, feeling the lactic acid set in, "We both know you would have won. You've always been faster."

"True." Vector shifts, switching which leg is extended, "But that wouldn't have made you feel any better."

Swallowing the bile rising in my throat, I rest my head against the grass and stare at the sky. It's turning pink with the afterglow of the sunset and the bright colours make me think of Lacey.

I shouldn't have run out on her today. It was cowardly and selfish, especially after she opened up to me about her past. Hearing what her ex-boyfriend did to her though... I couldn't help it. The anger detonated inside of me, and like always, I panicked.

But the anger isn't here anymore.

Shock washes over me when I register the rage controlling every thought is gone. My control is safely locked in place, and even though it hurts to breathe, I feel like myself again.

I look over and find Vector watching me with a satisfied smile.

"How did you know that would work?"

He shrugs, "Because I'm brilliant."

"You're a lot of things, Vec, but brilliant isn't one of them."

Vector bursts out laughing and the crack in my chest splinters.

Before I met Lacey, my brother was one of the few people who understood my sense of humour. He was one of the few people who could see past the boy who didn't use his face to smile.

He wipes the sweat off his brow and flicks it at me.

"You're such a little asshole, Sky."

"I know."

I stare at him, seeing the piece of my heart that has been missing for too long.

"Do I need to buy bleach and a body bag?" He raises a brow, "Those were some fucked up drawings even for you."

Shame heats my cheeks and I quickly look away.

"I don't want to talk about it."

"Good. I didn't want to hear about it."

Rolling my eyes, I glance over and see Vector studying me carefully.

"Just let me know if you need to hide a body. I've got a few places in mind."

"I'm sure you do."

He stares at me for another beat before climbing to his feet and heading inside. I don't say anything when he goes, my silence as familiar as the disappointment filling my chest.

My brother may have been the one who made the decision that changed everything, but I was the one who enabled it.

And now I don't know where that leaves us.

Chapter 16

Lacey

He bought me a book.

He bought me a *romance* book.

Giddiness fills my stomach as I stare at the adorable floral cover in Skylar's hands. I wasn't sure what to expect when he said he wanted to see me tonight, a few days after my mental breakdown, but here he is.

Casually holding my personal form of kryptonite in his hand.

"It's an apology. For rushing out the way I did." Skylar chews his lip, temporarily distracting me, "You might have already read this one, but I thought it could be a project as well."

"Project?"

He nods slowly before passing over the treasured item.

"I went ahead and covered up the sex scenes with sticky notes. I tried to label some of the sections so you can work your way up without taking a sharpie to the page."

Opening the book with shaky fingers, I flip through the pages until I find the sticky notes. Skylar didn't just label the sex scenes for me. He drew an entire symbol table that carefully explains what each colour of sticky note hides and what intensity level he associates with it.

It's simple and thoughtful and so perfectly Skylar.

"Thank you." Pressing the book against my overflowing heart, I can barely stop the tears from spilling over.

Skylar shrugs, shuffling his feet, "Like I said, it's an apology. I shouldn't have run out on you like that. Not after you opened up to me."

"It's okay."

"No. It's not." He blows out a breath, "I grew up seeing the consequences of my father's anger and now the thought of being out of control scares me. When things go sideways, my normal response is to turn and run but that isn't fair to you."

I frown, "You don't have to worry about hurting me, Skylar. Hurting people is a choice and that is not one you will ever make."

"You don't know that."

"Yes. I do."

Shaking my head, I grab his hand and pull him further into my dorm, "You don't give yourself enough credit. I've seen the way you extract yourself from situations when your temper flares up. It's cautious and thoughtful and not the actions of a violent man."

Skylar reaches up and brushes a wayward curl behind my ear.

"I don't know how you do it, but you give me hope. It's a dangerous feeling, but it feels safe when it's from you."

"Of course it does. I'm a reliable source."

He huffs out a laugh and my smile grows wider. Skylar's laughter comes out even less than his smile does and it makes me appreciate it that much more.

Skylar looks at me with the smallest of smiles, both irises sparkling with the afterglow of his mirth. My heart feels full as I stare back, the weight of my new gift digging into the palms of my hands.

"I know it's late, but would you want to watch a movie with me?"

"Do you want me to stay?"

I bite my lip and nod, watching his gaze flick from my face to the single bed against the wall.

"I'll stay then."

Quickly grabbing my laptop from my desk, I steal a couple of extra blankets from my closet before settling down on the bed. Skylar joins me soon afterwards, his frame just small enough so that we both fit on the bed side-by-side.

I pull him down so we're lying together, using a spare pillow to prop the laptop on my lap. Skylar's arm sneaks around my stomach as he shifts closer, wrapping himself around me.

"What do you want to watch?" My voice comes out breathless, the sudden proximity making my hands a little shaky.

Every time I'm around Skylar, I feel like I'm home. But the moment our skin connects, it's like suddenly I'm on the edge of a cliff, staring at the waves below, wondering if I'm going to make the jump or not.

It's exhilarating and petrifying all at the same time.

Skylar brushes my ear with his lips, causing a shiver to race through me.

"I'm not sure. I don't watch a lot of movies."

"Do you have a favourite?"

"Not really." His breathe is warm and inviting and it takes all my energy to focus on the choices laid out in front of us.

"What about genres? Favourite or least favourite."

Skylar goes silent for a moment.

"I like everything but action."

A flush creeps up his cheeks when he catches the look of surprise that crosses my face.

"I know it's weird." He swallows, dropping his gaze to the screen in front of us, "I just don't like blood. Or violence."

I am such an idiot.

Scolding myself for not putting the pieces together sooner, I quickly bypass the action section and find something that is bound to have a happy ending.

"How does *Grown Ups* sound?"

Skylar relaxes against me with a nod of approval. Pressing play, I snuggle down and escape into Adam Sandler's world of comedy.

It doesn't take long for me to start laughing at the ridiculous antics playing out on screen. Skylar stays silent beside me, but I can tell he's enjoying it. There's a lightness to him that I haven't seen before, and with every laugh I make, it grows and expands into something more.

About halfway through the movie I feel Skylar's fingers dance across my skin.

There's nothing expectant about the touch, nothing sexual about the way he mindlessly draws on my arm as the movie plays out in front of us. Despite the way my heart is racing, the innocent touch doesn't feel like the pressure I'm used to. It doesn't feel like Skylar is being calculating about his movements to ensure something happens tonight.

Sneaking a glance at him, my feelings are confirmed. Skylar's eyes are glued to the screen, his head tilted toward mine as his fingers lightly sketch invisible pictures on my skin.

It hits me right then, that this is what a healthy relationship looks like. Being able to hang out with your partner without the burden of guilt or the fear of malicious words.

When I'm with Skylar, there are no expectations sexual or otherwise. He simply accepts me for who I am and doesn't question the ridiculous schemes I come up with.

I might not be complete, but he makes me feel about as close as I'll ever be.

"I should probably go."

His voice draws my attention back to the final credits rolling on the screen.

"Sleepover tonight. You can drive home in the morning."

"Are you sure?"

I nod, shifting my laptop so I can sit up in bed.

"I have a spare toothbrush you can borrow. Give me five minutes."

Sliding off the bed, I grab my sleepwear and face cream before slipping into the bathroom. I stare at my reflection in the mirror, barely recognizing the girl with the excited eyes and permanent smile. For the first time in a long time, I look genuinely happy.

And not just on the outside.

Beaming at my own reflection, I quickly perform my ablutions before hunting down the toothbrush I promised Skylar. The entire routine takes less than five minutes, and I find him patiently waiting for me back in my room.

He takes the toothbrush without a word and disappears into the bathroom. The book he gifted me sits unopened on my desk and I walk over to grab it.

Flipping the pages to the symbol table outlined on the first page, I read the cursive handwriting and start to blush.

Yellow: Heavy petting with clothes on.

Blue: Basic finger foreplay.

Green: Oral sex.

Pink: First moment of entry. Missionary.

Red: Repeated intercourse. Mirrors and props.

"Everything okay?"

I snap the book shut and look up to find Skylar studying me. The heat in my face blooms, spreading down my neck and chest as I stare at the boy who outlined fictional orgasms for me.

His eyes flick down, following the blush to the exposed edges of my loose tank top. I squeeze my legs together, trying to ignore the ache building between them.

"Everything is great!" The high pitch of my voice has me cringing. My mind is stuck on the list of sexual acts he wrote out for me.

Was he thinking about me when he read those scenes?

I swallow thickly, wishing I was brave enough to ask the question out loud. Skylar hasn't moved from his spot in the doorway, his eyes carefully guarded as he looks at me.

"Do you want me to leave?"

"What? No. Not at all." An awkward laugh slips out, "Just the opposite."

A faint smile hits Skylar's face and the ache between my legs increases by tenfold. His hair is messy and a little wild from our movie and it makes me wonder what it would look like if we had watched the movie like a normal couple.

What it would look like if we hadn't watched the movie at all.

Heat pools between my legs as I think about the list he wrote out for me, the casual description he left for each colour. There's a quiet confidence about Skylar that makes me think he has a decent amount of sexual experience, but when it comes to knowing what he likes and desires, I am completely clueless.

"What are you thinking about, Flower?"

Caught mid-thought, heat flames my cheeks, "Well, uh, I was just wondering..."

I trail off, heart pounding when I make eye contact with the boy studying me from across the room. Skylar doesn't say anything, he patiently waits for my thought process to finish articulating.

"I was wondering if you have done any of those things. The ones you listed." I stutter the last bit, pointing to the romance book as if that might distract him long enough for me to run into my closet and hide from embarrassment.

"Is that a polite way of asking if I'm a virgin?"

My eyes go wide, "No! No, not at all. I mean, it's okay if you are but I didn't assume..." Catching sight of the humour flashing through Skylar's eyes, I stop mid-sentence and point accusingly at him.

"Deadpan humour is not allowed when we're talking about virginity."

He tilts his head, "Who said I was joking?"

"I know you are." Marching over to where he's standing, I point at his blue iris, "This one sparkles when you're joking while the other one," Jabbing my finger at the brown iris, a smile breaks across my face, "Turns into a pool of melted chocolate. I *know* you, Skylar. There's no fooling me with a straight face."

He smiles then, a real smile that chases away the shadows of his face and sets my soul on fire. We're close enough to touch and suddenly, I can't think of a single reason not to.

I reach up and trace the divots of his smile from his lips up to the crinkles of his eyes. My fingers brush over the edges of his cheekbones, silently thanking the fine bone structure that frames his face.

Skylar might spend his time making art, but he might be the most beautiful work of art I have ever seen.

"I'm not a virgin, Flower." He presses a soft kiss onto the palm of my hand, "And yes, I have done most of the items listed on there."

Skylar grabs my wrist and turns it slowly, tracing a finger over the pulse fluttering beneath the delicate skin. It's hard to remember how to breathe when he's touching me like this, making me feel like a new design he wants to memorize.

"The main character approached a few things differently than I would have." Running his finger from my wrist to my elbow, Skylar watches every micro shiver that goes through me, "I didn't like how fast he went through the green stage. I would have taken it slower so I could enjoy it more."

I swallow, watching Skylar's finger inch up my shoulder. His movements are precise and steady, exactly how you would expect an artist to be.

"Y-You enjoy oral sex?"

The stupidity of my question hits me immediately.

"Never mind, of course you like receiving-

"I didn't say receiving." He flicks his eyes to mine and I snap my mouth shut, feeling my panties dampen with the words left unsaid.

Skylar enjoys giving head.

Skylar

When I was reading the sex scene I outlined for Lacey, I had to stop to jerk off three times.

Not my proudest moment, but I hadn't realized how graphic those scenes were. The words were crude enough, but they were nothing compared to the pictures that got painted inside my head. Pictures that didn't feature the blonde heroine and the muscled up hero.

When the main character laid his partner down on the kitchen table to eat her out, it wasn't blonde hair I was picturing. It wasn't even the uncomfortable surface of a kitchen table.

Instead, it was dark curls splayed out on my bedspread while bright green eyes watched me from above. Flushed skin and freckles dancing along the pale stretch of her thighs while I slowly dragged my tongue over every inch of those impossibly long legs.

It might have been fictional characters getting off in the novel, but it was my flower that got me off in real life.

Lacey blinks rapidly, her cheeks flushed bright red. She looks nervous, unsure, and more than a little turned on.

"Have you ever been eaten out before, Flower?" I ask the question softly, trying not to scare her. My finger is still trailing up her arm, closing in on the bumps of her collarbone. I should stop touching her so she can have a moment to breathe, but her skin is so soft I can't help myself.

"No." She swallows, her eyes glued to mine as my finger reaches the thin strap of her tank top, "But I have given a blowjob before."

I pause, taking a moment to let her words sink in.

"You went down on your boyfriend but he didn't go down on you?"

Lacey bites her lip and nods, "He thought it was gross. Said it was too messy."

If I didn't hate this guy with every fibre of my being, I would feel bad for him.

Staring at the girl in front of me, I can't think of a single place I would rather be then buried between her legs. I would give up sketching in a heartbeat if it meant getting a single taste of her sweetness.

I lean in and press a kiss against her cheek. Her breath hitches when I press another one lower, on the edge of her jaw, before moving down to the tender flesh of her neck.

"You could never be gross, Flower. And messy is just the reality of sex."

Reaching the base of her throat, I flick out my tongue to taste the splatter of freckles decorating her skin. She lets out a whimper and I glance up at her.

"Tell me to stop and I will."

Lacey whips her head back and forth so fast it makes me laugh. Turning back to the precarious gift in front of me, I do what any excited kid before Christmas does.

Touch every inch of it before unwrapping.

Keeping my pace slow, I run my fingers down her ribcage, counting each one as I go. I drop my head and press a kiss right between her breasts, choosing to ignore the erect nipples pushing through the fabric. My fingers round the curve of her waist and dance back up her spine, memorizing every bump and dip of her vertebrae.

I want to strip her bare and study every inch of her body, but I don't want to push her too far tonight. Especially now that she's trying something new.

Carefully keeping her shirt in place, I gently push her back towards the bed. Lacey sits down clumsily, her eyes wide as she watches me sink to my knees and press a featherlight kiss to her stomach.

"Is this okay?" I whisper against her shirt, my hands already wrapped around the bare skin of her ankles.

"Y-Yes."

She trembles against me, her restless fidgeting growing stronger the closer my face gets to her centre. Nipping her hip bone gently, I sneak past her pulsing core and kiss the outer part of her thigh instead. She hisses out a frustrated breath and I smile, working my way down to where my fingers are wrapped.

"I think you missed a spot."

I glance up at the flushed cheeks and bright green eyes staring back at me.

The fantasy that wouldn't stop haunting me the other day is nothing compared to reality. Having her tender skin under my fingertips is a thousand times better than anything my imagination could conjure.

And I'm going to make sure she knows it.

"I told you I didn't like how fast the characters went." Flicking my eyes to the covered pussy waiting for a taste, my dick starts to stiffen, "So, I'm going to show you what I would do. Is that okay?"

Lacey blinks, her eyes glassy, "That's okay."

I bend down and press a kiss against the inside of her ankle. The bone juts out against my lips, so to make sure I cover every inch, I flatten my tongue against it.

Lacey jerks against my hold, her breathing growing heavy as I lick the seam of her ankle all the way up to her calf. My hand on her other ankle follows a similar trail, making sure both sides get an equal amount of attention.

By the time I reach the uneven bump of her knees, Lacey is clenching the bedsheets and squeezing her thighs together. It's adorable, seeing her fight for control, but the current position is blocking my trek upward.

Removing my tongue from her skin, I softly tap the back of her thigh, "Can you open for me?"

"Oh, sorry." She blushes and spreads her legs. I resume my path, letting my tongue mark every freckle and dimple on the way.

"Don't be sorry." I murmur, relishing in the fresh taste of her skin, "There is nothing to be sorry for."

I reach the edge of her shorts, the upper part of her thigh, and that's when I almost break. A damp spot peeks through the light pink colour and I can see the outline of her panties pressing through the thin material.

My dick was hard before, but now it's fucking painful.

Resisting the urge to hump her leg like a stray dog, I reach up and tug the end of her pyjama bottoms.

"I'm going to take these off now."

She gives me a shaky nod and I drag the shorts down her legs. Black lace panties await me, the red roses dancing along the material momentarily distracting me.

"Flowers on my flower." Brushing the pretty design with my fingers, I lean in to get my first taste, "How fitting."

"Skylar, wait."

I rip my hands from her body and sit back on my heels. It physically hurts to stop touching her, but nothing matters more than Lacey being able to trust me.

Even if it almost kills me in the process.

She bites her lip, suddenly looking shy, "What if I don't taste good?"

Is she joking?

Torn between wanting to laugh and wanting to cry, I can only stare at her, seeing the genuine concern etched across her face. She looks so defeated already that I don't know how to undo the damage Jerrell fucking Thompson left behind.

It's inconceivable to me that Lacey doesn't understand how badly I want her. How much time she spends in my head every second of every day. How many times I wake up in the night thinking about her smile. Thinking about her laughter.

She has me wrapped around her finger and she doesn't even know it.

"Flower." I meet her down casted gaze, hoping that she will understand, "It doesn't matter what you taste like. I'm going to enjoy it."

"How can you be sure?"

I sigh, "Because you're it for me, Flower. There is no one else."

The truth echoes around her bedroom, the weight of my words dropping like an anchor between us. Lacey starts blinking rapidly, tears shining through the lust in her eyes.

"You're it for me too, Skylar."

She whispers the secret tying us together, the unbreakable bond connecting our shattered souls. A thread engraved with Lacey's name pierces through my chest, tugging the fractured pieces back into place and sewing the bleeding lacerations closed.

I stare at her, unable to say anything else as my patched up heart beats painfully in my chest. A hint of uncertainty slips through her tender expression, the slight shift of her legs drawing my attention back to the question of whether I'm going to like what she tastes like.

As if I'm not going to like what she tastes like.

Reaching up, I press my finger against her damp panties. The wet edge of the lace has me letting out a groan and the sound only gets louder when I suck my finger into my mouth.

Lacey's gasp fills the room as she watches me, the flush on her cheeks quickly shifting from self-conscious to aroused. I meet her gaze and slowly pull out my finger, letting my tongue flick over the tip for good measure.

"You like it when I'm honest, so I'm going to be honest with you." I clear my throat, trying not to stare at the flush racing down her body, "You are fucking delicious and I am really looking forward to this. Do you have any other questions?"

She stares at me with dilated pupils, the desire painted in them reflecting the same one tenting my pants.

"I-I think I'm good."

"Is it okay if I continue?"

Her head drops in a nod and I let my fingers sink back into the soft flesh of her legs. Pushing her legs wider apart, I run my tongue up the inside of her thigh and press my nose against the black lacy material.

And then I breathe her in like she's the oxygen I've spent the last eighteen years waiting for.

"Oh my God." Lacey squirms against me, the material against my face growing damper by the second.

Fuck. She smells so fucking good.

I drag my tongue from the edge of her taint up to the flowers decorating the front of her panties. Lacey lets out a gasp, her bud swelling through the flimsy material. Using my teeth to grab the edge of the fabric, I drag the panties down over her legs.

She lifts her hips to help the process and I use the opportunity to tug her closer to the edge of the bed. Her breathing is heavy and uneven by the time I make it back to her pussy, and the sight almost makes me come on the spot.

I groan, reaching up to spread the glistening folds, "You're so wet."

"I'm so-

"Do not apologize." I cut her off, pulling one leg over my shoulder, "This is the best compliment a guy can receive."

Lacey blinks down at me, the vibrant shade of her eyes confirming its place as my new favourite colour.

I press a kiss against her swollen clit, "All I want you to do is tell me what feels good, okay?"

She shudders, her hands already back gripping the comforter.

"Okay."

Chapter 17

Lacey

Skylar is really good at giving head.

The clues were there, like when he pulled off my panties using just his teeth, but it still came as a shock when he swiped his tongue across my clit like he owned it.

My hips haven't stopped bucking against his mouth, but Skylar doesn't seem to mind. He murmurs quiet encouragement against my core, continuing the slow and steady torture of his strokes. The ache between my legs builds with each pass of his tongue, the hot pressure of his mouth making me desperate for more.

"Faster, Skylar. I need you to go faster."

He responds by slipping his tongue inside me and I moan, reaching out to grab his hair. He makes a satisfied sound when I thread my fingers through the white strands, gripping them tightly.

Skylar flicks his eyes up to mine, the lust filling each iris knocking the breath right out of my chest. His mouth is fused to my pussy and he's looking at me like there isn't a place he would rather be.

His fingers slide up to play with my clit while he continues to fuck me with his tongue. Another moan slips out of me and I rock against his face, trying to increase the pace. His fingers respond in earnest, rubbing the sensitive bud exactly how I told him to the last time.

"Oh my God." I gasp at the pressure building inside of me, unlike anything I have ever experienced before.

Skylar leans forward and captures my clit with his teeth. He bites down gently before sucking it back into his mouth, triggering my pending release to arrive.

I cry out his name, gripping his hair like it's the only thing tethering me to the ground. Skylar keeps going all the way through, only slowing down after my orgasm has passed and I'm left shaking and unable to hold myself upright.

He kisses my swollen bud one last time before pulling away.

"You did so well, Flower. I'm so proud of you."

I blush at the praise, watching Skylar lick the last bit of residue off his lips. All I did was let him eat me like a main course and yet he makes me feel like I did something special.

He makes me feel like *I'm* something special.

"I didn't do anything."

Skylar shakes his head, "Not true. You did the most important part."

"What's that?"

"You trusted me."

My face breaks into a wide smile as the broken pieces of Skylar's heart weld onto mine.

"I, uh, might need to take a quick shower before going to bed."

He shifts uncomfortably on the ground and that's when I notice the erection tenting the front of his pants. My eyes go wide as I take in the outline of his dick, the tip of it pressing angrily through the beige material of his pants.

It looks really painful.

"Do you me want to..." I trial off, waiting for him to finish the sentence. Compared to Skylar's quiet confidence about sex, I feel awkward and inexperienced when it comes to things as simple as a blowjob.

I have done it before, but only because it was expected. I never got the opportunity to discover my partner's pleasure because it was never an option for me. Jerrell made the rules clear and firm, using guilt and manipulation to force my hand or my mouth to do the things he wanted.

It sounds pathetic, but at the time I didn't know any better.

I do now.

Skylar studies me silently, his eyes seeing far more than they should.

"No. You've done enough tonight." He pushes himself off the ground with a wince and walks to my door, "I'll be back soon."

I watch him leave, feeling the humiliation of my past crashing down on me. It's been over two years, and I still can't get my ex-boyfriend out of my head.

It's been over two years and I'm still not normal.

Closing my eyes against the surge of tears, I hear the shower turn on just outside my bedroom door. I listen to the sound of water running, picturing Skylar stripping off his clothes and hopping in to jerk himself off.

All because I let some douchebag pressure me into sex.

Anger cuts through me, targeting the cowardly state of my current self. I just had the best sexual experience of my life, and here I am, letting the shadows of my past keep me from discovering the kind and thoughtful boy who buys me romance books.

Skylar deserves better.

I deserve better.

Swallowing the fear rising in my throat, I snag my shorts from the ground and wiggle them on. I tiptoe from my bedroom to the bathroom door, hesitating before I slip inside.

The dorm's bathroom separates into two stalls, one for the toilet and one for the shower. A quick glance confirms my roommate isn't hiding out in the bathroom stall. I take a shaky breath and knock on the closed door of the shower.

"Skylar?"

There's a moment of silence, then, "Is everything okay?"

"Yeah, I just..." An abundance of nerves hit me and it takes me a moment to swallow the lump in my throat.

"I was wondering if I could join you."

The lock clicks open and Skylar peeks his head out. Wet hair is plastered against his forehead and water droplets slip down his face. He looks younger like this, less like the haunted boy I've gotten to know and more like the one I've always seen.

"You want to shower with me?"

His eyes rake down my face, peering through the mask nobody else seems to get past.

"Yeah." Breaking eye contact, I look down at my chipped fingernails, "If that's okay."

"I'm not wearing any clothes."

A laugh slips out, "I think that's the point of a shower."

Skylar studies me for a moment longer before disappearing back behind the door. I stare at it, at a loss for what to do, when it shifts open. Steam sneaks through the crack, the hot humidity washing over my skin in the most inviting way.

I'm trembling when I slip out of my clothes and kick them over to where Skylar's lie neatly folded. Refusing to give myself a second to think, I pull open the door and step inside.

The steam of the hot water smacks me in the face, enveloping my naked body as I shut the door gently behind me. Skylar is watching me, his eyes carefully trained on my face.

I stare back at him, struggling to remember how to breathe. Nerves and fear have me glued to the spot, and now I'm wondering if maybe I do have asthma from the way my lungs have stopped working.

"So... do you come here often?"

He delivers the line with a straight face but it works to break the tension. A giggle slips out of my mouth and the humid air flows back into my lungs.

"About once a day. How about you?"

He shrugs, "First time."

I laugh and inch a little bit closer. Skylar flicks his eyes down my body, the slow perusal making my skin flush with awareness. He swallows and it suddenly dawns on me that there is not a lot of space in this shower stall.

"Are you shaking because you're cold or because you're scared?"

"Both." I admit sheepishly, crossing my arms over my chest, "I've never done this before."

"Had a shower? It's actually pretty easy."

I laugh, "No, I've done that. Showering is the one thing I am good at."

Skylar tilts his head, "You're good at a lot of things, Flower. But maybe you could show me how it's done."

He reaches up and grabs the shampoo balancing precariously on the shelf above us. I study the harsh lines of his body, admiring the lean juts of bone and muscle pushing through pale skin. Nico was right, Skylar is on the skinny side, but I wouldn't want him any other way.

My eyes drop to the one part of him I haven't seen yet.

The books I read put a lot of emphasize on size, but honestly, I've never really given much thought to a guy's dick size before. My one and only sexual experience was so traumatic that I didn't have time to wonder if the anatomy hurting me was above average or not.

Staring at Skylar's dick though, I can see why people get hyper focused on size. He's not big but it still manages to bring a blush to my face.

Because I think it might be the perfect size.

"Hold out your hands."

He smiles, clearly having caught me checking out his junk. Giving him a sheepish smile, I hold out my hands and he pours shampoo on them.

"Are you going to watch me wash my hair?"

"No." Skylar takes my hands and pulls me closer, "I'm going to wash your hair and you're going to wash mine."

"Oh."

I close my eyes as he guides me into the stream of hot water. Goosebumps raise along my skin as the warmth rushes through me. Gentle fingers tilt my head back, ducking my head under the water. The cool slide of shampoo hits my hair before Skylar starts massaging it in, his wet body gently pressing against mine.

Lathering the liquid in my hands, I reach up and thread my hands through his damp hair, watching the way his eyes flutter down at my touch. Rubbing my fingers against his scalp, I scrape my nails over his ears and down the back of his neck, leaving a trail of bubbles in my wake.

Giddiness rises up inside me and I scoop up more shampoo to smear it along his chest. Laughter escapes as I dab bubbles along his torso, casually decorating his nipples and belly button with white foam.

"Someone's caught her second wind."

Amusement dances through Skylar's gaze when he looks at me, the smile in his eyes almost as beautiful as the one painting his face.

I give him a modest shrug, "Just practicing my art skills."

"Uh huh."

Skylar steals a clump of foam from his chest and smears it on mine. I shriek and jump back, but he manages to trap me in the corner and smear more bubbles across my cheek. I'm so busy laughing that I don't notice how close we are until I feel the nudge against my stomach.

I look down and see the tip of his cock pressing against me.

Skylar

My dick is becoming a serious problem.

It used to be a piece of my anatomy that laid low and didn't cause any issues. I would almost go as far as to say I had admirable control over it.

Not anymore.

The moment Lacey gives me a lingering glance or brushes my skin with her fingers, it's game over. I have absolutely no control when it comes to my flower, and evidently, my dick feels the same way.

The hot water pounding against my back is doing nothing to help the boner I am currently rocking. I can't tear my eyes off the bubbles dripping down Lacey's naked body, the pink buds of her nipples pretty enough to draw.

The stiffness in her posture quickly snaps me back to reality. Making a hasty retreat, I'm about to crank the water temperature to cold when Lacey reaches out and stops me.

"Don't go." Her fingers wrap around my arm and she tugs me closer.

The problem with being the same height is it means our bodies align perfectly. All it would take is one shift and I would slip right between her legs.

My dick throbs at the thought.

Lacey slides her hands around my neck and smiles. That's all she does and yet it feels like she just took my heart and ran it over with a freight train.

"Flower." I whisper, wishing I didn't feel so out of control, "I really want to kiss you right now."

"Then kiss me."

She doesn't have to tell me twice.

Leaning forward, I run my tongue along her bottom lip, licking off the water droplets before pressing my lips to hers. Her nails dig into my neck as she pulls me closer, the pointed end of my erection pressing into the soft tissue of her stomach.

She's so soft I can't stand it.

The wet slide of her tongue meets mine and a strangled sound escapes me. Shampoo runs down my back, the soapy texture coating Lacey's hands as she marks my body with her fingertips.

It feels like she's lighting me on fire, the teasing dance of her purple fingernails igniting the fibres holding me together.

My hands weave into her wet hair, pulling her mouth closer so I can taste every inch of it. She bites down on my bottom lip and my hips jut forward, thrusting without my consent.

I pull away to apologize, but Lacey is already sliding her soapy hand between us and squeezing me gently. My brain stops working as her hand slides up and down my shaft, learning everything there is to know about the most irrational part of my body.

"Can you show me what you like?"

Lacey looks at me from under wet lashes and my legs almost give out from beneath me. Her green eyes are glowing against rosy cheeks, her naked body flushed with heat marks and the lingering trails of shampoo.

She's a living, breathing masterpiece. A breathtaking combination of darkness and kindness that I will never find in one perfect person again.

"Yeah."

Swallowing hard, I reach down and wrap my hand around hers, guiding her hand back up and twisting at the top. A groan slips out when Lacey's fingers brush the sensitive underside of my tip, her grip tightening as we work to get me off.

I bury my face in her neck as the pace picks up, keeping my free hand pressed against the wall to keep us from slipping on the wet tiles. My balls are tightening with a pending orgasm, but I'm not the only one breathing heavily.

Lacey's erect nipples rub against my chest on every inhale and the noises she's making are enough to convince me she's as turned on as I am.

I thrust into her grip, letting her take the lead as my hand trails down to the dark triangle between her legs. Water is the world's worst lubricant, but that doesn't stop me from feeling the slickness coating her upper thighs.

She's fucking soaked.

The realization has me coming faster than I would have liked, my hips thrusting feverishly as her hand continues to pump. My whole body shudders as the orgasm hits, my come shooting out to coat the soft skin of her stomach.

I'm expecting her to shriek and pull away, but all she does is pull me close. I can feel the sticky residue between us, but it doesn't take away from the feeling of being held.

From the feeling of being seen.

I close my eyes against her damp skin, breathing in the floral scent of the leftover shampoo. It takes a while for me to catch my breath, but it's worth it to see the smile waiting for me.

"How were my shower skills?"

She's looking at me with those playful eyes and I can't look away.

"Excellent. Would come back again."

"Glad to be of service."

She's still smiling when I take her hand and pull her under the stream of water. Gently washing her stomach clean of my seed, I let my fingers drift up and brush the hard peaks of her nipples.

Her breath catches, "We should probably get out. There will be no more hot water soon."

"We will. There's just one more thing I want to do."

Lacey arches her back in response to my touch, pressing her small breasts into my hands. I toy with the pink buds before sinking to my knees.

She looks down at me with a frown, "You just ate me out half an hour ago."

"I sure did. Can you open for me?"

By the time I have Lacey's leg thrown over my shoulder, she's gripping my hair and letting out quiet moans that has a smile spreading across my face. My flower deserves to be worshipped every minute of every day, without exception.

And maybe I deserve to be the one who gives it to her.

"Harder baby! Hit me harder."

The shout of ecstasy has me blinking open my eyes. An unfamiliar ceiling stares back at me, the warmth of Lacey's body pressing against my right side.

An exaggerated moan fills the room and a smothered giggle hits my ear. Rolling over, I turn and see Lacey covering her mouth with her hand. Her laughing eyes meet mine just as a loud smack echoes through the wall beside us.

I had heard Taber University's residence buildings were on the cheaper side, but this really puts things into perspective.

Another smack sounds through the wall and I wince.

"Sounds like it's going well."

Lacey bursts out laughing, "I should have warned you. Sunday mornings are louder than most."

"This happens more than once a week?"

"Yeah. I tried wearing earplugs at the start of the semester but they were too uncomfortable. It's mostly background noise for me by this point."

Loud grunts start up on the other side of the wall and Lacey blushes, "Well, not all of it is background noise."

We fall silent, staring at each other while the sex marathon continues one wall over. Lacey's face is flushed and sleepy and it's easily the prettiest thing I have ever seen.

Reaching out, I touch the freckles lining her nose, lightly connecting them all with my fingers. She scrunches her nose, trying to impair my progress, but I manage to sneak past the crinkles and mark every brown dot.

Lacey shifts closer, sliding her leg between mine and bringing our bodies that much closer. I savour the sensation of having her skin pressed against mine, knowing for a fact this is the only slice of heaven I will ever get to experience.

"Is that what sex normally sounds like?" She frowns, "That may be a silly question."

"It's not a silly question. Every person has their own preferences, as do every couple, so it's hard to say. Some positions can be louder than others, and if you bring props like whips and stuff, that will also change things."

Her eyes go wide, "Have you ever whipped someone?"

"No. I don't find pleasure through my partner's pain." I chew my lip, debating how much to share, "I've never been in a long-term relationship, so I haven't gotten the chance to branch out much."

Lacey mulls over my words, "Is there something you've been wanting to try?"

I fall silent, wondering how much is too much when talking about sex with a rape victim. There is no doubt in my mind that what her ex-boyfriend did was rape, but that makes it tricky to know what grey areas to avoid.

I want to help her grow but I don't want to scare her.

She nudges my shoulder, "Come on, Skylar. Share your dirty secrets with me."

Tearing my gaze from her face, I look down at the duvet covering our intertwined limbs. I can see the outline of Lacey's leg draped over mine and it looks too perfect to be real.

Before I can begin to doubt myself, I let the truth spill past my lips.

"I want to draw you naked on my bed. After we finish making love and the evidence is everywhere."

Lacey sucks in a breath and I flick my eyes back to her face, "And then I want to put ink on your body. Connect every freckle I can find and turn you into a living constellation that I can wish on every night."

She's staring at me with wide eyes and shame hits me immediately.

"Not that I'm expecting you to pose nude for me. It's just something I've been thinking about."

"So, your biggest kink is... wanting to draw me?"

I flinch at the pitiful description. I've read the romance books Lacey loves so much. I know exactly how short I fall from those standards.

"Yeah." Embarrassment heats my cheeks and I quickly look away.

"Skylar. Look at me."

Lacey waits until I meet her eyes before sliding a hand across my chest. The simple touch has my heart beating faster, the pathetic organ desperately trying to break through my rib cage to reach her fingers.

"Your passion for art is one of the things I love most about you. There's no need to hide it from me." Her face breaks into a grin, "Besides, it was really hot when you drew on me last time. My skin is yours to use anytime you want."

I swallow thickly, "You would let me draw on you?"

"Of course. My body can be your personal canvas."

I kiss her without thinking.

She gasps in surprise and I slip my tongue inside her mouth. I coax a gentle moan from her as she slides her fingers through my hair, tugging me as close as our clothed bodies can go.

My body can be your personal canvas.

The heartbreaking words echo through my mind as I lose myself in her, surrendering to the colour and warmth she's brought back into my life.

My flower. My lifeline.

Long legs wrap around my waist and soon I'm rolling on top of her. Lacey's nails scrape down my back as I press into her, savouring the soft whimpers disappearing from her mouth into my own.

"I really want to have sex with you." Lacey whispers against my lips, her voice breaking right at the end, "But I… I'm not ready. Not yet."

Pressing one last kiss against her lips, I gently untangle myself from the soft invitation of her body.

"You don't need to explain yourself, Flower. I will take anything you're willing to give and nothing more."

She searches my face, sad eyes looking for expectations that aren't there.

"I don't know how long it's going to take, Skylar."

My shoulder lifts in a shrug, "Ten months, ten years, it doesn't matter. I'm not going anywhere."

Her bottom lip starts to tremble and tears spill over. Gently kissing away each one, I wrap myself around her, trying to help her find the thing we both need the most.

To not feel alone.

Chapter 18

"I need your help."

Vector grins, passing the gravy to his mother, "I need you to convince Sky to join the track team."

Amber beams, taking the jug from his hands, "That is a wonderful idea! Skylar, honey, I didn't know you were thinking about trying out for the team."

"I'm not."

"But think of how much fun it would be! You could meet more kids your age." Excitement fills Amber's voice, "You could even train with Vector to get ready for the competitions."

Skylar shoots his brother a glare before turning back to his mom, "Tryouts ended back in September. Even if I wanted to join the team, which I don't, I wouldn't be able to."

She purses her lips, "You could start training for next year?"

I stifle a laugh by taking a bite of Shepherd's Pie. I still don't know if this meal is Skylar's favourite, but his mom makes it every time I'm invited over for dinner.

Not that I'm complaining. Amber Vin is a wonderful cook.

"Yeah, Sky. You could start training for next year." Vector throws me a wink, "I'm sure Lacey would love to come watch your meets."

Amber claps her hands, "We could all go!"

"No one is going anywhere because I'm not joining the track team." Skylar's hand finds mine under the table, "I've already had my opportunity to be a varsity athlete."

I smile down at my food, knowing exactly what he's referring to.

Vector shrugs, "I could talk to the coach. Get you on the team this year."

"I don't want to be on the track team."

Amber sighs, "You used to love cross country running. I just don't know what changed."

"The people I enjoyed doing it with changed. So did I."

Skylar stares down his brother and irritation flashes across Vector's face. I shift uneasily in my chair, glancing between the two brothers as they silently argue with each other across the kitchen table. Vector grows more agitated by the second, the muscles in his arms twitching with every inhale.

He catches me staring and the anger quickly melts into a smile.

"You've got nice long legs, Lacey. Are you a runner?"

Skylar stiffens beside me and Vector gives him a satisfied smirk. Whatever went down during the silent exchange ignited a fire between the brothers and the older one seems keen on handing out a punishment.

Oblivious to the tension, Amber turns to me with a smile, "You must have been an athlete with that remarkable height of yours."

"Um, not quite."

"Really? I would have guessed you played basketball in high school."

"Unfortunately, Wesley stole all the athletic genes in the family. But I did spend a few years playing-

"What about a model?" Vector cuts me off, leaning his elbows on the table, "Those legs would easily put you over the height requirement for that."

A flush creeps up my neck and spreads across my face. Amber looks embarrassed by her son's question while Skylar looks like he's about to explode.

"Uh, no. I was never a model."

Vector smiles, "Such a waste. You have the most enticing figure."

"Stop it." Skylar's voice slices through the room, "Stop objectifying her."

Vector ignores him and shakes his head with a sigh, "A pretty face and a pretty body. There isn't much more a guy can ask for."

Humiliation drips through me as I stare back at him, slowly removing my hand from Skylar's tight grip.

"Vector! That is not how we speak to our guests." Amber shakes her head before turning to me, "I am so sorry, Lacey, I don't know what's gotten into-

"May I be excused? I need to use the washroom."

"Of course, dear. Just around the corner by the front door."

I can feel the weight of Skylar's stare when I get up and leave, but I don't acknowledge it. Keeping my head down, I hurry from the kitchen, fighting back tears every step of the way.

The staircase to go upstairs is just across from the main bathroom and I take it without thinking. There's another bathroom just across from Skylar's room and right now I need a floor between me and the hurtful words that were spoken by his brother.

I make it into the bathroom just before the dam breaks. Collapsing against the door, I slide to the floor, crying into my knees as Vector's taunts bring back a wave of memories, harsh reminders of how cruel people can be when they no longer see you as a friend.

Did she really think her long legs were going to be enough to keep him around?

She's never been much more than a pretty face.

Can she at least pretend to be okay? It's not our fault she wasn't what he was looking for.

I hug my knees closer, letting my past stain the dark material of my leggings. The cold tiles of the bathroom floor dig into my ass and I use it as silent encouragement to pull myself together. Hiccups float out of my mouth as I glance around the small bathroom, noticing for the first time the artwork hung along the walls.

Pushing my trembling body off the ground, I amble towards the closest one. It's a landscape of Silverwood University, the metallic dome rising up like a wave about to crash down on the idyllic town below.

The cruel voices start to fade as I travel to the next one, Skylar's confident strokes of colour such a contrast to the grey setting he uses for most of the drawings. His artwork is a mesmerizing blend of darkness and hope, the seeds of his own life planted within each picture.

I know nothing about art, but even I can tell Skylar has incredible talent.

There's one last picture hanging above the bathroom mirror, so I hop up on the counter to see it. My knee cracks the sink base cabinet and the sound of breaking glass hits my ears.

Now I've done it.

Feeling like the worst guest in the world, I quickly drop to the floor and pry open the cabinet door. Bottles of hair and shaving products got toppled over during my climb, but nothing screams broken.

Once everything is back in place, I gentle close the door. It snaps shut with a thud, and I hear the sound again.

Glass knocking against glass.

I frown, opening up the cabinet and taking another look. Everything is how I left it, the plastic bottles are undamaged and there are no leaks in sight. Shifting the door to get a better look inside, I hear the sound again.

What the hell?

I crouch down and study the back of the cabinet door. A molding juts out about halfway down, the colour painted to look identical to the rest of the plywood. Prying my nail inside the opening, the entire thing comes loose in my hands.

There's a small white bag tucked between the molding's grooves, and I can just make out the rigid outline of glass through the material. Pulling the bag from its hiding spot, I open it and peer inside.

And suddenly nothing makes sense.

Being careful not to break anything, I pull out the syringe and set it on the bathroom counter. It's medical grade, the type you would expect to see in a hospital setting, but that isn't the part that has me confused.

Turning the bag over, a small vial drops into my hand.

"Flower? Are you in there?"

I jump at Skylar's voice, my heart racing with adrenalin as I snatch the syringe from the counter and clutch the vial tightly in my other hand.

Walking on shaky legs, I go and open the bathroom door. Skylar is standing on the other side, his eyes glowing with frustration as they rake over my tear-stained cheeks.

"I'm so sorry, Flower. There is no excuse for what he said, but I want you to know…" His eyes drop to what I'm holding and the blood drains from his face.

"Where did you find that?"

"Under the sink." Nausea is climbing in my throat but I swallow it back down. Dropping my gaze to the items in my hands, I read the letters on the vial's tiny label.

"I don't understand… what is this?"

I don't want to accuse Skylar of taking drugs but the evidence is quite literally in my hands. My chest aches as I look back at the boy unravelling in front of me, his mismatched eyes darkening with an internal fire.

"He fucking promised."

Biting off a snarl, Skylar stalks into the bathroom and drops onto the edge of the tub. Within seconds, his anger deflates and he hunches over like he's in pain.

"He *promised*."

The word breaks on a sob and I quickly shut the bathroom door. Putting the incriminating evidence back on the counter, I join Skylar on the edge of the bathtub and pull his shaking body into my arms.

My mind is stuck on a loop, my heart screaming with betrayal and confusion as the same thought pounds through my head.

It just doesn't make sense.

None of it makes sense.

I stare at the vial on the counter, the small black print that changes everything. Skylar is trembling against me, the bony ridge of his shoulders digging into my chest doing nothing to help solve the puzzle in front of me.

He doesn't even play sports. Out of all people, why would Skylar be taking...

Oh my God.

The answer slaps me across the face so hard it stings.

"Skylar." My voice trembles, the one question I never thought to ask mocking me from the bathroom counter.

"Why is your brother so much bigger than you?"

Skylar

I have a lot of bad memories in this house, but walking in on my brother injecting steroids into his ass was one of the worst.

I didn't know what it was at the time. I had just turned thirteen and could barely find the strength to get out of bed after helping my mom patch up her skin every night.

There weren't many good days back then.

"It's my fault." I choke on the words, unable to breathe from the guilt clogging my throat, "Everything is my fault."

Lacey's arms stay wrapped around me, her warm embrace the only thing keeping me from shattering into a million pieces. I should have known Vector wouldn't stop taking the drugs. That he would do whatever it took to stay the strongest predator in Silverwood.

I should have known he was going to break my heart all over again.

"Tell me your secret, Skylar."

There's a shake to Lacey's voice and it rips at the stitches holding my bleeding heart together. A metallic taste fills my mouth as the events that happened four years ago pierce through the carefully constructed silence.

"He was going to kill her. He was going to kill her and somebody had to stop him."

"Who are you talking about?"

"My father." Gagging at the memory, I can barely keep the nausea down, "He pushed her down the stairs and the fall broke her tibia. Mom was going to be on bedrest for the next six months. She was going to be a sitting duck for the next six months."

The drive home from the hospital was the longest ride of my life. Vector wouldn't stop shaking, the anger trying to claw its way out of his skin.

We were the same size back then. Just a couple of skinny kids cursed with a volatile temper.

"Vector had a plan. He didn't tell me what it was, he just said I needed to take care of mom and he would deal with Vincent. The next day he went to the gym for three hours. The next week he started counting his proteins."

Lacey blows out a shaky breath, "He was trying to get bigger."

"And stronger. Our dad wasn't that big, but he was strong. Vector needed to put on at least fifty pounds to even stand a chance. He would have gotten there eventually but our father's temper couldn't wait that long."

A strangled sound slips out of my mouth, "He ruined her recovery. Three months in, he re-fractured the injury. That's why she limps. He fucking broke her already broken body."

My shoulders hunch as I start to fall apart. The bathroom tiles swirl together as tears slink down my cheeks and Lacey pulls my shaking body closer.

"W-We didn't think she was going to make it. The doctors had to put her in a medically induced coma for two weeks. By the time she came out, I had started planning her funeral arrangements."

Lacey strokes my tear-stained face, her trembling fingers gently wiping away the scars of my past.

"Your brother took the drugs to get bigger faster."

"I didn't know about it at first. But then I did and I..." My gasping words trail off as a wave of self-loathing pours through me, "I agreed to keep quiet."

Lacey takes my face in her hands. Her eyes are filled with a compassion I don't deserve, her fingers stroking my cheek with a love I shouldn't crave.

"You must have been so young."

I was. But that doesn't change the fact I chose silence over action.

"It doesn't matter. I should have fought back. Pushed for another solution."

She frowns, "Your brother made his own decision. There was nothing you could have done."

And there it is. The moment of truth.

Squeezing my eyes shut, I block out the kindness radiating from the only person who ever cared enough to piece me back together.

"It didn't stop after Vector kicked him out, Flower. He was taking them up until last year. Taber's home opener was supposed to be the first game he was clean."

Lacey freezes, her hands tensing on my face, "That can't be true. Varsity athletes get tested for performance enhancers."

A choked laugh slips out, "In Canada they only test the winning teams. The top competitors."

"But that... that doesn't make sense. Silverwood always makes it to the finals."

I blink my eyes open, seeing the girl who stole my heart with a simple note.

The girl who goes to the rival school.

"Taber University has beaten Silverwood for the past six years. Every championship banner the Tigers brought home ensured Vector wouldn't get tested for another year."

Lacey stares at me in horror and the irony of the situation is not lost on me. She's finally peeling back the layers and seeing the red stains hiding underneath.

I meet her gaze with a heavy heart, "Do you know what the major side effect of anabolic steroids is?"

There's a long list of potential side effects and repercussions an athlete can sustain when using testosterone supplements, but there's only one that really matters.

"Aggression."

Her gasp echoes around the bathroom housing the dark secret tying the Vin brothers together.

My father was the first person Vector put in the hospital.

But he wasn't the last.

"Oh my God." She whispers, her hands slipping from my face, "That's why so many players have been injured."

The absence of her touch burns my skin, reminding me exactly what kind of a person I am.

"Every person he hurt was because of me. Because I chose to stay silent. Cody Ellsworth..." Tears burn my eyes, "Had to give up lacrosse because of me."

The hideous truth wraps around my ankles and drags me back into the depths of darkness. I can't see, I can't breathe, I can't feel anything except the girl beside me.

Silence blooms between us, and with each passing second, I fall further from the flower that brought me back to life.

"Skylar." Her voice sounds far away, like a distant dream I can picture but can't quite remember, "Cody didn't give up lacrosse because of his injuries. He stopped playing because he wanted to spend more time with Stella."

"That... doesn't make sense."

I think my heart is pounding but it's hard to be sure. There's a strange sensation in my chest, something that feels too light and hopeful to be true.

"Vector broke his cheekbone and a couple of ribs. I saw the photos."

"Maybe he did, but that's not why Cody stopped playing lacrosse."

It wasn't because of me.

The crashing wave of relief has me collapsing against Lacey. Fresh tears leak out as one of my countless demons slip away.

She sighs, gently brushing back my hair, "I don't blame you for keeping quiet. He's your brother, and despite how cruel he can be sometimes, I know he loves you. And I know you love him too."

I can feel my body start to shut down, but I fight it. I fight to stay in this moment, to hear her voice and feel her touch for just a little bit longer.

I should have told her sooner. I should have told her the first night we met.

I open my mouth to apologize, to say all the things I should have said, but Lacey steals the breath in my lungs before I get the chance.

"I love you, Skylar Vin. And I think it's time you did too."

She presses a kiss against my forehead and I pass out in her arms.

Chapter 19

Lacey

I tried and failed to carry Skylar back to his room.

To be fair, his slender frame is a lot heavier than it looks. It took less than two minutes for my arms to give out and for us both to go crashing to the floor. It was pathetic on all accounts, but the worst part was going to find someone to help.

"What the fuck did you do to him?" Vector glares at me before bending down to pick up his brother's unconscious body.

I glare back at him, the earlier taunts not forgotten, "He's been dealing with a lot lately."

"Apparently."

Shaking his head, Vector lifts Skylar off the ground and cradles him against his chest. I stare at the arm muscles flexing with the movement, the abnormal size difference screamingly obvious now that I know the truth.

It all makes sense now. The inflated muscles, the disfigured jaw, the irritated skin. If you know what to look for, Vector's steroid use seems like the most obvious thing in the world.

I sneak a glance at the cabinet sink holding his dirty secret. Returning the drugs to their hiding spot seemed like the right thing to do even though a part of me wanted to interrogate him. Ask why he would willingly take a drug that makes it impossible to control his temper. Why he would risk his varsity career just to be the biggest player on the field.

But in the end, I decided against it. Vector is allowed to have secrets, just as he is allowed to choose who to share them with.

Hurrying ahead to open Skylar's bedroom door, I wait until Vector has passed to slip inside. I watch as he gently lowers his brother onto the bed, his touch surprisingly tender as he pulls the bedsheets over his brother's small frame.

It hits me then, that it would be easy to hate Vector Vin.

The bully who can't control his temper, the lacrosse player who puts his opponents in the hospital, he's the perfect villain until you peer past the mask. Until you see the son who started taking testosterone supplements to protect his mom. The older brother who uses his strength to protect his younger one.

Then suddenly it doesn't become so easy after all.

"Do you need a ride home?" Vector glances at me before looking down at his sleeping brother, "I don't think he's up for the drive."

"No. I'm going to stay."

"He's not a fighter, you know. Never has been and never will be."

I frown, "Who said I want a fighter?"

"Your books do." Vector lifts a brow, pointing to the romance novel sitting on Skylar's desk, "Don't fool yourself into thinking he's a fictional character who will change for his true love. He's not some scarred hero you can fix."

Anger bubbles up inside me, fuelling a sudden need to confront the man who made too many assumptions about me tonight.

"Skylar doesn't need to be fixed. He's my friend, not my hero." I blow out a breath, unused to the bold adrenalin coursing through my veins, "And I don't appreciate the comments you made at the dinner table. You know nothing about me or my life, so don't go throwing statements that are based on nothing except superficial features. It's rude and unbecoming."

My heart is pounding as I wait for his reaction.

His face breaks into a smile as a chuckle slips out, "Now I see why he's so fond of you. Looks like you might be the fighter in this relationship."

"Just because he's small doesn't mean he's weak. Skylar is stronger than you give him credit for."

"Maybe." Vector closes the distance between us with a few strides. Even with my height, I have to tilt my head back to look at him.

"We have a rule here in Silverwood. A rule that I implemented when it became clear Sky would never hurt another person. Not even to defend himself."

I swallow drily, feeling my anxiety spike as he trails his eyes down my body. I'm used to having wandering eyes on me, but that isn't what this is.

This is a predator deciding which spot to attack first.

His eyes flick back to my face, a quiet anger simmering just beneath the surface.

"Break him and I will break you."

"Are you threatening me?"

He smiles then, a smile that does nothing to stop the fear from racing through me.

"It's not a threat. It's a promise."

I've seen firsthand just how many promises Vector has broken, but there is no doubt in my mind this is one he will see through.

"I'm not going to hurt him."

"We'll see." Vector brushes past me but pauses at the door, "Oh, and do me a favour. Don't leave him crippled on the floor next time."

He shuts the bedroom door before I can respond.

God. I think he's worse than my roommate.

Blowing out a breath, I walk over to check on Skylar's unconscious form. His face is pressed against the pillow, the tension drained from his features as sleep chases away the demons of today.

He normally sleeps in just his underwear, so I quickly tug off his jeans and carefully remove his shirt. He doesn't stir when I slide my hand across his chest, feeling the reassuring beat of his heart.

"It's okay, Skylar. You're safe now."

I whisper the promise before shedding my clothes and pulling on his discarded shirt. Sliding under the covers, I snuggle up beside him and let the warmth of his body soothe the anxiety from my mind.

It was a hell of a night, but Vector was right about one thing.

I will always fight for Skylar.

Skylar

She stayed.

My heart feels full as I drag my eyes over Lacey's sleeping frame, watching the way her chest falls with each breath. Dark curls cover half of my pillow as well as her own, and I can't help but touch a strand just to make sure she's real.

I can't believe she stayed.

Closing my eyes against the memories of last night's train wreck, I'm willing myself to fall back asleep when something wet presses against my nose. It happens again and the giggles that follow suit has my face breaking into a smile.

"Are you having fun?"

I open my eyes just in time to see Lacey try and lick my nose for a third time. She shrieks, pulling her tongue back into her mouth.

"You weren't supposed to see that."

"Uh huh."

Before she can blink, I lean forward and lick her lips. A loud gasp fills my room as big green eyes accuse me of initiating the game in the first place.

"You can only do it when the person is sleeping! It doesn't count if I can see you."

"There are rules?"

She smiles, "Of course. If the other person catches you, you lose by default."

I lean forward and lick her lips again.

"Skylar! I just told you that's how you lose." Her scolding tone breaks off in a laugh when I try and do it again, "What are you doing? The game is over."

My chest feels impossibly light when I look at her, the crinkles around her eyes putting the same ones in my heart.

"I wanted to taste your smile."

"You're such a weirdo."

She's smiling when she says it, and unlike the other times I've been called that, it sounds like something positive. Like maybe she likes my peculiar parts.

Maybe she loves them.

I stare at the girl lying beside me, the girl who told me she loved me. She said it after I spent thirty minutes crying out years' worth of guilt and grief over my brother's drug use. It's the last thing I remember before blacking out and that fact alone confirms the one thing I know about myself.

I am fucking pathetic.

"Flower." I swallow, wishing I had anything more to offer this girl than baggage, "I'm sorry about last night. From the comments Vector made to the way I broke down in the bathroom... I'm so sorry. You didn't deserve any of that."

She frowns, reaching over and bopping my nose, "We have a rule about apologizing. Don't go breaking it now."

"You deserve better."

"No, Skylar. *You* deserve better." A soft sigh escapes her, "You can't love someone else if you don't love yourself. It just doesn't work that way."

Shame has me breaking eye contact and looking down at my duvet.

"It's not that I don't love myself. It's just hard to look in the mirror sometimes."

"I know. But those are the days when you have to see someone else. You have to look past your own reflection and see the person you are getting out of bed for. The person you are choosing to live for."

She blows out a breath, "After the incident, I had to learn how to stop seeking ways to leave this world and start searching for ways to live in it. It took me a while but eventually I found a new appreciation through silly little things and it was enough to keep me going."

"Is that when your plant collection started?"

She nods, "And my romance addiction. As ridiculous as it sounds, I found peace in the predictable endings. In the simple routine of taking care of my plant babies. It doesn't have to be some great passion that pulls you out of the darkness. Sometimes all it takes is one friend who helps you forget about the scars lining the inside of your skin."

"Who was it for you?"

"Nico."

I glance at her in surprise and she lets out a laugh, "He made me this friendship bracelet when we were kids, told me to keep it until he could save up enough money to buy me a promise ring. This was before he knew he liked men, of course."

Lacey shakes her head with a smile, "None of the colours matched and most of the letters were different sizes, but it was the most beautiful thing I had ever seen. It was my most cherished possession until I lost it a few years later. I was so devastated that Nico bought me a new one as a replacement, but it just wasn't the same."

She pauses, staring at my ceiling like it might take her back to a different time.

"I ended up finding it two days after I tried to commit suicide. I hadn't seen it for seven years and it turned up 48 hours after I tried to leave my best friend behind."

There's an ache in her voice, the unbearable weight of regret filling each word. All I can do is look at her, look and see the strength of a survivor who chooses to get out of bed every day.

"Do you still have it?"

She nods, "I keep it in the pill bottle that almost killed me. It serves as a reminder of just how much I stand to lose if I choose to stop loving myself."

Gentle fingers run through my hair, pushing the strands back from my forehead. Lacey looks at me with eyes shining with grief and regret, but even in the darkness, a glimmer of hope remains.

"You deserve to be happy, Skylar. You deserve to be happy with me."

I stare back at her, clinging to that sliver of light in her eyes.

Since that very first message, this girl helped bring back the colours I stopped seeing. She became the light in a world gone grey, and with every correspondence, she slowly glued my broken pieces back together.

She helped me forget about the scars lining the inside of my skin.

"I love you, Flower." I whisper, trying not to break down into tears again, "I always have and I always will."

"I know." Lacey smiles, that same smile that stitched mine back together, "But now it's time to learn to love Skylar. He's pretty fucking awesome but sometimes he forgets that."

An unexpected laugh rips from my chest.

"I'll work on it."

"Nope. Not good enough." She grins, pressing a kiss to my cheek before sliding out of bed. I turn and watch her creep over to my desk.

"Are you wearing my shirt?"

A blush stains her cheeks as she snatches up my sketchbook and scurries over to jump back under the covers. Her long legs brush against mine as she awkwardly fumbles back into bed.

"I didn't want to be uncomfortable in my clothes. I hope you don't mind."

Her choice of words make me pause.

Turning over, I peer over the edge of the bed and spy the pile of discarded clothes on my floor. It doesn't take me long to spot the floral panties peeking out from the crumpled skinny jeans. I let out a quiet groan, replaying the image of my shirt brushing the top of her thighs.

"You shouldn't have told me that."

"Are you mad?"

"No." I blow out a breath, trying to keep my morning wood from becoming a real one, "My shirt fits your perfectly."

"You fit me perfectly."

Before I can react, Lacey steals my pillow and uses it to prop herself up. My head falls flat against the mattress but I'm too busy staring at the loose material covering her naked body to notice.

I want to peek so badly.

"Here you go." She thrusts the sketchbook at me and I take it, trying to tear my gaze away from the teasing outline of her breasts.

"What am I doing?"

"Art charades." She grins, tugging my arm until I'm sitting up beside her, "I'm going to describe something and you have to draw it."

"Do I get a hint of what it's supposed to look like?"

"Of course not. That would ruin the game."

A huff of laughter slips out as I unclip the mechanical pencil from my sketchbook. Turning to a fresh page, I give her a nod of approval.

"Ready."

"Okay, let's start with two circles."

I start to draw, letting my pencil spoil the clean surface of the paper.

"One is dark, the other is light. Shade in the dark one to be textured, like it's an endless number of layers that could go on forever. The other one should be bright, like how it feels when the sun finally escapes the clouds."

"How big are these circles?"

Lacey purses her lips, "Not big. Like a couple of quarters, maybe?"

I adjust accordingly and wait for the next round of instructions.

"Okay. So, these two circles are inside a bigger one." She forms the shape with her hands, "Like this, but bigger. A little sharper too."

I stare back at her, deadpan, "You want me to draw a sharp circle."

She laughs, "That's right. Don't question my logic."

"Okay."

We keep going for an indefinite amount of time, Lacey's specific descriptions making it easy to follow along. Eventually she peeks over at my progress and claps in excitement.

"We're almost there! Okay, this is the most important part. I want you to draw two orange slices tilted upward... No. More curved. Picture a crescent moon, but one that's sideways."

I frown, staring at the paper in front of me. The dismantled parts had me confused but now I'm starting to see the connection. Erasing the curved surface of the so-called orange peels, I pull the corners up and connect the two halves to make a pair of smiling lips.

"That's it! Now, draw a speech bubble and I'll add the final part."

Dutifully, I hand over my sketchbook and watch Lacey scribble a sentence down. By the time she passes it back, there's a satisfied gleam in her eyes.

"Now you have a reminder too."

I look down and read her handwriting.

I'm something special.

My heart starts to pound as I stare at the familiar slant of her calligraphy, the familiar sound of her words.

"You got me to draw myself."

I stare at the mismatched circles that are supposed to be my eyes. Lacey's description made them seem like two sides of the same coin, the opposition of each one bringing out the beauty in the other. The sharp circle is supposed to be the edges of my face, the hard lines of my cheekbones cutting through the page where a couple of orange slices smile back at me.

I look happy. I look *loved*.

"Now you can see how I see you." She nudges me gently, "A beautiful combination of pieces that make up the boy I love."

A swell of emotions rush to the surface as my heart cracks right open. Blinking hard against the surge of tears, I can only stare as the image in front of me melts into an indistinguishable web of lines and pencil marks.

"I-I'm something special."

Lacey reaches over and takes my hand. She squeezes my fingers with the same amount of love as the picture she got me to draw.

"That's right, Skylar. And this time don't forget it."

Chapter 20

Lacey

NICO: If you don't get your cute butt over here, I'm letting Wes pick the movie.

NICO: Which will mean another HSM marathon.

NICO: Don't make me do it. There's only so much Troy Bolton a man can handle.

I snort a laugh and quickly type a response. The weekly movie nights have been a nice addition to my weekly routine, although I do wish they didn't fall on the same night as Skylar's night shifts. Trip has started to join our movie nights as well which means Nico and I get to be the third and fourth wheel all night long.

Grabbing my residence access card from my desk, I snag an extra blanket and head out. My roommate's bedroom door is open, the steady tap of her keyboard filling the otherwise silent dormitory.

I hesitate before walking past her room. Cecelia hasn't been going out as much lately, and if the endless stream of profanity is anything to go by, I'd say midterm season is hitting her pretty hard. It hasn't stopped the sex marathons she manages to squeeze into her schedule, but it does make me wonder whether her mental health is doing okay.

Of all people, I tend to be a little more cautious when it comes to keeping a healthy school-life balance. It helps me appreciate the time and effort that goes into assignments and classes, but it also ensures the stress level won't bleed over into other aspects of my life as well.

Taking a courageous breath, I knock softly against her door. Muttered curses flow through the crack above the doorframe, the angry undertone making me nervous before she opens the door.

"What?"

Cecelia glares at me, her usual spunky hair pulled back into a messy ponytail. Her black tank top is stained and caught on the waistband of her grey sweatpants, officially confirming my theory.

As soon as exams hit, even the most fashion-oriented students succumb to the anxiety of midterm season. Freshmen and seniors alike have to re-organize their schedules and priorities to make sure a passing grade is reached.

Basically, we all look like shit from the moment exams start until the end of the semester.

"I was wondering if you would like to join a movie night with me and some friends?" I clear my throat, trying not to sound nervous, "There's no pressure, of course. Just thought I would offer in case you needed a break from studying."

"Since when do you have friends?"

I try not to flinch, "Technically, it's Nico, my brother and his girlfriend, but I consider them my friends."

An embarrassed flush creeps up my neck, the sorry state of my social life composed of blood relations and childhood friends.

Well, besides Skylar that is.

"Oh." Cecelia blinks, staring at my face like she's never seen a tomato before, "That's kind of sad."

"It's not sad to me." Clamping my teeth to keep from screaming, I turn and walk away.

Sometimes it feels degrading trying to be nice to people who don't want to be nice back. Sometimes it would be nice to not care as much. To shrug off the insults and continue on with my day like nothing ever happened.

"Lacey, wait."

My feet and train of thought slow to a halt. Turning from the door, I look and see Cecelia pulling on a sweater and a pair of shoes. She gives me a smile that looks more like a grimace.

"A break would be nice right about now. Even if it is with your annoying friend."

I blink, watching her readjust the sloppy ponytail. She catches me staring and sighs, letting the dyed strands fall down her shoulders.

"Look, I didn't mean to insult you. I can be a blunt sometimes and it can come off as rude."

"Sometimes?"

The snarky remark slips past my lips and Cecelia lets out a surprised laugh.

"Fine. I'm always rude. But someone has to be the bitch and it certainly isn't going to be you." She pulls a face, "You're a little too sweet for my taste."

Despite the earlier humiliation, my lips tug into a smile, "I'm going to take that as a compliment."

"You should. It wasn't an insult."

I huff out a laugh and together we head over to the residence building reserved for varsity athletes.

Nico and Wesley live on the second floor, and although they are sophomores now, their dorm room isn't any bigger than my own. Most students move off campus after their first year to find bigger living spaces and more privacy, but both co-captains vetoed the larger beds to stay close to their teammates.

Although knowing Wesley, he probably wanted to stay in vicinity to Trip as well.

The door swings open before I can knock and Nico's exasperated face steps into view.

"What took you so long?! I swear to God, those two haven't stopped touching since Trip got here... Oh, shit."

He stares at Cecelia in horror, "I didn't prepare any conversational contingencies and my self-esteem is at an all-time low after history of rock and roll kicked my ass this morning. Please don't hurt me."

She eyes him warily, "I left my weapons at home."

"Babe, we both know that tongue of yours is weapon enough." Nico shudders before waving us in, "Just give me a warning before you insult me. I'm achingly fragile right now."

My roommate rolls her eyes and I stifle a laugh. We follow him into the dorm where mismatched blankets are strewn along the ground. Trip is lounging on one of the couches, watching my brother do some sort of reenactment.

"All I'm saying is there was *this* much room on the board. Jack totally could have survived if Rose had shifted a couple inches over."

Nico throws his head back and groans, "Dude. You need to let that go. That movie came out before you were born."

He shakes his head solemnly, "It doesn't matter when it came out. That story will forever live on in us."

"You know it was fictional, right? Based on a true story does not make it real."

My brother gasps, swinging his gaze from me to Cecelia, "Tell me it's not true. The greatest love story of all time has to be real."

Cecelia blinks, "You think *Titanic* is the greatest love story of all time?"

He drops his head in a sacred nod, "Second only to *High School Musical*."

Nico pulls a face, "It's embarrassing how many romance movies you watch."

"How is that embarrassing? Now I know exactly what to say to get Trip to swoon for me."

Trip rolls her eyes and I bite back a smile. Cecelia looks visibly disgusted, flicking her eyes from the girl on the couch to the class clown that is my brother.

"How long have you two been together? If you're still in the honeymoon stage, I'm leaving."

Wesley grins, "Going on one year and two months today."

Nico mouths *pathetic* behind his back and I laugh.

Trip sighs, walking over to introduce herself, "Please excuse Wes. He tends to overplay the dramatics whenever other people are around."

"Do I?"

She ignores him and holds out her hand. Cecelia stares at it for a moment before reaching out and taking it.

"It's a good thing he's cute."

Trip smiles, "Tell me about it."

Wesley holds up a hand with a frown, "Excuse me, but I think I fall into the more than cute category. Someone definitely called me sexy yesterday."

Nico smirks, "Sure it wasn't your own reflection?"

My brother flips him off and wanders over to give me a hug. I squeeze him tight, the familiar embrace putting a warm glow in my chest.

"What movie are we watching tonight?"

He sighs before releasing me, "Nobody is letting me pick, so I think it's up to you."

I smile, glancing over to find Cecelia watching us closely. This is the first time we've hung out outside of the Silverwood excursion and I find myself hoping she enjoys herself tonight. Our relationship might not have started off the best, but that doesn't mean we can't find a comfortable friendship for the rest of the semester.

"Actually, I think my roommate should pick the movie tonight."

Cecelia blinks in surprise, "Are you sure?"

"Of course."

Nico looks mildly terrified as he passes her the remote. My roommate pinches her brows together before addressing us.

"Does it have to be romance?"

"Hell no." Nico interjects before my brother can open his mouth, "It would be nice if it *wasn't* romance this time."

She nods, pressing the remote and flicking through the options.

"How about the new *John Wick*?"

"Now we're talking." Nico pumps his fist in the air before settling himself down on the pile of green blankets, "Keanu Reeves could fuck me any day of the week."

Cecelia points the remote at him, "This may be the only time I ever agree with you."

"Babe, you're speaking my language."

Trip laughs, watching the interaction before settling herself down beside Nico. To my surprise, Cecelia takes the spot on his other side, leaving me and Wesley to join the end of the line.

My roommate and my closest friend strike up a shockingly long bucket list of celebrities they would do given the chance, while Trip chirps in the occasional comment.

It's a scene I never could have pictured happening at the start of the year. The only thing missing is Skylar and his deadpan jokes that seem to confuse Wesley more than anything.

Pulling out my phone, I read the last message he sent me.

SKYLAR: I'll be off by eleven if you want to come by for the rest of the movie.

ME: That's a long drive just for a movie.

The hardware store must be slow tonight because it takes less than ten minutes for a response to buzz in my pocket.

SKYLAR: I don't mind.

"He puts in a lot of effort, hey?"

I look up to find my brother reading the response over my shoulder. Pulling my phone closer to my chest, I tilt it so he can't see the screen.

"It's not nice to spy, Wesley."

He grins, "I was making sure you weren't sexting right next to me."

"Ew! Who would do that in public?"

Both Cecelia and Nico raise their hands from across the room. I stare at them in horror, pretending I can't see the red flush staining Trip's cheeks.

Wesley shrugs, "Like I said. Just making sure you weren't sexting next to your brother. That's wrong on so many levels."

"Is it wrong to sext someone else's brother while sitting right next to them?" Nico muses the question out loud, "Because I have definitely done that with Stella."

Cecelia glances at him in surprise, "You're still fucking the assistant coach?"

"You know it, babe. I locked that fine ass down."

She nods in acknowledgement, "Nicely done. He's hot."

"Wait. Mighty Mo gets called hot but I only get cute?" Wesley frowns, looking at his girlfriend, "That doesn't seem right."

Trip smiles, "Your dimples are cute, Wes. Don't read into it."

His jaw drops, "You did it again. You called me cute."

Nico snorts, "My alpha is hands down the hottest lacrosse player at this school."

"Whoa, wait a second. The guy doesn't even play anymore..."

I tune out the bickering friends and pull out my phone to quickly type a response.

ME: Actually, I have something to show you tonight (and it's not the movie). Maybe you could stay over afterwards?

SKYLAR: Sounds good. I'll let you know when I'm on my way.

His response has a smile staining my face. My brother was right, Skylar does put a lot of effort into our relationship. There has never been a time when I didn't feel like his number one priority, and as selfish as it sounds, it feels really nice.

A loud gasp pulls my attention back to the conversation going on around me.

"... I am totally an alpha! Trip, tell them what I did last night." Wesley puffs out his chest, "Tell them how I alpha-ed you."

Nico snorts, "The fact you just made up a verb proves exactly why you are not an alpha. Accept it, man. You are nothing more than a cinnamon roll."

My brother slumps next to me, "I don't want to be a cinnamon roll."

I nudge him gently, "I always thought you were more of a golden retriever."

"Is that better?"

Nico looks like he's about to burst a kidney laughing while Trip shakes her head and walks over to her boyfriend. He immediately brightens when she climbs onto his lap and presses a kiss against his lips.

"Stop being ridiculous and maybe I'll let you alpha me again tonight."

I shudder and shift away just as a couple of dimples pop out. "Yes ma'am."

Skylar

She's wearing makeup.

That's my first thought when Lacey opens the door.

Besides the first night I met her, I have never seen her wear makeup. It's not something that bothers me, her natural beauty is more than enough, but now I am having a hard time looking away from the shockingly dark lashes.

The slight addition has made it so her already sparkling eyes are downright magnificent, the dark emerald colour popping against the eye shadow smeared along her lids. Her lips look redder than usual as well, less pink and more dangerous.

I swallow thickly, trailing my eyes down to the exposed skin between her crop top and skinny jeans.

"Was the drive okay?" Lacey smiles, recapturing my attention with the bright shade of her lips, "Those roads are kind of sketchy at night. They really need to put in more streetlights."

"It was fine."

"Good."

She leads me to her room and I try not to stare at the sliver of skin peeking out above the curve of her ass.

"Thank you for driving here tonight. I really appreciate it."

"If you want me here, I am happy to make the drive." Clearing my throat, I tear my gaze away from her body, "What was it you wanted to show me?"

"It seems silly now, but..." Lacey walks over and picks up the romance book I got her. She hugs it against her chest before passing it over to me.

"Look how far I got."

I take it gingerly, noting the freshly painted fingernails as well. The new colour is darker than the last shade of purple, and it makes me wonder if she chose it for me.

Flipping open the book, I skip to the section I annotated for her and find most of the sticky notes gone. My heart skips a beat when I read the first moment of entry without any trace of black sharpie.

"This is amazing, Flower. How did it feel?"

"The first part was pretty easy. Especially since we've done most of it." She blushes prettily and breaks eye contact, "But the pink stage was tough. I cried the first couple of read throughs but by the fifth time it was okay."

The thought of Lacey crying alone in her room has a spark of anger igniting inside me. There's so many things wrong with the way her ex-boyfriend treated her that it hurts to even think about.

"I am so proud of you."

The blush spreads to her neck, the smile taking over Lacey's face dousing my simmering rage with a bucket of cold water.

"I'm trying, so it's nice to see results." She hesitates, running a finger along the spine of the book, "I was hoping maybe you could help me with the red stage."

"Do you want me to take off the sticky notes?"

She blows out a breath, "No. I was hoping you could read one of the passages to me."

I blink, "You want me to read a sex scene to you?"

"If you don't mind. I think it might be easier than reading it alone."

There's no way I'm going to be able to make it through one sentence knowing that Lacey is sitting next to me while some couple fucks through ink on the page.

I should say no. I need to say no.

Repeating the mantra to myself, I'm about to say it out loud when those big green eyes lock on mine. Uncertainty and hopefulness shine back at me and it's enough to throw my rationality back out the window.

"Okay."

She beams at me, knocking away the rest of my uncertainty. Taking my hand, she pulls me towards the bed and climbs on top of the covers. I follow her, gently resting my body next to hers before taking the book from her hands.

"Do you normally dress up for movie nights?"

I'm trying to keep the conversation casual as I flip to the page decorated with red sticky notes. My handwriting screams back at me, my letters calm and collected as they describe the sex scene I am about to be reading.

Fuck. I should have chosen a different book.

"Oh no. I did this for you." Lacey lets out an awkward laugh, "I figured it was time I put in some effort."

I put the book down with a frown.

"You never have to dress up for me, Flower. You take my breath away the moment you walk into the room. It doesn't matter what you're wearing." Hesitating, I look at the sparkles decorating her eyes, "But you do look lovely tonight. I really like what you did to your eyes. And your lips."

She grins, "Did you notice the new nail polish too?"

"I didn't want to assume it was for me."

"All of it is for you, Skylar."

Lacey looks down shyly and I can't stop myself from reaching over and stroking her cheek. She blinks in surprise, bringing those sparkling eyes back to mine.

"You asked me what my favourite flower was and I finally have an answer."

The warmth of her gaze has my face breaking into a smile.

"You."

She gasps softly and I kiss her before she can respond. Erasing any trace of self-doubt in her mind, I wait until her nails are digging into my neck before breaking away.

"Are you sure you're ready for the red stage?" Resting my forehead against hers, I search her eyes for the trepidation buried within, "It's okay to wait. I can read it to you another time."

She closes her eyes before giving me a nod.

"I'm ready."

Taking a deep breath, I turn and look down at the page. I can't remember what I was thinking when I picked this book off the shelf, but I definitely wasn't expecting to be reading it out loud.

Bracing myself for discomfort, I clear my throat and begin reading.

"She rocked back and forth against my jeans, her moans growing louder with every shift. "That's it, baby." I said, thrusting up against her, "Let me feel that pussy leaking through those panties."

The fact that I picked a book written through the male character's point of view is really coming back to bite me in the ass.

"By the time she finishes screaming my name, I have her on her knees with her ass in the air. Her soaked panties are the next thing to go and her needy whimpers make me smile. "That's it, baby. Tell daddy how much you want this cock."

I pull up short, rereading the passage a few times before turning to my blushing flower.

"That was more aggressive than I remember."

"You haven't been called daddy before?"

"I sure hope not."

Lacey's laughter fills the room and the tension between us starts to diffuse. It was starting to get hard to breathe, but now it almost feels bearable.

Once she gets herself back under control, Lacey wipes her eyes and looks at me.

"I'm ready, Daddy. Please continue."

It's my turn to laugh before I return to the page.

"She whines when my dick slaps the round cheeks of her ass. I spread her legs wider, pulling her hips back so I can rub the tip against her clit. It's dripping wet, the arousal coating my cock without a moment's hesitation. Reaching down, I spread her folds and..."

I'm starting to get turned on, but that doesn't stop me from sneaking a glance at Lacey. She's biting her lip and staring down at her jean-clad legs. There's a stiffness in her body that wasn't there before, a hidden anxiety radiating from the way her hands clench the pillow beside her.

It destroys me to see her like this. To lay witness to the scars another guy left on her body before breaking her heart to smithereens. No one has the right to break the clear cut lines of consent for this exact reason.

The violation of nonconsensual sex doesn't just damage a person's body. It takes away their ability to seek pleasure without having to hurdle a million invisible barriers. It stains a person's psyche in ways that can never be explained.

Biting my cheek to keep my anger in check, I turn my attention back to the page and skim the next few lines. The amount of manhandling this character does to his partner is as impressive as it is horrifying, so I make a rash decision to go off-script.

"...and I roll us over so my back is against the mattress. Those long legs wrap around my waist, straddling me gently as I smile up at her, "That's it, baby. Ride me the way you want to." She grins, pressing her lips to mine before sinking down on me slowly. Rocking back and forth, she takes every inch, letting out a soft moan when she finally gets to the bottom. I reach down and brush her swollen clit, rubbing it softly to help ease the tension from her body."

Ignoring the erection rapidly growing in my pants, I sneak a glance beside me and find Lacey's eyes closed, her lips pressed together as she listens to the scene play out. The tension seeping through her features makes me want to stop speaking altogether, but she looks so determined that I don't want to take this moment away from her.

Looking back down at the page, I ignore the pinch in my chest and continue reading the words written only in my head.

"I let her set the pace, watching the way her body moves against mine. The sweet seduction of her hips keeps me trapped in place, the sensual grinding driving me closer to the edge. She's in complete

control, pleasuring herself like she would if my body was a toy. The rhythm of her hips grows frantic the closer she gets to finishing and I grab her hips, doing what I can to help her get there. She finishes with a cry, squeezing me so tight I can't help but come myself, feeling the soft strands of her dark hair brush my chest."

My heart is pounding by the time I close my mouth, desperately hoping Lacey didn't notice the slip up of the hair colour. Shutting the book quickly, I clear my throat and try not to think about the dark strands currently brushing my shoulder.

"Red stage complete."

Holding my breath, I look and see Lacey blinking her eyes open. She doesn't look at me for a long time, just stares at the wall standing opposite to us.

"Can I tell you a secret?"

"You can tell me anything."

She exhales heavily, finally turning to look at me. Her eyes are brimming with tears and there isn't anything I wouldn't do to make them go away.

"I wish my first time had been with you."

Swallowing the lump in my throat, I reach out and wipe away the tear slipping down her cheek.

"I do too."

Chapter 21

Lacey

There's a surprise waiting for me after my therapy appointment today.

Trip gives me an awkward wave from the parking lot. A wide smile breaks across my face as I pull her in for a hug.

"I didn't know you were picking me up today!"

She nods against my shoulder, "I asked Wes if it would be okay. There's a cute plant shop I thought you might like just around the block."

"You've explored Silverwood?"

Trip pulls away, looking embarrassed, "Well, no. I just saw the little boutique and thought you might want to go for a visit."

I give her a reassuring smile, "That sounds perfect. Lead the way."

We follow the gravel path all the way to Silverwood's main strip. The prairies serve as a soft backdrop for the little mom-and-pop shops, their faded signs and rusted paint adding to the quaint charm of the rural town.

"Have you explored Silverwood much?" Trip glances at me, her grey eyes curious, "I heard you've been spending a lot of time here."

"A little bit. Skylar has taken me to a few places he thought I would like." I smile, remembering the bookstore, "But most of the time we're hanging out at his house."

"It's going well then? You and Skylar?"

"I was actually just talking to Karen about that."

Trip looks at me in shock, "You talk to your therapist about Skylar?"

"I talk to Karen about most things. She helps me sort out my thoughts and feelings in a way that doesn't make me feel judged. It can be tough, especially when we go into the deeper stuff, but today I got to share something positive with her."

I glance at her with a smile, "So, I guess the answer to your question is yes. Things are going well with Skylar."

"I am so happy to hear that." Trip clears her throat before looking down to play with the end of her baggy t-shirt.

"I know you only met me because I'm dating your brother, but I hope you know that I will always be there for you."

I smile, "Does that mean I get to be your bridesmaid even if Wesley isn't the groom?"

She laughs, "Absolutely."

My heart feels full when we come to a stop in front of an adorable plant shop.

A faded green sign screams *Bella In Bloom* while mason jars full of fairy lights sit along the steps leading up to the doorway. I've already fallen in love before we make it inside and find an entire folding table dedicated to succulents on sale.

"I didn't know there were so many plants in Silverwood." Trip wanders over and picks up a pot, "This is so cute. What are the chances I keep it alive for more than two weeks?"

I laugh, "Follow the instructions and you might make it to six months."

"Sold. I'm getting it."

Trip snatches up the cactus and wanders to a nearby display table full of colourful pots and accessories. I continue scanning the table, wishing I had enough money and dorm space to bring them all home with me.

Pulling out my phone, I snap a picture and send it to Skylar.

ME: I found a greenhouse bigger than mine.

"Oh my God! This one has a little guitar painted on it." Trip sighs happily and adds the pot to the stack in her arms, "You've officially converted me to planthood."

Another laugh slips out just as my phone buzzes with a new text message.

SKYLAR: I like yours more.

ME: That is an extremely biased answer, but I like it.

SKYLAR: You're welcome.

My cheeks are aching from the strength of my smile by the time I put my phone away.

I was worried Karen would have a problem with two of her patients seeing each other, but she seemed to think we had both showed significant improvement over the last few weeks.

At the thought of Skylar, a new mission comes to mind. Studying the row of succulents in front of me, I start looking for one that would fit his life. A compatible plant baby doesn't just look pretty, it needs to have a sunlight consumption and water schedule that matches your lifestyle.

By the time I find the perfect one, Trip has her arms full of plant accessories that have nothing to do with the cactus in her hand.

"I think I like the pots more than the plants. Is that weird?"

I laugh, "Not at all. They help brighten your room."

She sighs, "Stella is going to have a field day with this."

Trip catches sight of the succulent I picked out for Skylar and does a double take, "Are you getting that one? I think it might be dead."

I stroke the pale leaves gently, "Not all of them are green. You just have to know how to take care of it properly so it keeps its unique colour."

"Right." Trip blinks, looking completely lost, "Is there anything else you want to look at before we go?"

The bell rings above the door, announcing a new arrival.

"Actually, I wouldn't mind going upstairs to see..."

My words die off and Skylar's succulent drops to the floor. The plastic pot breaks on impact and soil splatters all over my leggings. Trip gasps, quickly abandoning her pile of painted pots to clean up the mess I just made.

"Oh no! Okay, let's sweep everything up and I'm sure the plant will be just fine... Lacey?"

She stands back up, holding the damaged plant, but I don't answer her. I can feel the blood draining from my face, the sudden surge of nausea making me thing I might be sick right here in this adorable plant shop.

"Lacey Williams. What the hell are you doing in Silverwood?"

The familiar voice slices through me and my body starts to tremble.

"J-J-J..." I gasp, feeling the panic flood my body. Trip shoots me a concerned look before turning to address the newcomer.

"Sorry, I don't think we've met. Who are you?"

The guy grins, the same flashy grin he used back when we were dating, "Jerrell Thompson. Lacey and I go way back."

My whole body is shaking as I stare at his face, that stupid face that humiliated me time and time again until finally I graduated and moved schools.

I was never supposed to see him again.

I never wanted to see him again.

"W-What are you doing here?"

Jerrell shrugs, drawing my attention to the Silverwood mascot engraved on the strap of his backpack, "Got sick of living with the parents, so I transferred schools. You know how it is."

I don't know how it is.

The response dies in my throat as his eyes flick down my body. His boyish good looks are parallel to the fictional characters I read about: the brown hair, bright blue eyes and well-kept body of an athlete was enough to fool me into thinking he was a boy with good intentions.

Jerrell always had intentions, but they were never good.

"I didn't expect to see a familiar face so soon." He grins and it makes me want to throw up right on his polished shoes, "Although I would have thought you grew out of the leggings and sweater stage by now. Aren't you taking business in university?"

"Y-Yes."

He throws Trip a wink before turning back to me, "Hate to break it to you, Lacey doll, but you aren't going to be able to wear oversized clothes to work every day. Don't you think it's time to update the wardrobe a little?"

My shoulders hunch on instinct and I have to bite the apology off my tongue before it can slip out.

Trip frowns, glancing between us, "The last time I checked, business clothes weren't mandatory for classes."

"My mistake." Jerrell turns and gives her a charming smile, "You're brave bringing this girl to a plant shop. Give her a leaf and she'll put you to sleep with facts about water dosage and sunlight in no time."

Trip shuffles her feet awkwardly, "Actually, I love learning new things. Lacey's knowledge is quite remarkable."

"Well, whatever you do, don't take her to the bookstore. She'll have you there for fucking hours." He lets out a laugh,

"Don't let the pretty exterior fool you. This girl is a bigger nerd than that guy on *The Big Bang Theory*."

I try not to flinch, but it's no use.

The excruciating memories come flooding back, the casual taunts made to seem innocent and playful when they were always meant to hurt. I used to think that maybe I was too sensitive, maybe I didn't understand his sense of humour.

By the time I realized the malicious intent behind the jokes and comments, it was too late.

Jerrell had gotten what he wanted and he didn't bother sticking around to pick up the pieces.

"Anyways, I better get going. Things to do, important people to meet..." He trails off, catching my eye, "You remember how it was when I moved to your town. All work and no fun until someone of interest comes around."

I swallow the nausea in my throat, remembering exactly who that person of interest was the last time.

"But hey, worse comes to worst I can always hit you up to keep me entertained." He grins, those horrible eyes locked on mine, "Take care of yourself, Lacey. I'll see you around."

Jerrell doesn't acknowledge Trip before turning and walking back out the door. I listen to the echo of his footsteps fade away, the same sound I heard after he shattered me into pieces.

"He's kind of a dick." Trip pulls a face, "No offence but I hope we don't see him around. How did you know him?"

"I need to go."

Trip's response gets lost behind me as I stumble out into the fresh air, desperately gulping down oxygen as I scan the street for Jerrell's build.

The street is completely empty, his presence gone except for the weight pressing down on me. I try to break into a run, but my fumbling movements send me face down on the ground.

The rough concrete scrapes my palms and knees, burning a hole through my leggings as the tears start to fall.

"Lacey? What's going on?"

Trip reaches out to touch me but I scream and jerk away.

The memories are too much, the pain is too much, and I crumble to pieces right there on the pavement. Sobbing into my knees, I curl up into the fetal position and let my tears stain the concrete beneath me.

"It's going to be okay. Lacey, just calm down-

"No." My voice breaks on a sob, "It's not okay. I'm not okay."

"Breathe Lacey. Come on, just breathe."

"STOP!" The scream rips from my throat as if I'm still trapped in the backseat of Jerrell's car, "Please stop. Just stop."

"Oh God. I don't know what to do."

Trip sounds like she's on the verge of tears herself, but I can't do anything to help. My mind is unravelling faster than the hole in my leggings.

"I'm going to call your brother, okay? He'll be here shortly and then we can figure everything out."

"I don't need Wesley." I choke out the words, knowing there's only one person who understands what it's like to not be okay.

"I need Skylar."

Skylar

"Skylar to the front desk, please."

My name gets paged over the intercom and I make my way to the front of the store. Mila loves paging people to keep her company during slow hours, but I'm surprised she would do it on a day like today. There's been a steady stream of customers and the upcoming lunch hour is sure to be slammed.

She's talking to someone when I arrive and my surprise only grows when I see who it is.

"Skylar. Thank God." Trip exhales heavily and Mila shoots me a questioning look. I offer her a shrug and turn back to the Tiger who drove a long way to see me.

"Were you picking something up today?"

"Huh?"

"From Brock's Bolts and Beams. The store you are in right now."

Mila flicks her hair over her shoulder, "It's the biggest hardware store in Silverwood."

I roll my eyes, "It's the only hardware store in Silverwood."

"No, sorry. I'm not here for the store. I'm here for you." Trip fidgets with the thick material of her t-shirt, "It's Lacey."

"Ooh, whose Lacey? Sky, you didn't tell me you have a new girl." Mila gives me a teasing smile but I ignore it.

"What happened."

Trip sighs, "I don't actually know. I took her to the plant shop after her therapy appointment and we bumped into this guy and then she freaked out. I managed to get her to the car, but she doesn't want to go home."

Every worst case scenario filters through my head, adrenalin and fear crashing through my system in the deadliest of combinations.

"Where is she?"

"I didn't know where to go, so I just-

"Where. Is. She."

Trip blinks at the unmistakable anger in my tone, the need to get to my flower overriding the need to be in control.

"In the parking lot. She's in really rough shape, so you might want to be careful..."

I'm already sprinting for the door before she can finish her sentence.

For how busy the store is today, there aren't many cars in the parking lot. The fact that most of our customers are local and within walking distance works in my favour as I go running past the parked vehicles, squinting through windshields to find Lacey.

Where is she where is she where is she.

The panicked loop keeps me going until I find the rusty red Honda sitting at the far end. I was expecting to find her in the passenger seat, but it's movement in the backseat that catches my eye. I slow to a stop in front of the door, peering through the window one more time to make sure somebody didn't just leave their dog in the car.

"Flower?"

There's another shift of movement and I use it as confirmation. Gently prying the door open, I slip inside and find Lacey curled up in a ball, pressed tight against the opposite door. Rage sweeps through my body as I take in the ripped leggings and cuts decorating her palms.

"Flower. It's me."

"I-I'm not okay, S-Skylar." She can barely get the words out, her breathing almost to the point of hyperventilation.

"You don't have to be okay. It's just me."

My hands are trembling when I reach out to touch her. She's shaking from head to toe, the grief wrecking her system almost as strong as the rage burning through mine.

"Come here."

Lacey lets me pull her into my arms, her sobs burning a hole right through my chest. Her skin is swollen and puffy, her vibrant green eyes painfully bloodshot.

Swallowing the ache rising inside me, I wrap my arms around her.

"You're allowed to break, Flower. I promise I will put you back together again."

She cries for a long time but I don't let go. I hold on to her, holding her together the way she has held me together these past few weeks. Every wrecked sob, every shudder has my rage creeping past the point of concern as I feel my flower fall apart in my arms.

"Name five things you can see."

It takes her a while to suck in enough oxygen to respond.

"B-Black jeans. S-Steering wheel. R-Radio."

Another sob breaks the list and I wait patiently for her to keep going.

"W-Window. Y-You."

"Now countdown from one hundred. Go by tens."

Lacey follows my instructions, and by the time she makes it to zero, her breathing is almost back to normal.

"That's it, Flower. Just breathe."

"H-How did you know that would work?"

Tucking her tight against my chest, I refuse to acknowledge the fury desperately trying to break through my skin.

"Because I've used that trick myself far too many times."

Lacey falls silent against me, her heavy breathing filling the empty space of the car. I press my lips against her hair, gently brushing my fingers through it to untangle the knots. She buries her face into my neck, her shaky fingers digging into my shirt.

"He hurt me, Skylar."

The rage surges to the surface and soon I'm digging a fingernail into my jeans to keep myself from exploding.

"Who hurt you?"

I swear to God, if Walsh or another lacrosse player cornered her again...

"Jerrell Thompson." Lacey trembles against me, "My ex-boyfriend is here in Silverwood."

I stop breathing.

"You saw him?"

"He bumped into us at the plant shop. Said he just transferred schools." She breaks down into tears again, her fingers clutching my shirt like it's a lifeline.

"H-He hurt me."

Caressing her face with shaky hands, I gently trace her tear-stained cheek with my thumb. Devastated eyes stare back at me and that's all it takes for me to finally understand what happened four years ago.

What pushed my brother to make the decisions he did.

"I made a vow, Flower." I swallow, feeling the last piece of my heart shatter, "I made a vow that I would never hurt another person. I would never turn my anger into a physical weapon that could be used to hurt someone else."

My voice breaks, "But if you want me to hurt him, I'll do it. I'll do it for you."

The wailing beat of my heart slams against the only person who means more to me than any moral ever could. Tears slip down my face as I stare at her, hoping she can see the hero I was never meant to be.

"No." Lacey whispers softly, her eyes never leaving mine, "That's not who you are."

"It doesn't matter."

"Yes it does." She brushes the tears off my cheek with a sad smile, "I would never ask you to change who you are. Not now, not ever."

"He hurt you."

"He did. But that doesn't mean you need to hurt him back." She blows out an uneven breath, "I will never ask you to be my hero, Skylar. Only my friend."

"I should be able to be both."

She shakes her head vehemently, "I'm not some damsel in distress who needs to be saved. I just need someone who is willing to listen and hold my hand during the hard times. And that person is you."

There's a spark back in her eyes, a defiant glint that has my heart piecing itself back together. Brushing back a piece of her hair, I press my lips against hers, silently promising to do whatever it takes to keep that light alive.

"Promise me you won't hurt him." Lacey murmurs before kissing me back, "I would rather see him walk free than have you break a vow."

"I promise." Breathing the words into her mouth, I take my time kissing away the rest of her sorrow. Her quiet gasp fills the car when I pull her onto my lap, her long legs straddling mine as I help her forget the past for a little while.

By the time we break for air, the windows have fogged up and our heavy breathing is the only sound in the car. Lacey starts to laugh, her breathless giggles replenishing my lungs without the need for oxygen.

"This looks way worse than it is." She leans over me and writes five words on the window. Laughter bursts out of my chest when I read what she wrote.

We're not fucking, I promise.

"I think you got the message across."

"Just making sure Trip doesn't think we're contaminating her backseats."

"Uh huh."

There's a giant smile taking over Lacey's face and I trace it with my fingers, relishing in the fact I helped bring it back.

"Is there anything I can do?" Scanning her face, I'm looking for a solution not yet found, "In case you see him again."

She pulls a face, "I hate that he's relocated to Silverwood. It's extremely inconvenient."

I blow out a breath and her eyes flick back to mine.

"But there is something you could do to help."

The hesitation in her voice has my stomach dropping. She glances at the words scrawled along the window and suddenly I know exactly what she's about to say.

"Have sex with me."

Chapter 22

Lacey

He said no.

Humiliation sweeps through me as I stare at the boy who just spent the last ten minutes kissing me.

"You... you don't want to have sex with me?"

I'm still straddling his lap, so I quickly scramble off and press myself against the opposite door. Tears are threatening to make a reappearance, but I force them down, refusing to be the girl who cries about rejection.

Skylar doesn't look at me, he just stares down at his lap, where I was moments before.

"It's not the right time."

"Since when do you get to decide when it's the right time?" Anger and hurt fills each word.

"I don't decide when it's the right time, but I can tell when it's the wrong one. And right now, it's the wrong time."

I fall silent, staring at the dirty carpet in front of me. Trip must not vacuum her floors because it is atrocious back here.

"I'm not doing this to embarrass you." He blows out a strained breath, "I'm trying to keep you from making a mistake. You know as well as I do that it's never a good idea to make a big decision after an emotionally draining day."

I scowl at the ground, hearing the familiar words of our therapist. Skylar leans over and tugs my pinkie, patiently waiting until I face him like a petulant child.

"You're trying to rush into things because of your encounter with Jerrell today and that's not a good enough reason to take the next step."

"Jerrell has nothing to do with this. I want to have sex with you."

Skylar sighs, "You're not thinking about me right now. You're thinking about your past and how you want to prove he didn't hurt you as much as he did."

My bottom lip starts to quiver as the truth of his words sink in.

"I don't want to be broken anymore."

"Everyone is broken, Flower. Some people just have a few more pieces than others." He tilts his head, watching my reaction, "When we have sex it's not going to be because you feel like you need to. It's going to be because you want to."

"But... what if that day never comes?"

He shrugs, "Then we find a different way to fog up car windows."

I pull my knees up to my chest and squeeze them tight. Everything he's saying makes sense, but my brain is refusing to accept rationality right now.

"Can't we just try and see what happens?"

Skylar closes his eyes and leans his head back against the headrest.

"Not for this, Flower."

"Draw on me then." I shove the words out of my mouth before the fear can sink in, "Like you wanted to. Use my skin like it's paper."

Heavy silence fills the car until Skylar opens his eyes and looks at me.

"You want me to draw on you?"

"Yes." He doesn't look away and soon a blush stains my cheeks, "Don't say no again. Let me give you this one thing."

"You don't have to give me anything."

"Don't say no, Skylar. Please."

My plea is what does him in.

"Okay." He sighs, looking down at his hands, "Not tonight though. I want you to take a few days to think about it and if it's still what you want then…"

Skylar swallows before looking at me. His irises are more contrasting than usual, the light one burning with quiet anger while the dark one smoulders with desire.

It's as though his body can't decide which passion to unleash.

"Then I'll draw on you."

My face splits into a beaming smile, "Really?"

"Yeah."

He sounds angry with himself and I can't help but reach over and take his hand. Smoothing my thumb over his knuckles, I bend down to give them a kiss.

"Thank you, Skylar. I promise I'll think about it."

"Ta-da!"

Nico pushes through the door to his partner's apartment and beckons me inside. By the time Skylar went back to work and Trip drove me home, I felt better but too emotional to be on my own tonight.

So, I asked my best friend if we could have a sleepover.

"Are you sure Mo won't mind?"

Glancing around the apartment, I take in the state-of-the-art home appliances decorating the lavishly furnished bachelor pad. It's no secret that Taber's assistant coach comes from money but it's still a shock seeing it up close.

"Maurice is on pizza duty. He'll be home soon." Nico throws my overnight bag on the granite tabletop and scoops me up, "Just wait until you see this man's curved TV. It's like watching a movie in virtual reality."

I laugh, wrapping my arms around his neck, "And you said you were only with him for his body. It's been his money all along."

"Babe, he's got the body *and* the money. Almost makes it worth the disgusting food he insists on eating."

"Good to know my redeeming qualities make up for a healthy diet."

The amused voice floats through the apartment and we both turn to see Taber's lacrosse legend standing in the doorway.

Nico grins, "It's not healthy if it would make a dog cry."

Mo raises a brow, "It's a good thing we don't have a dog then, isn't it?"

"The key word there is yet. We don't have a dog *yet*."

Laughter spills out of my mouth and Mo glances over at me with a warm smile, "It's good to see you, Lacey. The guest bedroom should be all ready for you."

"I still haven't told him." Nico whispers loud enough for Mo to roll his eyes, "He's being replaced as my body pillow for tonight."

My best friend sets me back on the ground before strutting over to his partner. The exasperated look on Mo's face morphs into something softer when Nico plants his lips on his.

"Sorry babe, I'm abandoning you for my favourite girl tonight."

"I'll try not to be torn up about it."

Nico throws his head back and laughs before stealing the pizza box from Mo's hands.

"Did you remember to ask for extra cheese?"

"Did you remember the conversation we had about healthy eating?"

Nico scoffs, waving the pizza box in the air like it's proof the conversation never happened, "I do enough cardio not to worry about that for another ten years."

I bite back a laugh, "Don't you skip the cardio components at practice?"

Mo smirks, "He does, but he wasn't talking about lacrosse."

Oh.

My cheeks flame and I quickly look away from the men who clearly have no problem fucking on the regular. The familiar ache of despair rises up but I force it aside and follow Nico to the mahogany kitchen table.

To my surprise, Mo doesn't take the seat at the head of the table. Pulling out a chair beside his boyfriend, he sits down next to Nico and steals a slice from the box.

I study him from across the table, watching the way his eyes roam over Nico's face while his partner chats about his day.

Trip confessed to me once that she thought Mo should be on the cover of a GQ magazine and she's not wrong. The expensive dress shirt molds to a muscular frame that's impressive even for varsity standards while the masculine lines of his face accentuate the intelligence shining through pale blue eyes.

By all definitions, Maurice O'Brien is a very attractive man.

But I still wouldn't pick him over Skylar.

"What would you like to do tonight, mi amor?" Nico captures my attention by throwing a piece of pepperoni across the table, "Tonight is all about you."

Shaking off the restless thoughts, I glance around the luxury apartment. There's an endless supply of entertainment at my disposal, but the idea that comes to mind doesn't require anything fancy.

"Actually, I was thinking maybe we could play some cards."

"Done." Nico snaps his fingers, "I just bought a bag of skittles that can work as betting chips. Maurice, go grab the cards."

Mo raises a brow, "I didn't realize this was your apartment, Montez."

"Babe, quit being cute. We got a card game to play."

He rolls his eyes and gets up from the table. I quickly clear the plates and by the time Nico is finished sorting the skittles into varying money chips, the rules of the game have been explained and everyone is dealt a hand.

It soon becomes clear that Nico and I are seriously outmatched. The careful calculations Mo puts into every move has it so we've both run out of skittles by the fifth hand.

"That's it. Two against one." Nico sniffs, standing up to join me on the other side of the table, "Team Redemption versus The Skittle Stealer."

I laugh, reaching over to refill our skittle pile, "I don't think it's going to help."

Mo smirks, "This reminds me of a pool game we played. Remind me, Montez, what was the outcome again?"

Nico lets out a growl and deals out the cards. Our combined strategies don't help in the slightest and pretty soon we're back in the same losing position.

"You couldn't let us win one round?" Nico groans, dropping his head onto the table, "All I wanted was a red skittle. Nothing more."

"It's not winning if the other person hands it to you." Mo gives his partner a pointed look and Nico flips him the bird.

"It's a good thing I'm sleeping in the guest bedroom with Lace tonight. Otherwise, your ass would be on the couch."

"Again, I return to the question: whose apartment is this?"

The scowl that used to stain Mo's handsome features is nowhere to be found when he shoots me a grin. I laugh, feeling the irreplaceable warmth that comes from being surrounded by loved ones.

"He's got you there, Nico."

"Babe, you can't take his side. Maurice never lets me live it down."

Mo smirks, pushing back his chair to stand up, "Enjoy the guest bedroom tonight. I'll enjoy having a bed to myself for once."

"Liar."

Ignoring his partner, Mo turns to me with a smile, "Have a good night, Lacey. Let me know if you need anything."

"Thanks, Mo."

Nico pulls a face at his retreating back, "He's in denial. He loves being my body pillow. That man is a fucking teddy bear come sunrise."

"I can still hear you."

Mo's voice echoes down the hall and I laugh.

Grabbing my hands, Nico pulls me to my feet and leads me down the dark hallway until we reach the guest bedroom. It's just as nicely furnished as the rest of the apartment, the dark blue drapes matching an equally tasteful bedspread.

"Now we won't have to squish on those sad rectangles our university calls a mattress." Nico grins, pointing to the king size mattress, "It gives you a new appreciation for comfort."

"I bet." Scoping out the rest of the room, my eyes catch the alarm clock sitting on the nightstand, "Why don't you use the bathroom first? I've got something I'd like to do."

"Sounds good to me." Nico grabs the fresh briefs lying on the bed, "Keep in mind the sacrifice I'm making for you tonight."

"Not sleeping beside Mo?"

"Hell, no. I'm talking about the fact I'm putting a layer of material between my body and these silk sheets."

I pull a face, "You normally sleep naked?"

"Have you seen the man I sleep next to? That would be an even bigger waste than these sheets."

He throws me a wink and saunters out the door. Shaking my head with a smile, I take another glance at the time blinking back at me.

I pull out my phone and press the call button.

Skylar

My phone rings at the same time it does every night.

After the events of today, I honestly didn't think she would call.

Pressing accept, I'm about to speak when Lacey's voice echoes down the line.

"I was being selfish. Earlier today when we were in the car together. I was being selfish and I'm sorry."

"You don't have to apologize."

"No, I do. You were right, Skylar. I wasn't thinking about you. I was thinking about myself when I asked you to have sex with me and that's not fair."

There's a shuffle of movement on the other end of the line and I can't help but picture Lacey lying in her bed, staring up at the ceiling like I'm doing now.

"It's okay, Flower."

"Stop being so nice. I'm trying to apologize."

The frustration in her tone has my lips pulling into a smile.

"In that case, I accept your apologize."

"Good." She blows out a breath, "Just so you know, I do want to have sex with you. I want to know what it feels like when you're inside me. I want to experiment and try weird positions so we can figure out what works and what doesn't. I want to do all of those things with you and only you."

Each word has me clutching my phone tighter, the ache in my chest growing until it encompasses every fibre of my being.

I've waited my entire life for someone to see past the broken exterior and still want the messy parts inside.

I've waited my entire life to meet someone I was convinced didn't exist.

And then my flower came along and proved me wrong.

"I want to do all those things with you too." I falter, feeling the honest truth press against my tongue, "But if we rush into things I could hurt you. And if that happens I would never forgive myself."

The thought of making Lacey cry, or worse, making her recovery process painful has resentment rippling through me. Shoving myself off the bed, I walk over to my desk and grab a fresh sheet of paper.

My fingers are shaking when I press the tip of my pencil down.

"You aren't going to hurt me, Skylar. Do you know why?"

The lines I'm leaving behind are sharp and merciless, the cruel twist of my pencil tarnishing the white sheet in front of me.

"Because I trust you. I trust that you will do whatever it takes to make sure I'm comfortable, and I trust that if I told you to stop, that's what you would do."

My pencil slows to a stop, the harsh beat of my heart pounding in my ears.

"That's the bare minimum a person should do for their partner, Flower."

"Then you should have no problem surpassing my expectations."

She's smiling. I can hear it in her voice and picture it in my head. She's smiling and here I am, destroying an innocent piece of paper because I'm terrified I won't be strong enough to help her.

Fuck. I'm such a mess.

Crumpling the piece of paper in front of me, I blow out a breath and start afresh. I sketch the outline of Lacey's smile, the untamed curls flowing over her shoulder and down her back. Colouring in the freckles and birth marks I've been able to find, I slowly create a silhouette of her body.

"Anyways, I should let you go. Nico will be back soon but I just wanted to get that off my chest."

"I'm glad you called." I hesitate, staring at the partial sketch in front of me, "About what we talked about earlier... don't feel like you have to do something you aren't comfortable with, Flower. Not for me."

Silence falls on the other end.

Chewing my lip, I pass time by shading in the edges of her collarbone, carefully leaving space for the splatter of freckles that sits at the base of her throat.

"There's no one else I would rather be uncomfortable for. Have a good night, Skylar."

I blow out a breath, "Goodnight, Flower."

Our call ends but my pencil doesn't stop moving.

Losing myself in the piece before me, I sharpen the crease of her smile, brighten the colour of her eyes, and shade in the juts of her elbows and knees. Outlining the shape of her breasts, I leave her body bare except for the thin edge of her panties hugging the curve of her waist. I colour in the flowers lining the band of the panties I remember taking off, the delicate petals bringing a smile to my face.

That was a good day.

By the time I resurface, it's long past midnight and my hand feels like it's about to fall off. Flexing my fingers against the ache, I stare at the drawing, noting the intricate dance of her freckles. They creep along her body like landmarks, disappearing only in the places I haven't explored yet.

Pushing back from my desk, I'm still thinking about those freckles when I notice the light shining under Vector's bedroom door. I pause my trek to the bathroom, remembering the demons Lacey has had to face these last few days.

She's so strong. So determined not to let the past drag her down. And here I am, hiding from the demons living in my own house.

Blowing out a breath, I turn and push open my brother's door. He's shirtless, lying on his bed with a textbook of some sort. I stare at the hard cut muscles running along his torso, the obnoxious six-pack rippling with every inhale and exhale.

"I know you're still taking the steroids."

I wait for the crash of anger to fill my system, but it never does. The only thing I feel is sorrow for the relationship we lost and regret for the boy who was forced to become a man.

Vector doesn't look away from his textbook, "Let's not do this tonight, Sky."

"You broke your promise."

"No. I didn't."

The first spark of anger hits and I take another step closer.

"You said you were going to get things under control before Taber's home opener. You promised me you were going to be better."

"Fine. You want to do this tonight? We'll do this tonight." Vector throws his textbook to the side and sits up in bed. His broad shoulders are completely in shadow, the only light burning from the fire in his eyes.

"I've only made two promises in this life, Sky." He glares at me, "Do you know what those are?"

I glare back at him, "You were going to kick out dad."

"And that's exactly what I did."

"And you were going to stop hurting people."

"No." Vector snaps his teeth together, "I never once promised that. I told you I was going to try and get a handle on my temper and you took that to mean I would stop taking the drugs."

Fury barrels through my body as the silence that kept me in the dark all these years comes crashing down.

"You couldn't control your temper when we were kids. How the fuck were you going to control it when you're injecting testosterone into your ass every week?"

"I wasn't planning on controlling my temper." Vector grinds out the words, his darkening expression locked on mine, "I was planning on keeping my promise."

"Bullshit. Everything you've done has been for yourself."

"You're such a fucking idiot." He snarls, pushing off the bed and striding towards me. I watch him with narrowed eyes, daring him to hit me.

Vector slows to a stop, his chest heaving as he stares down at me.

"I promised to protect *you*, Sky. I promised I would do anything it takes to keep you safe."

"I don't believe you."

"Jesus Christ, Sky. Look at you." He growls, the ugly truth reflecting in his eyes, "How many times did you get bullied in junior high? How many times did people make fun of your eyes and the sketchbook you were always carrying around?"

I can't breathe as I stare back at him.

"Did you think it was a coincidence the taunts came to an end in high school? That the same day I injured the biggest player on the lacrosse field was the same day people stopped picking on you?"

He lets out a bitter laugh, "I didn't mean to hurt him, but once I saw the way people started treated me, the way people started treated *you*, I couldn't go back."

"I didn't ask you to do that."

"Of course you didn't." Vector shakes his head, tearing his eyes away from my face, "I was trying to be your fucking hero. Do you know what I got for my efforts?"

Tears burn my eyes as the consequence of my actions finally catch up to me.

"I got treated like a villain since the first day I kept my promise."

The regret spills onto my cheeks, streaming down my face as I stare at the brother I've shamed and avoided for the last four years.

I should have talked to him. I should have questioned his decisions more, not fallen back on the assumption he's just like our father.

I should have known better.

"I've missed you." Choking out the words, there's nothing I can say to fix the mistakes we've both made, "I've missed you, Vec."

"Come on. Don't cry." He groans, wrapping those large arms around me, "This is exactly why you got bullied in the first place."

"Fuck off." My watery laugh is muffled against his chest, but it doesn't stop Vector from squeezing me tighter.

"I've missed you too, Sky."

We stay like that, clutching each other for a long time. The pain in my heart doesn't go away, but the tears on my cheeks start to dry.

And maybe that's good enough for today.

Vector pulls away first, his oversized hands gripping my face tightly.

"I don't break my promises, Sky. Even if you don't like what I have to do to keep them."

I scan his face, looking for any sign of remorse. Any regret of the violence he's unleashed to sustain a reputation.

There isn't a single trace.

"I can't come to your lacrosse games anymore. Not if you won't put in the effort to get clean." I swallow thickly, "It's not fair to every other player on the field. Especially when you struggle with anger issues."

Vector lets go of my face, studying me silently.

"I'll work on getting clean if you start sharing your artwork again."

"What?"

"Your art." He says it slowly, like it's the words and not the comment that has me confused, "I want to see it."

I stare at him, waiting for the punchline.

Vector sighs, "Stop making this a big deal. You used to show me your projects and I would like to see them again."

"Are you serious?"

"No. I'm joking." He rolls his eyes, "Of course I'm serious, dumbass. Your girlfriend isn't the only one who thinks you have talent."

Warmth explodes through my chest as I smile at my brother for the first time in four years.

"I'm still not joining the track team."

He grins, soaking in the happiness radiating through my features.

"We'll see about that."

Chapter 23

Lacey

Mo is in the kitchen when I stumble in for a glass of water.

He's scowling at his laptop, a sweat-stained gym t-shirt plastered to his body. I eye him warily, unsure of how he's already worked out and fully functioning this early in the morning.

"I didn't know you worked on weekends."

He grunts, not taking his eyes off the computer, "I don't. Some moron pulled the wrong dataset for the quarterly report and now someone has to fix it."

Besides being the assistant coach for the university's lacrosse team, Nico's partner also works as a financial advisor for an international corporation. From what I've heard, most of the work is virtual and pretty flexible, although apparently not when someone pisses him off.

"Can you fix it?"

"Of course I can." Mo sighs, pinching the bridge of his nose, "But if people did their jobs correctly, I wouldn't have to."

I wince at the harsh tone and return my attention to rehydrating and crawling back into bed.

My mission becomes more difficult when my search for a cup turns up empty. Hesitating by the sink, I'm debating whether I should just drink straight from the faucet when Mo shoots me an amused glance.

"Bottom right cupboard. Don't be afraid to ask questions."

"Oh. Right." I clear my throat, bending down to open the right hiding spot, "Thank you."

"You're welcome."

Mo returns his attention to the computer in front of him but I can't bring myself to leave the kitchen. Staring down at the glass in my hands, my thoughts stray back to the conversation with Skylar last night, and I can't help but feel sad all over again.

Everyone makes it look so easy. Being in a relationship. Taking that intimate step with their partner. Nobody talks about the painful moments, the flood of self-consciousness that always comes with a lack of experience.

The frustrating part is I can't tell if it's because people don't like talking about the ugly moments or if I am just the exception.

"Did you have another question?" Mo's voice startles me, and I quickly look up to find him staring at me. I shake my head then pause, rethinking my answer.

"What was your first time having sex like?"

If he was surprised by my question, he doesn't show it. Thinking over the question carefully, Mo takes his time responding.

"I thought of it more as a milestone that needed to be checked off. The experience itself was fine, so I can't say I put much value on it."

"Right." My shoulders slump with disappointment. Turning to walk back to the bedroom, I'm about to drown in a pool of self-pity when a throat clears behind me.

"It wasn't until my second semester of university that I had sex with a guy for the first time."

I pause, turning back around. Mo flicks his eyes at me, a ghost of a smile crossing his face.

"Scariest moment of my life."

"You were scared?" Disbelief oozes through my tone as I stare at the man who holds the record number of varsity championship banners.

Mo nods, "Terrified. Thought I was going to pass out at one point."

"No way." Wandering closer, I pull out a barstool and sit down beside him, "Were you the bottom?"

"Of course not."

The candid answer has my laughing and Mo shakes his head with a smile.

"That didn't make it any better though. I knew that once I took that step, I could no longer label myself as straight."

I frown, "But nobody knew you were bisexual until you and Nico started dating."

"It's not so much what other people think but what you think of yourself." Mo tilts his head, his eyes finding mine, "The most powerful perspective is always your own. It has the ability to change, to adapt and rearrange to fit a new piece of your identity, but at the end of the day it's up to you to make that change."

I mull over his words, taking a moment to let them soak in.

"Was it a good experience? Your bi awakening?"

He grimaces, "Do not use that term on me again. That is the worst thing I have ever heard."

"Sorry. It's a book trope."

He chuckles, "It's fine. I wouldn't say it was a bad experience, but looking back, I should have approached it differently."

"Do you mind me asking how?"

"Well, to put it simply, I did it for selfish reasons. My mother had just died and I wanted to feel like I had control over one aspect of my life. I didn't care about the guy I was doing it with, I couldn't even tell you his name. It was a jump in the deep end without a second thought about his feelings or my own."

He pauses, glancing at me, "I guess the lesson to be taken away is don't rush into things just because you feel broken inside. Once the sweat dries, you're stuck with the same problems you were trying to run from in the first place."

I fall silent, studying the man beside me.

He's strong in every sense of the word, but at the end of the day he's only human. A man who makes mistakes and does his best to learn from them.

"You've given me lots to think about. Thanks, Mo."

"You're welcome, Lacey."

I smile at him and he smiles back. There's something special about the people who enter your life through those you love the most and I think I can confidently say that I made a new friend today.

"I was going to go back to bed, but I have a better idea."

He raises a brow, "If you're going to keep banging my cupboards, I might have to go work in the office."

I laugh, "I was thinking more along the lines of ambushing Nico with a pillow fight. Would you like to join me?"

Mo glances at his work computer before looking back at me. After a moment, he reaches out and closes the laptop in front of him, putting a pause on the hard deadlines of the corporate world to help me wake up the man he loves.

"Absolutely."

I risk life and limb and borrow my brother's car.

Driving to Silverwood isn't the most scenic drive at the best of times, but when the car you're driving is making concerning noises, suddenly the drive feels unbearably long. Every splutter the vehicle coughs out has me clenching the steering wheel in panic, certain Lola is about to crap out on me.

Somehow we make the 45-minute drive without a call for help and by the time I'm pulling into the dirt parking lot, my palms are sweating for a completely different reason.

Scanning the street for any sign of Jerrell, I hop out and make my way inside the plant shop.

I make my purchase and force myself to walk back to the car. Jerrell has had a hold over me for too long and I am not about to let him ruin the town I've grown to call my home.

Despite the mental pep talk, relief still crashes over my body when I finally clamber back inside the manic vehicle. It takes a moment for the panic to subside, but once it does, I feel a tiny surge of victory.

I did it.

Jamming the gear stick into drive, I let the smile break clear across my face as I head over to the little house four blocks down.

Amber is in the front lawn, working on her garden when I get out of the car. Dropping her gloves to the ground, she limps over to greet me.

"Lacey, honey, I didn't know you were coming over! What a lovely surprise."

She immediately wraps me in a hug and I squeeze her back.

"I was hoping to surprise Skylar. Is he home?"

"He just came back from a run with his brother. Try the kitchen and if not, I'm sure he's in his bedroom." Amber grins, her eyes flashing mischievously, "Be sure to tell him how excited you are to go watch his track meets next year."

I laugh, "I'm not sure that will make a difference."

"You would be surprised. Go on, now. Don't let me keep you."

Planting a kiss on her cheek, I go racing inside the house. The kitchen turns up empty and I go running up the stairs, adrenaline and excitement fuelling my stamina just long enough to make it to Skylar's bedroom.

It's genuinely embarrassing how much I'm panting from that small amount of physical exertion. Forcing the thought aside, I knock gently against his door.

"I don't think he's home."

The voice comes from behind me and I scream, throwing up my hands and nearly hitting Skylar in the process. He ducks just in time, saving himself a black eye.

"Oh my God." I clutch my chest, panting in earnest now, "You need to give me a warning next time."

"That was my bad. I forgot to put on my bell."

I laugh, throwing my arms around him. Damp skin meets my hands and that's how long it takes for me to realize he just got out of the shower.

And he's only wearing a towel.

A blush stains my cheeks as I quickly pull away and try not to stare at the water dripping down Skylar's bare chest. I've seen him naked on more than one occasion, but there's something about a freshly showered body that should not be allowed.

It's too tempting. Even for someone like me.

"I didn't know you were coming over today." Skylar flicks his eyes over my face, the edge of a smile pulling at his lips, "But I'm glad you did."

My desire to check out the abs peeking out of the towel is nothing compared to the need to soak in the face smiling back at me.

"I wanted to surprise you with a present."

"You didn't have to do that."

"Hush until you see what it is."

My scolding tone has his smile growing even wider. Taking my hand, he pulls me into his room and shuts the door. He lets go of my hand, presumably to go put on some clothes, but I don't let him.

Grabbing his shoulders, I pull him flush against me, needing to feel that smile pressed against my own. It takes less than two seconds for him to kiss me back, the hard surface of his bedroom door digging into my back.

The bag that was hanging around my arm slides to the ground. Reaching behind me, I turn the lock on his bedroom door before running my hands down the naked torso in front of me.

"Flower." Skylar hisses out the word, his breathing uneven, "I can't take it when you touch me like that."

"You mean like this?" I smile, trailing a finger down those abs before stroking the bulge that's growing beneath the towel.

"Exactly like that."

He goes to put his lips back on mine but I swerve, pulling a trick from his book and nipping the edge of his jaw. Skylar shudders, closing his eyes as I keep going, slowly kissing my way down his neck to his shoulders.

My fingers tug the edge of the towel and it comes loose, falling to the ground between us. Skylar's eyes snap open when I start kissing my way down his torso, my hands stroking him the way he taught me to.

"Maybe we should slow down. I don't want you... *Fuck*."

The curse comes out when I press a kiss against the tip of his cock. Flicking out my tongue, I taste the pre-cum glistening there and look up with a smile.

"It's been a while, so bear with me."

"Flower. You don't have to do this."

My smile widens, "I want to."

And it's the truth.

I've lost count of the number of times Skylar has gone down on me. He treats me like a queen, worships my body like it's a religious temple, and never asks for anything in return.

He's so kind and thoughtful and always puts me first.

But today I want to put him first.

"You can stop anytime." Skylar swallows, staring at me with glazed eyes. I can feel his erection throbbing in my hand and yet he's still worried about my own comfort.

"I know."

Not giving him a chance to say anything else, I take him in my mouth. Gliding my tongue along his ridge, I swallow as much as possible before sucking my way back to the top. It helps that he's not that big, I can almost make it to the base before my gag reflex kicks in.

"Easy, Flower. Don't hurt yourself."

He strokes my jaw and I relax, focusing less on the deep pulls and more on the sensitive underside of his tip. Skylar's breathing grows heavy as I play with the spot he showed me in the shower, the suction of my lips and teasing pressure of my tongue making him come undone.

"*Fuck.*"

His hips thrust forward and I take him to the back of my throat again. Another curse slips out when my tongue hits the same spot, his hands threading through my hair as I suck him off.

"I'm about to come."

The warning doesn't impair my progress and I keep going until the salty stream shoots down my throat. Skylar is shaking by the time I sit back on my heels, his eyes glowing against the flushed state of his cheeks.

"That wasn't your present." I blurt out, suddenly self-conscious, "It doesn't seem that way, but I promise I didn't drive all the way here to give you a blowjob."

Giving me a heart-stopping smile, he bends down and presses a kiss against my lips.

"You never need a reason to see me. I will always be waiting."

Skylar

She bought me a plant.

I study the white tinge of the leaves, the unusual colour making me wonder whether she picked it because it matches my hair.

"It needs a lot more sunlight than most succulents, but your window faces the south, so I thought it would be okay." Lacey gives me a bright smile, "You only have to water it a couple times a week and there's a fertilizer sample in the bag in case you want to replant it with new soil."

"Is it okay in this pot?"

"Yeah. I already transferred it from the original plastic container." She bites her lip, "If you don't want it though, there's no pressure to keep it."

"This is my first plant. Don't go stealing my firstborn now."

She laughs and the sound has my lips pulling into a smile.

We're both sitting on my floor, leaning against my bed while Lacey explains the intricacies of owning a succulent. Her face is alight with unbridled excitement as she walks me through the different watering techniques and I can't help but ask more questions just to keep her passion alive.

"I have this little watering can that is more of a mister... oh my God." She claps a hand over her mouth, staring at me with wide eyes, "Why didn't you say something? I've been talking about plants for the last half hour."

"I like hearing you talk about plants."

A flush creeps up her cheeks and she quickly looks away, "You can't let me go on tangents, Skylar. I'll put you to sleep in no time."

There's a shift in her voice, a quiet vulnerability that makes me think this isn't the first time those words have been spoken.

"Flower." I wait for her to look at me, "You could talk to me about plants for hours and I still wouldn't fall asleep."

"I'm such a nerd. I'm so-

"No." I cover her mouth with my hand, cutting her off, "Don't say that like it's a bad thing. You have the confidence to share your passion with the world and I have the privilege of witnessing it. It's a gift to be cherished, not an apology to be delivered."

Lacey blinks, her eyes glistening with unshed tears as I give her the last shred of reassurance inside me.

"I love all your pieces, Flower. The broken ones, the hopeful ones, the romantic ones. They all come together to form the mosaic you are and I love every single piece."

The tears spill over and I kiss away each one, cherishing the best present I have ever received. Her arms wrap around my neck, pulling me close enough to feel her fractured heart beating in time with my own.

I clutch her tightly, knowing there will never be anyone else. No matter what the future holds, no matter what decisions come to play, there will only ever be my flower.

For now, and for always.

Lacey sighs, "For someone who insists he's not a romantic, you have a terrible tendency of making me cry with beautiful words."

"Just trying to live up to your book standards."

She pulls away, brushing away the last of her tears, "You are the farthest thing from a book boyfriend a girl can get, but that might be my favourite thing about you."

I stare at her, unable to fathom how that would be something positive. Fictional billionaires and hot jocks sound a lot more promising than a tortured artist with anger management issues.

As if reading my thoughts, Lacey leans over and takes my hand. She squeezes it, giving me a smile that wipes the cobwebs of doubt clear from my mind.

"You're real."

Her words wrap around my heart in an unbreakable clasp of hope and joy. The sharp edges of my past are still there, slicing through the tissue every time I breathe, but the love flowing through my veins takes away the sting.

It takes away the pain of being broken.

"Sometimes I don't think you're real." I whisper, unable to tear my gaze away from her bright eyes, "Sometimes I'm worried that one of these days I'm going to wake up and this was all a dream. That you were nothing more than a dream."

"This isn't a dream, Skylar. I'll prove it to you."

She sits up and pulls her t-shirt right over her head. I can only stare as a sea of creamy skin marked by freckles becomes exposed, the teasing sight stretching from the waistband of her leggings to the black cups of her bra.

Taking my hands, she places them on her bare torso. I stroke her without thinking, my greedy fingers craving the soft texture of her body.

She shivers, "This is going to be more difficult than I imagined."

"What's going to be difficult?"

Lacey exhales slowly, watching my fingers dance along her skin.

"Having you draw on me."

I freeze, staring at her with wide, stupidly hopeful eyes.

"You still want that?"

She gives me a shy smile, "I'm ready if you are."

Nodding slowly, I push myself off the ground and wander over to my desk. I grab my sketchbook and the packet of body markers and return to my spot next to Lacey.

My hands are shaking when I open my sketchbook to the drawing I did the other night.

"Oh my God. Is that me?" Lacey lets out a gasp and leans closer.

Her mostly naked body is displayed in front of us, the sparkling smile lighting up her face from the edge of her lips to the crease of her eyes. It's some of my best work, but that doesn't change the fact I drew her nude without her permission.

"I should have asked if this was okay." I chew my lip, staring at the freckles on the page, "It's from memory so it's not perfect."

"It's so…" She trails off, staring at the lines of her body, "Beautiful. I love it."

"You're not upset I drew a naked picture of you?"

"Of course not." She sighs, reaching out to brush the pencil marks, "You made me look so confident. Effortlessly sexy."

"That's how I see you. Confident and sexy and nothing less than a masterpiece." I clear my throat, "There are a few designs I thought might work, but we can use this as a guide so you can show me where you want it done."

"Okay."

Pulling out my phone, I open the photo album I created the other day. It felt presumptuous making it before Lacey confirmed she wanted me to draw on her, but I didn't want to be empty-handed in case she did.

"Ooh, I like that one." She leans over and points to the silhouette of blossoming azaleas surrounded by falling leaves.

"There are a few things I can do with this one." Flipping back to the sketch of her, I run my finger over the lines of her body, "We could keep it small and simple, on your arm or your leg for instance, or I could expand it to cover the surface of your back."

She falls silent beside me, watching my fingers trace the outline of her body.

"Where would you want to put it?"

"It's not my body, Flower."

"But what if it was?"

I swallow thickly, looking down at the sketch in my lap. There are so many things I want to do, but only one has been haunting me from sunrise to sunset.

"I would start here," I tap the edge of her finger, "And work my way up, using your freckles as a guideline." Trailing my finger along the sketch, I hear Lacey suck in a breath, "Until I make it to your heart. Then I would head south," I brush the peak of her nipple before cutting across her torso to the opposite hip, "And take my time here. I would finish by working my way down to your toes, so there isn't a part of your body that I haven't marked."

"Wow." Lacey exhales heavily, "You've given this a lot of thought."

"You could say that."

She laughs, a breathless sound that has my blood simmering.

"Do you have enough markers to do that? Mark me from head to toe?"

I should tell her no. I should tell her it's a ridiculous fantasy that will never come true because it's too much too soon.

"Yeah."

Cursing myself for being a selfish bastard, I can't bring myself to look at Lacey while she thinks over her answer.

"Okay. Let's do it."

"Are you sure?"

"Yeah." She blows out a breath, giving herself a nod, "This is going to be fun."

I shut my sketchbook and climb to my feet. By the time I have everything ready, Lacey looks more excited than nervous, and the sight calms the racing pace of my heart.

Helping her strip off her clothes, I gently lay her down on my bed.

"Are you okay?"

I'm trying not to stare at her naked body lying on top of my duvet, but it's no use. My eyes drink in the sight of the pale skin glowing against my bedspread, the dusting of dark hair between her thighs, the hesitant smile painting her lips.

"I think so. Is this going to hurt?"

Reaching out, I brush the constellation of freckles running along her torso.

"It shouldn't. I bought special markers that are supposed to be better for skin."

Sliding my finger up her body, I observe the way she reacts to my touch. There's an initial flinch, a slight tension when I reach a new spot, but it shouldn't be a problem as long as I take it slow.

Lacey bites her lip nervously and the sight has me quickly pulling away my hand.

"We don't have to do this."

"No. I want to." She hesitates, looking me in the eye, "I'm just a little scared right now."

The words pierce my chest and I have to bite my tongue to keep from calling this whole thing off. My flower wants to do this, so I have to honour that.

But first I need to ease her mind.

Taking a marker out of the packet, I uncap it and offer it to her. Lacey takes it with wide eyes, watching me pull my shirt over my head.

"I'll go first then."

Chapter 24

Lacey

I am the world's worst artist.

Giggles escape as I draw a stick figure on Skylar's back. He's lying face down on the bed while I'm straddling his waist, precariously balancing over him as I attempt to add another stick figure to the collection.

"How long does this take to wash off?"

He shifts beneath me, "A couple days, normally. A week at most."

The thought of Skylar walking around with my hideous drawing for a week has laughter bursting out of me.

"Do I want to know what you're doing back there?"

"Shh, I'm working."

When Skylar offered me the chance to draw on him, I didn't know what to think. It was obvious he was doing it to help me relax, but I didn't see how scribbling ink all over his body was going to reduce my anxiety.

Turns out, drawing on someone else is really fun.

A smile lights up my face as I give my stick figures some clothes. It wasn't just the art that helped to reduce my stress, it was Skylar himself. He didn't just give me free reign to mark his skin, he also gave me time and space to get comfortable being naked around him.

There isn't a scrap of material on my body and yet the discomfort from earlier is nowhere to be found.

More giggles float out of my mouth as I write our names under each one. Drawing a little heart to connect the two, I re-cap the marker with a flourish.

"All done."

He shifts beneath me and I quickly scramble to the end of the bed so he can sit up. The stick figures ripple along his back as he pushes himself off the bed and the sight has my face breaking into a wide smile.

"I think I outdid myself."

Skylar glances at me with bright eyes before walking over to the mirror hanging on the far wall. He studies the drawing, twisting his spine so he can read the two names scrawled underneath each figure.

"Am I the one on the left or right?"

I laugh, climbing off the bed and walking over, "You're the one with short hair. Here, let me show you."

He watches me through the mirror, his eyes following my fingers when I gently brush stick figure number one.

"This is Skylar. He's an unbelievably fast runner but pretends he doesn't exercise very often."

He huffs out a laugh and I feel it vibrate through my fingertips. Trailing my hand along his skin, I gently tap stick figure number two.

"And this is Lacey. She's a terrible runner but pretends reading counts as cardio." I smile, tracing the warped shape linking the two figures, "And this is our heart. Broken when we're apart but perfectly complete when we're together."

Skylar meets my gaze in the mirror, his eyes a beacon of happiness when that beautiful face breaks into a smile. My heart slams against my chest as I stare at him, stare at the boy I saw in that photograph all those weeks ago.

The one who shared his joy with every facial muscle.

"You have the prettiest smile." I whisper, wrapping my arms around his waist, "It takes my breath away every time."

Pressing a kiss against his neck, I wait for those mesmerizing eyes to meet mine.

One brown. One blue.

Each one glistening with an untold story, the sacrifice and struggle of a boy learning to love himself again.

"You're the real work of art, Skylar Vin. I hope you know that."

He swallows, looking at me like I just sliced his chest open and stole the organ beating inside. Pressing another kiss against his neck, I slide my hand up to his heart, leaving my own mark on his body.

"This is my favourite part of you. This ugly thing that keeps us alive." Pressing my fingers down, I can feel the fragments of my own heart beating underneath, "I know it hurts sometimes but that's what makes it beautiful. That's what makes it mine."

Skylar slowly turns around, his eyes alight with so many emotions it's impossible to distinguish a single one. My hand is still pressed against his chest, the accelerated beat of our heart thundering against my fingers.

"I've always been yours, Flower." His eyes are locked on mine, the light and dark iris teasing me with endless opportunities, "I just didn't know it until I read your handwriting for the first time."

I laugh, feeling my eyes start to well-up, "I thought for sure my pen pal was a girl."

"A middle-aged cat woman, if I remember correctly."

I laugh again, the tears flowing freely as I look at the perfectly broken boy who had been waiting for me.

"Do you want me to tell you a secret?"

"Always."

"I'm really glad you didn't turn out to be a girl."

Skylar starts to laugh, the boisterous sound echoing off the walls of his bedroom. It's a beautiful sound, loud and carefree, and soon I'm laughing right alongside him.

"Alright, it's your turn."

"You want me to tell you a secret?"

I shake my head, wiping the tears from my eyes, "Not this time."

Grabbing his hand, I pull him back to the bed. I snatch up the marker from the duvet and pass it over.

"It's your turn to draw on me."

Skylar takes the marker without a word. Making myself comfortable on his bed, I lie flat on my back and brace myself for the fear to set in.

But it never does.

My breath flows easily through my lungs as I watch Skylar study me quietly. There's an unspoken question in his eyes, the need for reassurance that I suddenly find myself being able to give.

"I'm ready."

The honesty of those words fall between us, the smile lighting up my face serving as encouragement for Skylar to start drawing. He takes a step closer, reaching out to take my hand. Pressing down the tip of the marker, he wraps a vine around my ring finger before starting the slow trek upward.

True to his word, he connects every freckle, branching them all together in a stunning array of blooming flora and fallen leaves. Tending to my body like I tend to my plant babies, Skylar devotes time and attention to each new piece of skin he comes across, treating me as though I am something to be treasured.

The marker glides across my skin in effortless strokes, leaving a beautiful design on a broken girl. Skylar doesn't say anything while he works, he simply lets his hands and ink serve as a reminder.

I am a flower worth waiting for.

Skylar

The sunshine tissue digs into my hands as I leave my therapist's building.

It's a habit I've gotten into, stealing a bright yellow tissue on my way out the door. I used to use them as a way to escape the dark thoughts of my past. It worked for a while, but then I met this mystery girl named Lacey.

And she turned my life upside down.

Nowadays, these tissues are only used for the floral drawings I gift her. I do it for selfish reasons, so I can watch the excitement light up her eyes, but I also do it as a thank you. A hidden message to let her know just how much colour she brought back into my life.

Just how much colour she brought back in me.

Winter has arrived in Silverwood and the crisp air bites through the sweater I stupidly decided to wear today. The walk from Karen's sessions to my house is less than fifteen minutes, but based on the goosebumps covering my flesh, it's going to feel a lot longer.

"Learn to ski this season, Ellsworth, and maybe your ass won't get so bruised."

I pause, hearing the familiar voice of Stella O'Brien. Turning towards the parking lot, I spy her standing in front of her boyfriend, hands planted on her hips. Taber's old lacrosse captain grins, his blonde fauxhawk standing just as tall as it did the day I bumped into him.

"If you didn't insist on finishing every ski day with a race, I wouldn't feel the need to impress you."

Stella scoffs, flicking a long braid over her shoulder, "You couldn't impress me if you tried."

"That's not what you said last night."

The couple stare each other down for less than five seconds before they both crack up. I still haven't been able to figure out the dynamics of their relationship, but arguing seems to be their preferred type of foreplay.

Forcing my feet to turn in their direction, I don't stop walking until I'm right in front of them.

"Vin." Stella gives me a cool nod, "Good to see one member of your family is getting the help he needs."

The words are sharp, but I don't let the sting deter me. Turning to Cody, I wipe my sweaty palms on my jeans and make eye contact.

"It doesn't make it right but I'm sorry. For what Vector did to you." I swallow, forcing myself not to look away, "My brother shouldn't have been on the field that day and you bore the consequence of his actions."

Cody blinks, his brown eyes just as kind as the first time I saw them.

"It's Skylar, right?"

"Yeah."

He smiles, "There's nothing to apologize for. Your brother kicked my ass on the lacrosse field, but that's part of playing a contact sport."

The familiar surge of guilt hits me.

"Vector takes contact to an extreme level."

"He sure does. But that doesn't change the fact he's an amazing player."

Stella grumbles something under her breath and he glances at her, "Getting my head bashed in helped me re-evaluate my priorities. I'm not going to thank your brother for cracking a few ribs, but if it wasn't for him, my own story would have looked very different."

"I'm still sorry you got hurt."

Cody shrugs, "I'm not. It meant I got to see how much my gym buddy missed me."

Stella crosses her arms with a huff, "I didn't miss you in the slightest."

"Is that why Stephen said you were always talking about me?"

"Stephen is delusional."

He laughs, looking back at me, "Anyways, the point is there is nothing to feel bad about. My face and ribs healed just fine and now I get to be tormented by the shortest girl at Taber University."

Stella gasps, reaching out to punch his arm, "I am not the shortest girl at Taber."

"You're right. Just the most competitive."

She goes to punch him again but Cody dodges with a quick step to the side.

He shoots me another grin, "I'll see you at the Tigers' next game, Skylar. Apparently you're the only one who understands lacrosse."

Warmth seeps through my chest, the sincerity in his tone making me want to pinch myself.

Stella sighs, turning to me, "I'm not as easy going as Ellsworth, but I'll try not to hate on your family as much. It was really thoughtful of you to apologize."

"It was the right thing to do."

"That doesn't mean you had to do it." She studies me for a moment, "You've come a long way, Vin. Don't go back to keeping your head down."

"I won't."

Turning on my heel, I walk out of the parking lot, leaving one less demon behind me. It doesn't change what I did, the repercussions my silence had on the victims of Vector's drug-fuelled temper, but it does lighten the weight in my chest.

My phone rings just as I'm walking through the front door, absolutely freezing and in desperate need of a hot shower.

"You won't believe what I found today."

Lacey's excited voice echoes through the phone and suddenly I can't think of a single thing more important than listening to her voice.

"A purple succulent?"

She laughs, "I already have one of those."

"A new purple succulent?"

More laughter flows through my phone as I take off my shoes, giving my mom a wave as I walk through the kitchen.

"No, silly. I found the spring sign up sheet for the track team."

I pause, "Silverwood doesn't have a second round of tryouts."

"That's because it would be in Taber. I already checked and students are allowed to compete from different schools because technically it's a club not a varsity team."

"Flower. You realize I'm the rival."

"You could be the Saber in disguise. Then come fall you could join the varsity team at Silverwood and kick ass."

Laughter bursts from my chest, "You want me to trojan horse the track and field team?"

"Why not? This way there's no pressure to keep going if you don't enjoy it."

"I'll think about it."

"Good." She blows a raspberry through the phone and hangs up. I laugh again, knowing the first thing she'll do tonight is apologize for not saying a proper goodbye.

Movement shifts in my peripheral and I turn to see my mom staring at me with glistening eyes.

"Mom. What's wrong?"

She limps closer, tears spilling onto her cheeks as she reaches out and touches my face.

"Nothing's wrong, honey."

"Why are you crying?"

Her hands cradle my face, those pale blue eyes glistening back at me.

"You're smiling."

I freeze, staring at the tears sliding down her face.

"I didn't know if I would ever see it again." Her fingers brush my lips, memorizing the upward curve, "My baby boy's beautiful smile."

Amber's tears continue to fall as I wrap my arms around her, pulling her close. It's a routine we used to do a lot, her sobs filling the kitchen while I stitched her back together, but this time it's different.

This time I'm different.

"It's okay, Mom." I whisper the same reassurance I did all those years ago, except this time I'm doing it with a full heart, "We're going to be okay."

She clutches me tightly, hearing the one thing that was always missing.

Hope.

Chapter 25

Lacey

"Are we inviting your roommate?"

"Of course we're inviting my roommate, she's the one who suggested a night out."

Cecelia's gruff voice floats through the dorm walls and I smile, hearing Maren's squeal of excitement.

"I'm so excited to see her! It's been so long."

"You literally saw her in the hallway last week."

"Yeah, but that's not the same as hanging out."

Closing my latest romance novel, I put it down on my nightstand before going out to greet Cecelia's friends.

"Are you ready to hit BEATS tonight?"

Maren squeals again, running over to throw her arms around me. I laugh, squeezing her back while Ava gives me a nod of acknowledgement over her shoulder.

After Cecelia joined my brother's weekly movie night, she declared we needed to instigate something similar for our own dorm. Two action movies later and Maren and Ava finally started acknowledging me in the hallways. Another three and suddenly I was cool enough to be considered a friend.

Although my relationship with Cecelia isn't a natural one, I realize now that our rocky start was a double-edged sword. I wasn't willing to put myself out there and she wasn't willing to look past the book nerd exterior.

The sex marathons are still a thing, but those nights I usually sleep over at Skylar's or we spend hours talking on the phone together. It might not be a perfect solution, but it's one that I can live with.

Maren grins, "This is my first time being the DD, but I think I can handle it."

Ava snorts, "You couldn't handle the alcohol last time, so let's hope this turns out better."

"I wasn't that bad."

"You made out with three different guys before passing out on the bathroom floor."

Maren shrugs, "You can't blame a girl for making her presence known."

I smile, adjusting the purse strap over my shoulder, "Actually, I have a surprise for all of you tonight. Especially you, Cecelia."

My roommate groans, "Don't tell me you bought me a romance book. That shit is not going to cut it tonight."

"There are quite a few dark romances I think you would really enjoy." At her pinched expression I let out laugh, "But no. That's not your surprise."

Cecelia narrows her eyes and Ava lets out a hoot.

"The virgin has a dark side to her."

"She's not a virgin." Cecelia crosses her arms, giving her friend a glare, "And she can be a bitch sometimes. Don't go sprouting shit you don't know."

I wouldn't say being called a bitch is a compliment, but looking at the smile Cecelia sends my way, I'm pretty sure it was meant to be one.

"Uh, right. Who's ready to hit the road?"

Maren claps her hands, "Let's do this!"

The four of us leave the residence building together, amiably talking about the fast approaching finals when my phone starts to buzz.

NICO: [image]

NICO: Is two chains too many?

NICO: Or should I push for three?

My face splits into a grin when I pull open the photo, studying the glittering chains marking his bare torso. It's hard to tell if he's wearing a shirt or if it's completely unbuttoned.

ME: How many buttons will be undone?

NICO: Mi amor, come on. Always three.

I laugh, quickly typing a response.

ME: Two chains is classy, three is slutty.

NICO: Slutty it is.

ME: Date night?

NICO: You know it, babe.

NICO: What are you up to tonight?

"We're going to leave your ass in this parking lot if you don't get in."

Cecelia shouts the threat from the passenger seat and I laugh, dropping my phone back into my purse and rejoining the group of girls I've grown to call my friends.

"Vector, I'd like you to meet my roommate."

Stepping to the side, I let her take over the introduction. Cecelia smiles coyly at him, flicking a strand of green hair over her shoulder.

"Nice to meet you, Vector. I heard you're quite the lacrosse player."

He grins, "And I heard you're from the rival school. Not scared to be in enemy territory?"

"I've always found enemy lines to be more interesting."

Biting back a laugh, I turn and see Ava and Maren staring at me with wide eyes. When I brought them over to meet the varsity team, it took them a second for them to realize I wasn't joking. Skylar had told me exactly what part of the nightclub the lacrosse team hangs out in, so it was pretty easy to introduce my roommate to her rival crush.

"Hey, Gorgeous. Remember me?"

I turn to see a dark-haired guy step forward. It takes me a moment to recognize him as the one who tried to corner me against the bar.

"Fuck off, Walsh."

The harsh voice cuts through the crowd, making the guy flinch. Vector smiles, his tone no less sharp when he speaks again.

"You know she's with Sky."

"Fine." He bites off the word, looking less handsome by the second, "Would you mind introducing me to your friends, Lacey?"

Shooting Vector a grateful smile, I turn and face the girls.

"Be careful with this one. He gets handsy when he's drunk."

Ava shrugs, tossing back her drink, "Sounds good to me. What's your position, pretty boy?"

He grins, "Forward. I'm the one who scores the goals."

Rolling my eyes, I turn to talk to Maren, but she's already chatting up a different lacrosse player. It's déjà vu, being back in Silverwood's nightclub without my girl squad, except this time I know exactly who I'm looking for.

Slipping into the crowd, I make my way along the edge of the dance floor, avoiding the mass of sweaty bodies dancing and grinding in time to the music. The shock of white hair stands out against the dim lighting, those mismatched eyes searching the crowd for my arrival.

I duck my head and creep past, sliding along the wall so I can shimmy up behind him. Carefully slipping my hands around his waist, I press myself flush against his back.

"Looking for someone?"

A quiet laugh echoes through him, the hard ridge of his shoulders digging into my collarbone.

"Just a girl with the worst coordination."

"How tragic. Any chance I know her?"

"Highly likely." Skylar turns around, a smile painting his eyes and face in equal measure, "She goes to the rival school. Same as you, I believe."

"Now there's a coincidence. Do you think she goes to therapy as well?"

"Odds are high."

I laugh, leaning forward and pressing a kiss against his lips. He's still smiling when he kisses me back, his fingers grazing the sliver of skin between my crop top and jeans.

"I like what you're wearing."

"I knew you would."

It didn't take me long to realize Skylar is a tactile learner. He touches and feels his way through life, using physical sensors to memorize the simplest of things.

And I just happen to be his favourite subject of study.

The nightclub's music is blasting through the speakers, the heavy base driving the hips of university students of all shapes and sizes. It's not the type of music I like dancing to, but that doesn't stop me from roping my hands around his neck and pulling him closer.

"I'm not a good dancer, Flower." He whispers the confession in my ear, his hands resting on the small of my back, "I failed this unit in gym class."

"That makes two of us."

Resting my head on his shoulder, I hear him huff out a laugh before taking my hand. Slowly we start to dance, our steps awkward and unsteady as the rap song blasts overheard.

The nightclub fades away as we hold each other, swaying to a beat that only the two of us can hear. I close my eyes, knowing with absolutely certainty that this is what my love story looks like. Not a fairytale ending, but a real moment.

One that exists only between Skylar and me.

"Hey, Skylar?"

"Yes, Flower?"

"I love you."

He pulls back to look at me, those beautiful eyes so much brighter than the first time I saw them. It's the perfect moment, so naturally I had to ruin it.

Tripping over my own two feet, I stumble into the person beside me. Skylar is quick to catch me, but not quick enough to stop the embarrassment from coating my cheeks.

"Oh my God. I'm so sorry. Are you okay?"

I'm so flustered that it takes me a while to look at the guy's face. When I finally do, that perfect moment evaporates into a distant memory.

Because the person staring back at me is none other than Jerrell Thompson.

Skylar

I hate him even more in person.

"Lacey doll, those clumsy feet of yours are always getting you into trouble." Jerrell flashes her a grin, "Don't go hurting yourself to get my attention."

"I-I'm not." She's flustered and stuttering and her anxiety has a spark of anger igniting inside me. It took less than ten seconds for Jerrell to introduce himself and crack a joke at Lacey's expense.

I really fucking hate this guy.

"I have to say, I'm surprised to see you here." He raises a brow, flicking his eyes down her body, "The girl I knew never went out past her curfew."

She swallows and I quickly reach over to grab her hand. Her fingers latch onto mine and I gently brush my thumb over her skin so she knows I'm not going anywhere.

"I-I..." Lacey gulps down a breath, squeezing my hand tightly, "I'm not the girl you used to know. Not anymore."

"Apparently not." He grins, as if the charming smile is enough to disarm her, "We'll have to reconnect so I can see what's different."

"No."

The simple word is spoken quietly but forcefully. Jerrell blinks a couple of times, as if he's not used to his ex-girlfriends rejecting him.

"No?"

"That's right." Lacey clears her throat, forcing her shoulders back, "I don't want anything to do with you, Jerrell. And I would appreciate it if you would leave us alone."

Jerrell glances at me for the first time.

"Looks like you aren't the girl I used to know." He flicks his eyes over my face, down my body, and lets out a laugh, "Especially if you went from me to this."

I stare at him, taking in the preppy clothes and athletic frame. He's a good-looking guy if you ignore the stench of entitlement and frat boy vibe he's got going on.

The rich boy aesthetic didn't come as a surprise, but his size did.

Given the fact Lacey has never once commented on my small frame, I figured her ex-boyfriend must have been similar in stature. It's not uncommon for tall girls to end up with shorter guys, so I didn't give it much thought when the conversation of my size never came up.

Clearly, that was a misassumption on my part.

Jerrell stands about three inches above me with an extra thirty pounds of muscle. He's nowhere near the size of a varsity athlete, but still big enough to tower over me.

Something which he seems to enjoy doing.

He lets out another laugh, "Could you not find an adequate replacement for me? Wanted to branch out and lock down the biggest freak in town?"

Lacey clutches my hand tightly, her cheeks flushed with anger, "Don't say that."

"No, I'm serious. Look at this guy." He grins, staring at my face like it's the punchline, "I don't even know which eye to look at. You know they invented coloured contacts for a reason, right?"

The question is directed at me, but I stay silent. It's nothing I haven't heard before and there's no use in adding fuel to a fire that's bound to burn out of control.

Besides, I'd rather have him attack me than my flower.

"Shut the fuck up, Jerrell." Lacey spites out the words, her voice more venomous than I've ever heard it, "You're being a dick for no reason."

"You're no fun anymore, Lacey doll. I was just meeting your new boo."

"She's not your doll."

It's the first thing I've said to him, and the anger in my voice has Jerrell taking a step back. The fear in his eyes quickly fades when he remembers the size difference between us.

"Oh yeah? Does that make her your doll?" He takes a step closer, looking down on me, "Or does that make you hers?"

My breathing goes shallow as I glare back at him, the familiar claws of anger sinking into my skin.

"Skylar, let's go home." Lacey tugs my hand, her fingers still wrapped around mine, "I don't want to be here anymore."

"Looks like your owner is pulling the leash." Jerrell flashes me a grin and it takes all my will power not to punch it right off his face.

"Skylar. Let's go."

The plea in Lacey's voice is what pulls me away, the unbreakable clasp of her hand keeping me from doing something stupid.

Shaking my head, I turn and walk away. We don't make it two steps before Jerrell's taunting voice breaks through the crowd.

"Oh, and Skylar? I hope you enjoy my sloppy seconds."

Ten seconds go by and nobody moves.

And then I explode.

My control shatters as I lunge for him, the rage in my bloodstream fuelling the need to make him bleed.

I'm going to rip every fucking limb off his body.

A hand yanks me back, the fingers clenched around mine refusing to let me get close enough to start shredding skin. Jerking against the hold, I try and rip my hand free from Lacey's grip, but she holds on.

"Skylar. Look at me."

"Let me go, Flower." I snap my teeth at her, but she doesn't release my hand.

"No. I'm not going to let go. Do you know why?"

My whole body is shaking as I look at her, the soft edges of her face staring down the monster inside of me.

"You made a vow, Skylar. And you promised me you were going to keep it."

"Let. Me. Go."

"No." She shakes her head, lifting her free hand to touch my face, "I'm not going to let you go, Skylar. Not now, not ever."

She runs a finger along my eyebrow and I freeze, staring into her glistening green eyes.

"Don't let him get into your head. Focus on me."

Her finger glides between my brows and down the slope of my nose. She follows it along the edges of my cheekbones, gently tracing my face.

Instead of getting me to draw, she's drawing me.

She keeps going, painting my skin with love even while I seethe from the inside out. Her fingers never stray from my face, the gentle touch reminding me of all the times we've had together, all the moments we've stolen for ourselves.

"Come on, Skylar. Focus on the art."

I can see the tears in her eyes, the tears that could easily turn into fear if I let my temper control me the way it did my father.

The way it does my brother.

The thought sobers me enough to suck in a breath and give her a nod. The pressure beneath my skin is enough to make me want to scream, but the fog in my mind has cleared to the point where I know exactly what I have to do.

Turning around, I clamp a lock down on my anger and face Jerrell fucking Thompson.

"Have you learned what the word 'no' means yet?"

He freezes and Lacey sucks in a breath beside me. Gently prying my fingers out of her loosened grip, I start closing the distance between us.

"It's only two letters. Usually taught by kindergarten."

His face contorts into an unflattering sneer, "Fuck off, freak. You don't know what you're talking about."

"I think I do, actually. Most rapists have a problem understanding the simplest of terms and you don't seem to be an exception."

A circle has formed around us, the tension rising with the murmurs going around the suddenly empty dance floor. Jerrell is visibly agitated, his jaw clenching harder with every word that comes out of my mouth.

"You think you're a hero? I'm about to kick your ass in front of all your friends."

I shrug, "I don't have any friends. And I'm not a hero."

He blinks a few time before recovering. Glancing at Lacey over my shoulder, he gives her a mocking smile.

"Found yourself a real winner, doll. Did you make him wait for bad sex too?"

I recapture his attention by tapping his chest.

"We're not talking about her right now. We're talking about you."

Jerrell responds by shoving me and I go stumbling backwards. The strength of my anger flows through me like a drug, but I fight it. I fight to stay in control, to keep the promise I made to my flower.

Because I'm not the only one who made a promise.

Walking back up to the guy I've murdered fourteen times on paper, I reach up and flick him on the nose.

"Learn to respect women, Jerrell, and maybe you wouldn't be such a pathetic piece of shit."

I don't get a chance to blink before he tackles me to the floor.

Chapter 26

Lacey

Skylar has lost his mind.

"Jerrell, stop it! He's not going to hit back!"

I go running for my ex-boyfriend who is pummelling my current boyfriend into the ground. I don't know why Skylar decided to start a fight he had no intention on participating in, but right now I want to kill both of them.

"Let him go!"

I'm about to jump on Jerrell's back when an elbow hits me right in the face. Staggering back, blood fills my mouth as I watch him land another punch, making Skylar's head snap back against the floor.

Now I'm pissed.

Cursing every male in the vicinity, I stumble forward, about to start my own attack when someone grabs me by the waist.

"Don't think so, mi amor." Familiar signature cologne fills my senses as protective arms wrap around me, "You're going to stay right here with me."

"Nico?" Shifting in his arms, my panic dissolves into shock, "What are you doing here?"

"That is an excellent question."

The deep voice captures my attention and I turn to see Mo standing three feet from us.

Nico grins, "We decided to see what you were up to."

"But why?"

"You didn't text me back. I got worried."

Glancing between Nico and Mo, I notice the expensive dress shirts and slacks both men are wearing. One of whom has three gold chains glittering along his neck.

"Wasn't it your date night?"

Nico squeezes me tighter, "You're more important than fine dining cuisine."

Mo sighs, "It took me two weeks to get that reservation."

"Babe, don't ruin the moment."

A gasp echoes through the crowd. Squirming against Nico's hold, I try and break free.

"I need to help Skylar."

He clutches me tighter, "No way. You are not participating in a bar fight on my watch."

Mo tilts his head, watching the ongoing fight, "Which one is Skylar?"

Nico winces, "The one on the ground."

I push against his arms, "Skylar doesn't hurt people. Please, let me help him."

"Absolutely not."

A frustrated scream rips from my throat and I start thrashing around, trying to loosen his hold. It doesn't get me anywhere, Nico keeps me locked against his chest, and soon the frustration gives way to tears.

"H-He's hurting him."

Nico shoots his partner a look, "That's your cue, big guy."

Mo sighs, rolling up his shirt sleeves, "You owe me a dinner reservation."

"Deal."

Blinking through my tears, I watch Taber's lacrosse champion break through the fight circle and grab the back of Jerrell's t-shirt. Mo drags him off Skylar, taking a few stray punches to the stomach as Jerrell tries to get in a few last shots.

A sob rips from my throat when I see Skylar still lying on the ground. His delicate skin is bruised and swollen, the pale strands of his hair caked with blood.

He looks every bit the broken boy I fell in love with.

I'm crying so hard that I don't notice the sudden silence that falls across the bar. I don't even notice Mo returning to our side with a smug looking Jerrell trapped in his arms.

It's not until a familiar voice cuts through the silence that I realize the lacrosse team has joined the circle.

"I didn't realize Silverwood was such a popular hangout for Tigers nowadays."

Vector steps forward, his gaze trained on Nico and Mo. There's a stillness in the air, a collective intake of breath as everyone watches the rivals face each other.

"Maurice O'Brien. Didn't think I'd be seeing you again."

Mo smirks, his arms still locked around Jerrell, "And I didn't think you'd still be in school."

Vector cracks a smile, "Looks like we're both disappointed."

The whispers start up around us, the Silverwood students shifting excitedly as Mo's reputation starts to spread.

"Holy shit. That's Mighty Mo."

"The lacrosse legend?"

"He holds the record number for championships wins."

Cecelia appears among the crowd, her expression annoyed as Ava and Maren pop up beside her.

Vector studies our group, his gaze lingering on the tear streaks lining my cheeks. His eyes narrow as he looks from me to the surrounding crowd.

"Where's Sky?"

A deathly silence falls upon the room. Nobody moves, nobody breathes as Vector flicks through every person in attendance. Walsh appears by his side and whispers something in his ear.

And finally, his eyes drop to where his brother lies broken on the ground.

"Looks like one of your cubs needs a cage, O'Brien."

Vector says each word slowly, spiking the tension in the room. His body is taught as his eyes stay locked on the bloody boy who isn't moving.

"He's not ours."

Mo gives Jerrell a shove and he stumbles forward. The smug look on his face has disappeared when he looks around the silent bar.

"What the fuck is going on?"

Nico's arms tense around me as Vector looks at the blood-stains coating Jerrell's fists. He doesn't say anything for a long time, just stares at the spilled blood as though it was his own.

"Get him off the ground."

The command slices through the room, the razor edge making a few people flinch. Walsh swallows and quickly walks over to where Skylar is laying.

"Come on, Baby Vin. Let's get you somewhere more comfortable."

More tears spill out as I watch Skylar get carried from the room, his beaten body limp and unresponsive. Jerrell whips his head around, glancing from the fear-stricken audience to the man twice his size.

"Can somebody tell me what the fuck is going on?"

Vector tilts his head and looks him dead in the eye. There's a stiffness in his posture, the hard clench of jaw that glimpses at the anger simmering just beneath the surface.

"What's your name?"

"Jerrell Thompson."

Those pale blue eyes flash dangerously, and suddenly I'm grateful for the barrier of Nico's arms. Despite the familiar edge of Vector's face, he doesn't look like the older brother I've come to know. He looks like the infamous Silverwood bully.

The monster who can't control his temper.

"You see, Jerrell, we have a rule here in Silverwood."

There's a long pause, and tension ripples through the crowd.

"Whatever you do to Skylar Vin gets done to you."

Vector steps forward, his massive frame making Jerrell's seem significantly smaller in comparison. My ex-boyfriend quickly stumbles back, trying to increase the distance between them.

"Look man, it was nothing personal. I didn't even know the kid."

"That's where you're wrong." A growl seeps into his voice, "This is very personal."

Bolting for the closest door, Jerrell doesn't make it past the crowd before another lacrosse player shoves him back. He stumbles back into the circle, panic filling his eyes as he searches for a way out.

Finding none, he turns and raises his hands in the air.

"He was a skinny kid looking for a fight and I overpowered him. No harm done."

"You spilled his blood all over these floors and you want to tell me it was no harm done? I don't fucking think so."

Grabbing Jerrell by the collar of his shirt, Vector's pale blue eyes ignite as he brings him up to eye level. Jerrell flails, the polished ends of his shoes scraping the ground as he tries to escape the monster's hold.

"Who the fuck do you think you are? Put me down right now."

Vector bares his teeth, "I'm the guy who's about to repay the damage you did to my little brother."

Jerrell goes still, his feet dangling in the air.

"He's your brother?" Catching sight of the unusual colour of Vector's hair, he pales, "I didn't know."

"Now, you do. And I'm going to make sure you don't forget it."

My ex-boyfriend starts to scream as Vector starts dragging him towards the side door. Nico lets out a gasp, his arms loosening around me, and I quickly break away.

"Vector, wait!"

He pauses, turning to look at me. Jerrell catches sight of me running towards him and gasps in relief.

"Oh, thank God. Tell this psychopath to put me down. This town is fucking crazy."

"Vector, could you please put him on the ground?"

He lowers him so Jerrell can touch the ground but doesn't let go of his shirt. His entire body is trembling with fear when he flashes me a grin.

"Do me another favour, doll. Tell him to let me go."

I stare at him, seeing the boy who bullied, manipulated, and violated me until I was stripped of my self-esteem and sense of self-worth. It took me over two years to find myself willing to love again, and even now, I can't shake off the past long enough to have sex with my boyfriend.

He ruined me in every sense of the word and yet the anger I feel towards him has nothing to do with the way he treated me.

"Lacey doll, anytime now. I'm not getting any young-

His words get cut off when I slap him across the face as hard as I can. Jerrell blinks, his mouth opening and closing as he stares at me.

"That's for Skylar."

Holding my stinging palm close to my chest, I turn and give Vector a nod.

"He's all yours."

"Wait. What? Lacey doll, think about what you're doing..."

Jerrell shrieks when Vector hauls him back up into the air.

"She's not your doll, dumbass. She's dating my brother."

Dragging him out the closest exit, Vector doesn't spare me or anyone else a second glance before the door bangs shut behind them.

A stunned silence descends on the crowd, the tension lingering until Nico breaks it with a hoot.

"Round of tequila on Mighty Mo!"

Cheers explode around the room while Mo turns to glare at his partner. Patrons start pushing their way to the bar and eventually the club's music gets turned back on. The nightclub slowly comes back to life as the dance floor refills and people start laughing and talking again.

The adrenalin finally leaves my body and soon I'm shaking, swaying uneasily on my feet as I start pushing through the crowd, looking for the most important piece of my heart.

Skylar

My brother always said one day I would be grateful for the person he turned out to be.

Turns out, he was right.

"I said I wanted to see your ass kicked, but this fucking sucks." Walsh sighs, pressing a washcloth against my face, "I don't like it when you're not a moody bitch."

My lips are cracked and bleeding, so I don't bother responding. The thunderous pain in my skull makes me think I have a concussion, but it could also be the swelling that seems to have taken over my face.

"Skylar? Oh my God."

Gentle fingers reach out to touch me and I instinctively lean towards her. Lacey brushes a hand through my matted hair and I smile despite the discomfort.

"Hi, Flower."

"What the fuck?" Walsh whips his head around, "You've been able to talk this whole time?"

I go to shrug but the sharp pain has me quickly rethinking that decision.

"I take it back. I don't like you even when you are a moody bitch."

Lacey shoots him a glare, "He's not a moody bitch. You can leave now."

He grumbles under his breath and makes his departure. She quickly takes his place by my side, gently lifting and resting my head onto her lap.

"I'm so mad at you right now."

"I know."

She sighs, stroking my bruised skin, "That was so stupid, Skylar. You could have died."

"I know."

"If Mo hadn't gotten Jerrell off you..." Her voice breaks and it hurts me more than any injury ever could.

"Don't cry, Flower."

"That was so stupid." She's crying in earnest now, "I told you not to try and be my hero. Why didn't you listen?"

Her tears drip onto my face, slipping down my cheeks as if they were my own. I can feel her heartache in each one, the fear and pain she went through by having to watch the fight.

Opening my mouth to respond, I suddenly notice the bruise blooming on her cheek. A brand new ache fills my body as I reach up and touch it.

"Did you get hurt?"

"I caught an elbow when I was trying to pull Jerrell off you." She shakes her head, wrapping her hand around my own, "Don't avoid the question, Skylar. Why did you start a fight that you didn't want to win?"

"I did win." My chest clenches painfully as I start to laugh, the sound coming out more as a wheeze, "A hero will charge into battle to save the one he loves but a villain will destroy anyone who touches them."

Lacey presses her hand to my chest, trying to get me to stop convulsing, "I don't understand what you're saying."

"You needed a villain, Flower. And I needed to be saved."

This whole time, I've been worried about falling short of being the male lead this girl deserves. Now, I know that it was never about the love I have for my flower.

It was about the love between two brothers.

Turns out, I didn't have to be a leading role because someone had already claimed that title. And with one flick on the nose, I made sure Jerrell would never bother Lacey again.

"You did it on purpose." She blows out a shaky breath, "Even though you didn't know if Vector would come for him."

"I knew he would."

"How?"

My face breaks into a painfully wide smile, "Because he promised."

Lacey blinks down at me, her bloodshot eyes tracing the curve of my mouth.

"I'm still mad at you."

"That's okay. Do you want to know a secret?"

She bites her lip, trying to contain her smile. Reaching up, I press my thumb on her bottom lip until it slips free.

"I love you."

"You're a terrible hero, Skylar Vin."

"That's true."

She laughs, bending down to press her lips to mine, "I love you too."

Closing my eyes, I'm about to soak in every second of this moment when a clap echoes beside us. Blinking my tired eyes open, I turn and see silk material and glittering chains approaching us.

"Don't worry, Expressionless Wonder, I bought the perfect remedy for you." Nico grins, plopping himself down beside Lacey and passing over a shot of tequila.

"He bought the remedy for the entire bar."

The grumble comes from my other side and I shift to see none other than my brother's biggest rival scowling at the ground.

Lacey and Nico help to push me into sitting position. Trying not to stare at the lacrosse legend, I take the alcohol offering with a nod of thanks.

"To the little guys." Nico clinks his shot glass against mine, "For not being afraid to lose."

"Nico!"

"What? I was going to say for not being afraid to get broken and bruised but that felt too soon."

I tap his glass and throw back the shot. Nico lets out a hoot and Lacey shakes her head with a smile.

The three of us sit together, watching the Silverwood students dance and mingle around the dance floor. The tequila helps to take the edge off, but the pain radiating through my body has me ready to find the cleanest spot on the ground and pass out.

"I think it's time we got you home." Lacey's hand wraps around mine, squeezing it gently. I smile at her, grateful for the executive decision when Nico lets out an excited shriek.

"Maurice, this is our song!"

"This is not our song."

"Babe, it totally is."

Mo crosses his arms, "Pony from *Magic Mike* is not our song."

Lacey lets out a laugh while I watch the interaction with wide eyes. Nico jumps up from the bench and shimmies over to his partner.

"Remember what happened the last time this song played?"

Mo's lips twitch, "I don't think this place has private rooms, Montez."

"See? It is our song." Nico glances back at me, "How conservative would you say this crowd is?"

I blink, "I'm not sure."

"Fuck it."

Nico grabs Mo's hand and drags him over to the dance floor. The handsome Latino immediately starts moving his hips in time to the music and after a moment, Taber's lacrosse legend joins him. It takes less than ten seconds for the two men to start grinding on each other, their sensual movements drawing envious stares from every other couple in the vicinity.

Clearing my throat, I turn back and look at Lacey.

"I wasn't expecting that."

She bursts out laughing, "They can be a lot sometimes."

"So... Mighty Mo is gay?"

"That's a story for another time. Come on, let's get you home."

Looping her arms around me, Lacey helps me stand up and hobble out of Silverwood's one and only nightclub.

By the time we crawl into bed, I'm covered in bandages and Lacey is wearing one of my t-shirts. Her long legs tangle with mine as we curl up together, our broken bodies and tattered souls welding together like two sides of the same coin.

As my eyes drift closed with my arms wrapped around the only girl I will ever love, I can't help but think today was a good day.

And tomorrow will be the same.

Chapter 27

6 months later...

Lacey

"He's not going to make it."

Amber is biting her nails next to me, her anxiety just as high as my own.

"He's going to make it."

Vector's confident tone cuts straight through my nervous energy. Wringing my hands together, I can't tear my eyes away from the group of men rounding the corner for the last lap of the race.

"Come on, Skylar!"

It's the first track and field meet of the spring season and it's Skylar's first track and field meet since high school. I've been sweating since I woke up this morning, the stress soaking through my sweater even though I'm not the one competing today.

"Run, Skylar!"

The flash of white hair makes it easy to spot him in the sea of orange and black. He's running in third place right now, but with the last corner coming up, all the guys are breaking into a sprint.

Screaming at the top of my lungs, I jump up and down, watching Skylar sneak his way to the front. Amber claps her hands over her eyes, only to peek between her fingers as the Saber disguised as a Tiger goes charging through the finish line.

"OH MY GOD! HE DID IT!"

I'm losing my shit, cheering and celebrating with Amber while Vector crosses his arms, looking smug beside me.

"I told you he would make it."

All the athletes who crossed the finish line have either collapsed on the field or wandered off to stretch, but not Skylar. He doesn't slow down as he goes running for the bleachers, and pretty soon I'm running too.

We collide on the platform between two levels, the stability of the bleachers just enough to keep me from falling over. Skylar wraps his arms around me, crushing me to his chest as he picks me up.

"You did it, Skylar! You did it!"

I'm screaming and he's laughing, both of us a sweaty mess. Those beautiful eyes are alight with endorphins and victory when he puts me back down.

I reach out and feel the elation radiating from that smile.

"I'm so proud of you."

He presses a kiss against my fingers, "Were you nervous?"

I smile sheepishly, raising my arms to show him my pit stains, "There were a few moments of stress."

"I'll run faster next time so you don't have to worry as much."

"Good. My stamina can't take the pressure."

Skylar shakes his head solemnly, "I wouldn't want that asthma to flare up again."

I burst out laughing, wrapping my arms around his neck and pressing a kiss to that deadpan face. He kisses me back, the laughter flowing through his body reminding me of just how far we've come since that first night at the football stadium.

"I guess this means you're a varsity athlete now."

He shrugs, "Not really. There was only one thing I was thinking about the whole time I was running out there."

"Bringing home the W?"

"Running home to you."

I start blinking rapidly, feeling the tears well up in my eyes. Skylar shakes his head, pressing his lips against mine one more time.

"Let's go home, Flower."

Shepherd's Pie has been confirmed as Skylar's favourite meal.

"Oh honey, you looked so fast out there!" Amber passes the dish to her youngest son, "I couldn't believe how easily you overtook those other boys."

"Mom. I was losing up until the last 100m."

She waves off his comment, "You were just trying to make the race interesting."

Vector grins, stealing the green beans from his brother, "Both mom and your girlfriend didn't think you were going to win."

Skylar shrugs, "Neither did I."

I lean over, tapping his shoulder, "Vector had no doubt you were going to win."

"That's cause he's brilliant."

Vector barks out a laugh, "You're such a little asshole."

Amber clucks her tongue, "Language."

I laugh, watching the two brothers exchange grins over the dinner table. A lot changed since that night with Jerrell, some for the better and some for the worst.

The Thompson family packed up and left Silverwood but not before filing an assault charge against Vector. Their timing was meticulously planned so Skylar's injuries were mostly healed and could no longer be used as evidence in the case. Vector will have to appear in court once the case comes up, but with the slow rate of the judicial system, that could take months or years, so none of us know how that is going to play out.

The positive that came out of the situation is it brought the Vin family back together. The unknown state of Vector's future has it so every moment together is one to be appreciated and cherished. That doesn't mean every moment is positive, I've witnessed more than a few showdowns between the brothers, but as a whole, the scars of the past seem to be healing and gradually fading from their everyday lives.

As for Skylar and me, well, our relationship is as stable and supportive as it always was. I had hoped that once Jerrell moved out of town, I would be able to take that final step and have sex but I couldn't bring myself to do it.

There were a lot of tears and frustration on my end, but Skylar just kept reminding me there was no need to rush. That one day, the time would be right.

And I'm hoping that day has finally arrived.

Slipping my hand inside the pocket of my sweater, I trace the edge of the sunshine tissue to make sure it's still there. It took me an atrocious amount of time to pick a quote that goes with my message, but Karen was kind enough to let me sift through the entire box until I found the perfect one.

Once dinner is over and we finish cleaning up, Vector has left to go hit the gym and Amber has settled down on the couch with a romance book. I introduced her to the genre a few weeks back and now she's obsessed and I love her that much more for it.

Skylar and I escape up to his bedroom, and by the time his door is locked, his shirt is on the floor and we're both gasping for air. His lips are back on my neck as we go stumbling towards the bed, our greedy hands pulling at clothes that have no business still being on.

"Wait. I have a surprise for you."

Pushing against his chest, I sit up and straddle his lap. Skylar's hands slide up my hips, casually shaping the contours of my body.

"Pretty soon my greenhouse is going to be bigger than yours."

I laugh, "It's not another succulent, although I really need to stop buying you those."

"I like them. They remind me of you."

Blushing at the compliment, I quickly pull the sunshine tissue out of my pocket. My heart starts to race as I pass it over, the anticipation and nerves mixing together in the most exhilarating way.

The sunshine tissue unfolds and I hold my breath, watching Skylar read the message I left for him.

Skylar

I've missed her handwriting.

I fall silent as my eyes soak in the familiar slant of her letters, the curve of her punctuation. It's simple in a way her physical beauty is not, the dark marks on the yellow material tarnishing my soul long before I read the words she wrote for me.

Be patient with yourself, nothing in nature blooms all year.

You've taught me how to be patient with myself, how to love the parts not yet in bloom. It's taken me a long time but I finally understand the difference now. Between having sex and actually wanting to. It's not about the physical act itself, it's about the meaning behind it, the love between you and the person you're doing it with.

The truth is, I don't want to have sex with you, Skylar. I want to make love with you. I want to feel your body inside mine, the same way your heart bleeds with mine. I want to become so intertwined I don't know where I begin and you end, sharing the same space until our souls can't help but collide. I want all of you, Skylar Vin. And I hope you will let me give you all of me too.

When I finally look up from the sunshine tissue, hopeful green eyes are waiting for me. I stare at her, seeing the girl who stole my battered heart, stitched it back together, and gave it back to me.

After Jerrell left Silverwood, she told me she didn't think the sex was going to be worth the wait. I told her there were a lot of things I've waited for in this life, but having sex was not one of them.

I didn't tell her that every morning I wake up waiting to see the smile on her face. That every conversation we have, every phone exchange, I hold my breath in wait, dying to hear the sound of her laugh. That every night I'm in agony, waiting for the moment when she crawls under the covers and buries herself between my arms.

I have never stopped waiting for my flower. And I have a feeling I never will.

Swallowing hard, I stare at the girl who helped me remember that I am something special. That I am someone worth fighting for.

"I want all of you too, Flower."

Epilogue

3 years later...

Wes

Did you miss me?

Of course you did.

We all knew who the fan favourite was, so it came as no surprise to learn my POV was nominated for the series finale. Nico was pissed, but he should have known the Troy Bolton of Taber University was going to outvote him.

Shit. I should have picked 14 as my varsity number.

"Wesley! Stop moving. You're ruining the shot." Lacey purses her lips at me, staring me down the way only a sibling can.

We're in the middle of taking grad photos and somehow my girlfriend ended up atop her roommate's shoulders. I offered to save Stella's spine and lift Trip into place, but the tiny O'Brien saw my chivalrous offer as a competition.

So now I have a 180-pound Latino balancing on my shoulders.

"Dude. You need to lay off the pizza." I groan, shifting under Nico's weight, "You're fucking heavy."

"Maurice never has a problem lifting me."

Mo looks over with a smirk, "Different builds, Montez."

If I didn't have a man crush on the guy, I might find that comment insulting.

Lacey snaps her fingers, recapturing our attention, "Say cheese!"

The four graduates echo back the response, our cheesy ass smiles and matching regalia looking like the perfect end credit scene.

Trip, Stella, Nico, and me. All graduated and unleashed into the adult world.

God help us all.

Cody and Mo are chatting off to the side while Lacey continues to harass us with photo opportunities. Her boyfriend Skylar is nearby, watching the scene from a careful distance.

Despite the fact he doesn't laugh at my jokes, I'm actually quite fond of the guy. He creeps me out sometimes with the lack of expression, but I've seen the way he takes care of my little sister and it's pretty fucking cute.

Stella carefully kneels to the ground and Trip slides off her back without a hint of elegance or grace. Her dress slips up her thighs and I grin, catching sight of the panties I bought her last week.

Best purchase ever.

"How's Nico getting down?" Lacey asks the question with genuine fear in her eyes. Considering how much I struggled to get him up here in the first place, the fear is not misplaced.

"He's going to jump." Interjecting confidence into my voice, I tilt my head to look at him, "It's all about the dismount, man. Don't let me down."

He stares back at me in horror, "Fuck that. I'm not about to break my neck for you."

I put my hands together in prayer, "It's okay if you don't believe in yourself because I believe in you."

"That's not helpful."

"Sure, it is. I just re-established your confidence."

Nico groans, "You're useless. Maurice, could you give me a hand?"

Pausing his conversation with Cody, Mo looks over with a smirk.

"I enjoyed watching Wes' knees buckle the first time."

For the record, my knees did not buckle. They may have been quaking at one point but they did not buckle.

"Dude. You gotta jump."

"No way. I didn't go through two years of braces just to knock all my teeth out now." Nico looks back at his partner, "Babe, I'm too young to wear dentures."

Mo rolls his eyes before walking over and lifting him from my shoulders, "If you didn't do stupid shit, this wouldn't happen so often."

"Where's the fun in that?"

I laugh, looking over to where Trip is talking to her friends from class. She's completely distracted so I quickly slap my best friend on the shoulder.

"Pass it over."

Nico smirks, "Imagine if I had jumped and this had fallen out."

"*I told you so* is not a good look on you."

"It's a better look than a wannabe alpha."

Let me take a quick second to clear something up.

I, Wesley Williams, am not a cinnamon roll. A man is allowed to be sweet and thoughtful and an alpha all at the same time. Anyone who says otherwise clearly hasn't met me because I am living proof that swoon-worthy boyfriends are just as masculine as grumpy assistant coaches.

Mo might be your stereotypical alpha, but I'm your adorable alpha.

Giving Nico the full force of my alpha glare, I sniff indignant-ly, "We agreed to never speak of that conversation again."

He grins, passing over the package I had given him the night before, "I agreed to no such thing. Ten bucks says you're going to cry."

"Please. I'm not going to cry."

"I'm upping the bet to twenty. Good luck, Alpha."

Flipping him off, I quickly walk over and grab Trip's hand. Stealing her from her friends, I bid them all promises of her safe return before tugging her towards the cobblestone path that leads us away from the hustle and bustle of convocation.

"Wes, we can't fool around right now." She glances over her shoulder, "We're definitely going to get caught this time."

I grin, hearing the excitement in her voice, "If you want me to bend you over outside the science building again, all you have to do is ask."

To all those students who use the winter gardens for actual studying, I am so sorry. Those benches have been contaminated on many occasions.

But hey, at least we're making the most of our school facilities.

Trip blushes, "Maybe on the way back."

My girlfriend is an equally dedicated citizen.

The university's manicured lawns gradually turn into rows of trees and flowers as we enter the courtyard. It's the one place we always seem to come back to, the one location on campus that never grows tired of our antics.

Trip squeezes my hand, "You didn't make meatless tacos again, did you?"

I laugh, leading her over to where that unfortunate dinner date happened, "Not this time. I do have something planned for dinner though."

"I'll start mentally preparing now." She looks around the empty courtyard, the memories of our freshman year reflecting in those gorgeous grey eyes, "I'm going to miss this place."

"Me too."

Clearing my throat, I do my best to ignore the swarm of butterflies attacking my stomach lining, "So, we've been dating for four years now."

"I didn't realize you could count so high."

God. I love it when she's mean to me.

"Four years ago, you decided to become the worst pack mule this school has ever seen and I got to experience first-hand just how much you packed in those boxes. Somehow, we ended up in the same psych class and I managed to find a way past that adorable scowl of yours."

Trip laughs, "Your dimples did most of the work."

She's not wrong.

Pulling the small velvet box out of my pocket, I get down on one knee.

"Miss One Trip, otherwise known as Lou Mackenzie," Swallowing the lump in my throat, I tell myself not to cry, "Crashing into you that first day was the best thing that ever happened to me. You've taught me so much and I want you to teach me so much more. You are the rom to my com and I am hopelessly in love with you."

Fuck. I owe Nico twenty bucks.

Blinking through the tears in my eyes, I give her a dimpled grin, "Marry me, Trip, because I don't want to spend a single day without you."

"Oh my God." She's covering her mouth, tears glistening in her eyes, "Did you seriously call me the rom to your com?"

"I considered the Gabriella to my Troy, but that felt a little too on the nose."

She laughs, those tears spilling over, "Of course I'll marry you, Wes. There is no one else I would rather spend the rest of my life with."

Beaming like a ray of sunshine, I carefully slide the ring onto her finger. The modest diamond shines back at me, the chain of daisies running along the band making Trip gasp in delight.

"It's so perfect!"

"Lacey helped me pick it out." Taking her hand, I sweep into a bow, "May I escort you back to the convocation, milady?"

She curtsies on cue, our routine well established by now, "That would be most gracious, kind sir."

Together, we walk back to where our friends and family are waiting with expectant smiles. Trip raises her left hand and cheers break out.

Looking around the sea of familiar faces, I can't help but think about the last four years. The laughs and tears we've shared, the lacrosse tournaments we've won and lost, the friendships and relationships we've formed. We all started freshmen year as young adults trying to find our place in the world, and now we're slightly older adults still trying to find our place in the world.

My eye catches on Lacey and Skylar, smiling at each other behind the crowd of people. My sister's midnight locks bring out the pale colour of Skylar's hair, the same way her presence seems to brighten his own.

Rumour has it that Skylar's brother was facing five years of jail time until someone swept in and bailed him out. Nobody knows who the person was, just that they were looking to employ the infamous Silverwood bully. Some people think it's a cult while others think it's an undercover military op for delinquent adults.

Personally, I think Vector is a guy who's been stuck with a bad reputation for too long.

"Expressionless Wonder! I heard you started working in a tattoo parlour." Nico grins, jerking his thumb towards me, "Maybe you could draw something up for the new groom."

"Absolutely not."

Skylar glances at me, "Afraid of needles?"

I puff out my chest like a proud peacock, "No. I get my flu shot every year."

Lacey laughs, "You totally are. Trip always has to go with you."

"Don't expose me like that, Garden Girl."

Skylar stares at me, unblinking, without a trace of a smile. I stare back, trying not to shrivel under his mismatched gaze.

Could you imagine getting stabbed by this guy in the name of art?

No, thank you.

Nico sniffs, pulling Lacey into a hug, "I'm going to miss you next year, mi amor."

"I'll miss you too, Nico. Make sure you come visit us."

That twenty bucks threatens to make a reappearance as I look at my baby sister whose all grown up. She's already made the decision to stay and start a life with Skylar in Silverwood after graduation. I always knew my sister was resilient, but seeing her bloom these last few years has truly been something special.

It's strange to think we are all going our separate ways now. Nico and Mo are heading to Vancouver while Cody and Stella are going to Lethbridge. Trip and I are currently undecided, so I guess that will be the first decision we make as fiancés.

Holy shit. I have a fiancé.

Grinning like a fool, I lean down to whisper in my bride-to-be's ear, "We still have an hour before the after party begins. Thoughts on making one last trip to the science building?"

She grins back, "I thought you would never ask."

Doing my best to look nonchalant, I cough up an excuse to use the bathroom and go walking for the closest exit. Trip shows two minutes later and I scoop her up, running and laughing all the way to our favourite hookup spot.

I could go into the dirty details of what happens next, but I think I'll just leave it at our happy ending.

Pun intended.

Author's Note

In the summer of 2021, I decided to embark on the journey of writing a novel. I didn't know whether I'd be able to finish it, never mind create an interconnected four-book series. Turns out, I'm a slut for fictional characters because by the end of my debut novel, I couldn't say goodbye to these characters. Not before they got the chance to have their stories told.

Lacey was originally introduced to help add depth to Wes' character. He was my first MMC and I had made him too perfect. From the dimples to the dramatics, I checked off every book boyfriend characteristic except for the most important one. Depth. The man was a gorgeous goofball who was completely surface level.

And so, I introduced Lacey. A younger sister whose traumatic sexual experience was enough to make Wes avoid relationships completely. I didn't give her much thought until the end of my debut when I realized she deserved to have a chance in the spotlight. The problem was, once I solidified my decision to cast Lacey as a lead, I had to find someone to help me piece this broken girl back together again. Someone whose darkness matched her own.

It was more challenging than I expected. The Tiger roster left me with Hunter or a new rookie – unfortunate on all accounts – so, eventually I cracked and made a list of all the male characters who were featured in the first book. And low and behold, one name stood out to me. Skylar Vin, aka the odd duck who drew a shockingly violent poster for the home opener. He was created to help highlight the rivalry between the two schools and emphasize the anger management stemming from the Vin household. He was never meant to be anything more than a background character but suddenly I had Lacey's perfect match.

There was a lot of heavy issues mentioned in this book, but the one thing they all had in common was the loneliness of struggling with abuse and mental health. The idea of being seen and heard was central to this novel, and although I am not a psychiatrist, I do believe that having a support system – whether it's a group of people or a friend who is willing to listen – makes a world of a difference. Everyone is fighting an invisible battle, and it's important to know that you are not alone. If any of these issues rung true to you or a loved one, please seek the resources and support needed to get through it.

Lacey and Skylar's story marks the end of my Taber Tigers series, and I hope that if nothing else, you found love within these pages. Personally, I cried my way through this story, so if you met the same fate, you have my deepest apologies.

Until next time!

Xo, Jade

Acknowledgements

I told my friends and family that this story was going to destroy me. I was right. All three of us – a broken boy, a broken girl, and a sobbing author – made it to the end a little more bruised than we started, but I can confidently say this was the most rewarding story I have yet to write.

Writing can be an extremely lonely process, but I am lucky enough to have a tremendous support system around me. I will do my best to include everyone, but if I forget your name, you have my apologies.

Mara – You are the only person who loves talking about my writing as much as I do, and no matter how many times I spam you with updates and potential graphics, you always respond with enthusiasm and endless support. You are a god-damn queen and I couldn't ask for a better reader or friend. Thank you for everything.

Mom – You do too much for this family, and I hope you know how much we appreciate you. Thank you for always taking the time to edit my writing and take gorgeous photos of my books. Love you.

Dad – If you read this book, I hope it made you realize that it is not a man's strength that distinguishes his character, but his decisions. Love you.

Dani – Your relationship with my brother has nothing to do with the love I have for you, and I hope that you recognized Trip and Lacey's relationship as a reflection of our own. Thank you for being the newest and brightest member of our family.

Taylor – You are my friend and my hero. Thank you for teaching me how to countdown from one hundred when everything else was falling apart. I cannot wait to see what the future has in store for us.

Angel – You read my last book in six hours, on a weekday, and took the time to send me feedback. Your enthusiasm for my upcoming novels has kept me going on more than one occasion. Thank you.

Grace – Your constant excitement is my favourite thing ever, as is your insistence that no matter how many published authors you read, you will always come back to my writing. Thank you.

Katie – You never cease to amaze me with the speed in which you read and the live feedback you provide warms my heart every time. Thank you for always insisting each book is better than the last.

Christine – You read IBTC as your first MM and took the time out of your Spain trip to read and celebrate it via spammed snapchats. Thank you for being an irreplaceable friend.

Jada – You were my favourite part of this last semester. Thank you for rekindling my love of swimming and for always waking up at the ass crack of dawn to workout with me. I couldn't think of another person who would willingly do a three-thousand push-up challenge with me. Twice.

Elizabeth – Another book for my non-reader! Thank you for all the love, support, and memories we've collected over the years.

Granny – You've always been the biggest supporter of my writing and are willing to read anything I write (including your first MM book at 80 years-old). Thank you for being the moon to my stars. Love you.

To the little girl I saw at Nationals last year – You looked at me with one blue iris and one brown iris and it was the most beautiful thing I have ever seen. Thank you for giving me a glimpse of a character not yet written.

To the people who have been with me since the beginning – Writing would not be possible if it weren't for readers, so I thank each and every one of you for taking the time to fall in love with someone else's words. You are the most important part of an author's journey and I hope you come back again soon.

To the wonderful bookstagram community – You have all made this journey so much better than I could have ever imagined and I am so grateful for the new friends I have discovered along the way. Thank you from the bottom of my heart.

To anyone who made it to the end – Thank you for taking a chance on Lacey and Skylar's story. I hope it made you cry less than it made me.

And lastly, celebrity shoutout to Tahereh Mafi for showing me how powerful a villain in a suit can be. It was an unexpected step in my research but an important one. Thank you for Aaron Warner, love.

About the author

Jade Everhart writes new adult romances to help her flawed characters find their happy ever afters. When she's not day-dreaming about book tropes, you can find her building Lego and plotting out the best way to seduce a villain.

Jade loves to hear from readers – connect with her on Instagram @authorjade_everhart or email her at jadeeverhartautho r@gmail.com.

Don't Miss Out on the Rest of the Taber Tigers Series!

I Blame the Dimples (Taber Tigers #1)

When the social butterfly falls headfirst into the girl who considers herself a social outsider, things are bound to get interesting...

Always the odd one out, Lou Mackenzie has never found a place that feels like home. Moving into residence feels like a step in the right direction, and that's before a gorgeous rookie plows her down on move-in day.

Wesley "Wes" Williams has never met anyone he can't befriend. Teammates, teachers, fellow students: when it comes to making friends, Wes is at the top of his league. So, when he accidentally body slams a pretty resident across Taber University's front lawn, it's only natural for Wes to keep an eye out for the sarcastic girl who knocked him down. Literally.

What starts off as friendship gradually becomes something more as Wes and Lou embark on the ups and downs of freshman year. Together they will face condescending professors, matchmaking roommates, and lacrosse tournaments that will put their connection to the test and leave them wondering whether the spark burning between is that of friends or something more.

I Blame the Alcohol (Taber Tigers #2)

When two gym buddies are forced to spend winter break together, they suddenly find themselves with a lot more in common than a love of gains...

Finally cleared to train after a brutal injury first semester, Cody Ellsworth finds himself back on the lacrosse field faced with a new problem: his gym partner is becoming more and more of a distraction. A fierce, stubborn distraction who also happens to be his mentor's younger sister.

Stella O'Brien is over the whole gym bro charade she's been playing with the lacrosse captain, so she's decided to make a move. The plan quickly backfires, however, when a kiss that leaves both their heads spinning has Cody more certain than ever that they can't be together.

But sometimes life and older siblings have plans of their own, and what was supposed to be a much needed break from each other soon becomes a winter break under the same roof. As cold nights and petty fights turn into heated midnight confessions, Cody and Stella will have to face ugly truths to finally decide if a future together is worth fighting for or if it's time they both walked away.

I Blame the Club (Taber Tigers #3)

When the lacrosse legend returns to Taber, he's in for more than a simple coaching position...

Maurice O'Brien is back at Taber University as the lacrosse team's new assistant coach. He is ready to start a new chapter and take a break from the pressure of the corporate world, but what he isn't ready for is the promiscuous goalie who infuriates him at every opportunity.

Nico Montez has a new purpose in life: annoy the hell out of Taber's lacrosse legend. A grumpy, smouldering assistant coach is exactly the kind of distraction Nico needs right now, and with every heated exchange, the stakes rise a little bit higher.

When a violent confrontation leaves Nico wounded and in the arms of his enemy, the lines between hate, lust, and love start to disappear. Demons will emerge and swords will be laid to rest as Maurice and Nico suddenly find themselves seeking comfort from the one thing they never could have predicted: each other.